SEDUCING SUMMER

by

SERENITY WOODS

DEDICATION

To Tony & Chris, my Kiwi boys.

CONTENTS

Prologue

Five years ago

"Whose stupid idea was this?" Neve grumbled.

Callie Summer glanced to her right and chuckled at the sight of her friend tugging up the bodice of her bridesmaid's dress. "Will you stop fidgeting? You've got a ton of tit tape on—it's not going to fall down."

"One sneeze," Neve stated, "and I swear my boobs will pop out."

"Along with the best man's eyes," Bridget said.

Neve snorted, and the rest of the bridesmaids laughed. The best man, Rhett, appeared to have the hots for Neve. They'd been teasing her all morning that he'd make a move on her by the end of the day.

"I understand why men can't take their eyes off us. I think we look fantastic," Rowan said.

Callie had to agree. When Rowan's twin sister had first told the four of them that she wanted them to be bridesmaids at her wedding, they'd all been super excited, as none of them had been a bridesmaid before. Then Willow had revealed that the wedding was to take place in Matamata, at one of the sets from the movie *The Lord of the Rings*.

"Please don't say you want us to dress up as hobbits," Bridget had begged.

"No, silly." Willow had rolled her eyes. "I thought you could be the four seasons, with gorgeous, flowing Elven dresses."

"There are six seasons in the Elven year," Liam, the groom-to-be, had pointed out.

Willow had thumped him. "We're not making a Tolkien documentary. I just want them to look beautiful."

"I'd rather be an orc than wear a bridesmaid's gown," Neve had grumbled. "Can't I have a pantsuit?"

But Willow had asked her sister to design their dresses, and as they stood together waiting for the photographer, Callie thought that even Neve couldn't deny what a marvelous job Rowan had done. All four gowns were the same style—simple and strapless with a tight bodice and a full-length satin skirt—but they differed in their color and in the pattern on the flowing layers of tulle.

With the surname Summer, Callie's choice of season had been obvious. She had a dress of sunshine yellow, and the tulle of her skirt bore a gold-and-orange pattern that looked great with her pale, English-rose complexion.

Between the four of them, they'd decided that Rowan should be autumn because the foliage of the tree after which she'd been named turned red at that time of year. A rich gold-and-red tulle covered her russet gown, complementing her brown hair.

"My name's Latin for snow," Neve had suggested. So she'd become winter, with a pale blue dress covered in a shimmering white tulle flecked with blue to make sure she looked different from the bride.

That left spring for Bridget, and as her nickname was Birdie they thought the season fitted her rather well. Tiny pink and purple flowers covered the tulle over her pastel pink dress.

Together, the four gowns made them look like a row of flowers, and Willow had cried when she'd first seen them all together at the rehearsal. Rowan had made her dress, too—a flowing white gown based on Galadriel's, with thousands of beads and glittering thread. She'd also made all their underwear—beautiful lacy, strapless bras and matching panties—and it was when Callie had stood in front of her mirror and admired the garments that she'd had a revelation.

"I've had an idea I want to talk to you all about," she said as they watched the photographer taking the final shots of the bride and groom. "I think we should go into business together."

The other three looked at her with raised eyebrows. "Doing what?" Neve asked. "Running a circus?"

"No, silly. The Four Seasons Lingerie Shop."

They all stared at her.

"What?" Bridget said.

"After we finish university, we should open a lingerie shop. Rowan can design the clothing, I'll manage the business side of things, Birdie—you can run the shop, and Neve can be in charge of promotion. She can hold naughty lingerie and sex toy parties and spread the word."

"I like it," Neve stated while the other two burst out laughing.

"You're serious." Rowan's smile faded when Callie didn't join in.

"Perfectly. Don't you think it would be fun? Between us, we have all the skills we'd need. We get on really well, and I'm sure we'd work well together, too. It would be fantastic. I can just see us all in five years' time—rich, successful businesswomen, happily married, babies on the way... It'll be great."

Rowan smiled, Bridget looked thoughtful, and Neve rolled her eyes, but Callie could see she'd sown the seeds.

She turned her gaze back to Willow and her new husband. The photographer had finished their shots and beckoned to the bridesmaids and best man to join them, so they all walked forward to surround the bride and groom. Callie watched Rhett bend his head and whisper something in Neve's ear. She shook her head, but a smile played on her lips.

Callie's stomach bubbled with excitement and hope. She knew the lingerie shop would be successful. With Rowan's artistic talent and the combined fashion and business knowledge the rest of them were amassing from their university degrees, they'd make it work through sheer effort and determination.

All the girls were warm-hearted and sincere, and Callie knew it wouldn't be long before some decent guys snapped them up. Bridget had her eye on one of the ushers, Callie herself had plans to chat up the hot guy in charge of the catering, and even Rowan—with all her hang-ups—was casting sidelong glances at one of Liam's cousins.

Five years, she thought as the photographer gestured for them all to move closer together. It would be five years, maximum, before their business was super successful, and they'd all settled down with roses around the door and babies in their arms. *Just wait and see.*

Chapter One

Present Day

Callie sat at her desk, her chin in her hands, and read the email that had just popped up on her computer screen. It was from Willow, thanking Callie for the anniversary card she'd sent the previous week.

"I can't believe Liam and I have been married five years," the email read. "Where does the time go? And yes, baby's due on February 29th—typical! The poor thing will only have a birthday every four years. Hey, I know my baby shower is going to be the day before Valentine's Day, but I really hope you can come."

Yeah, Callie thought, she'd go. It wasn't as if she had anything better to do.

She pushed her chair away and walked over to stand at the window of her office, looking down at the bustling city center of Wellington, capital of New Zealand. Many of the shop windows were decorated with red hearts and Valentine's Day gifts, and the usually quiet boutique chocolate shop across the pedestrianized high street had a queue out the door.

Love was in the air. Allegedly, anyway. Callie had yet to see any evidence of the fat baby archer and his bow.

So much for her predictions on the day of Willow's wedding. She couldn't have been more wrong if she'd tried. She sighed as she contemplated not just her own disastrous love life, but also the failed relationships of her three friends. Maybe she'd jinxed them with her prophecies.

Neve's brief fling with Rhett had ended abruptly—Callie had never discovered why, and since then Neve had moved from one relationship to another without any sign of them being serious. Rowan had proven useless with men, having no clue as to what made them tick, and had yet to stay with any guy for more than a few months. Bridget's on-off relationship with her boyfriend seemed more off than on lately. None of them appeared close to settling down and having families.

Callie's own love life also seemed doomed. After a couple of failed relationships, she'd eventually moved in with Jamie, and she'd thought things were going well right up until the moment she'd walked in on him in bed with his secretary.

Her eyes stung, and she swallowed hard. She'd done her crying over Jamie Verne—over any man, in fact.

She lifted her chin. Not every prophecy she'd made had been wrong. The Four Seasons lingerie shop in Wellington had not only come to fruition, it had been hugely successful. They'd leased a shop toward the busy end of Cuba Street, and although it hadn't been cheap, it had proved to be a worthwhile investment, especially as it came with a couple of rooms above, from which Callie was able to run the business. As well as selling well-known brands of lingerie and swimwear, they distributed Rowan's own brand that specialized in lingerie for "real women," built on the belief that all women liked to wear pretty undergarments, no matter what their shape or size.

And now she was about to embark on the next phase of the business. Today was Thursday, and on Monday she was setting off for a countrywide tour of high street clothing shops to promote Rowan's Four Seasons brand of lingerie with the hope that a large proportion of the shops would agree to stock it. It was an ambitious move that could propel their brand from small scale to nationally recognized, and might even mean expansion to Australia and beyond.

She had far too much on her plate to even think about romance. She should have been thanking her lucky stars that Jamie had shown his true colors before she'd done anything really stupid like gotten married or—horror of horrors—fallen pregnant. Now she could concentrate on the business, which was what she was best at, when it came down to it. Finding love would stay at the bottom of her to-do list, where it belonged.

Checking her watch, she realized that several minutes had gone by since she'd buzzed Neve to send in the next interviewee. Becky, her heavily pregnant PA, had unfortunately had to start her maternity leave early when her blood pressure had shot up, and Neve was sitting in for a day or two until the temp agency came up with a replacement.

Callie turned and, to her surprise, saw someone waiting in the doorway.

She'd expected a middle-aged woman with graying hair, glasses on a lanyard, frumpy clothes, and possibly a hairy lip.

This person was neither middle-aged nor frumpy. He was about six-foot-two with short brown hair, and wearing what looked like a tailored charcoal three-piece suit with a sparkling white shirt and a stylish sky-blue tie. He stood with his hands behind his back, his head tipped a little to the side as he surveyed her, suggesting he'd been there for a while.

He was also the most gorgeous guy she'd seen in… well, possibly ever, if you liked your men hard and rather dangerous. He looked as if he could complete a million-dollar business deal for a piece of land, build a shelter on it with his bare hands, and drag a woman to it by her hair. Callie hadn't thought that kind of guy appealed to her, but she had to admit that if she'd ordered herself a late Christmas present, or an early Valentine's Day present, or indeed any kind of present, this was the kind of parcel she would have hoped for. All he needed was a bow tied around… somewhere interesting.

"Oh," she said, confused, and flustered at his steady gaze. "Can I help you?"

"I'm here for the interview."

She stared at him. Part of her was aware that her jaw was sagging, but her brain couldn't process the information he'd just given her.

He raised a hand to scratch his cheek. "Ma'am? Is there a problem?"

Ma'am. That one word melted her a little inside.

She looked at the name she'd scribbled on her notepad. "I understood that the next candidate was called Jean Bond." She looked back up, confused. "As in Simmons, Harlow. Miss Brodie— the Prime of."

"It's G-e-n-e," he clarified. "As in Hackman, Wilder. Kelly—who sings in the rain." He brushed a hand down himself, drawing her attention to his suit again and the undoubtedly male physique that lay beneath it. "I'm a guy, in case you hadn't noticed."

As it happened, Callie *had* noticed. And that was where the problem lay.

She put her hands on her hips and pursed her lips. "Neve, get your butt in here!" she yelled.

Gene's eyebrows rose, and then he moved a few steps to the side to leave the doorway clear.

Neve's head appeared around the door. Her innocent expression informed Callie that she was well aware of what had just transpired. Neve sidled in and cast a quick glance at the man still standing in the center of the room before saying, "How's the interview going? Not progressed to sitting down yet?"

"I'm supposed to find a replacement for Becky today," Callie pointed out.

Neve nodded and gestured with both hands at the man standing by her side as if he were a magician and she was his assistant. "And here he is... Ta da!"

"It appears that 007 here is a man," Callie stated.

"007?" Neve queried.

"Mr. Bond."

"Ah." Neve looked him up and down. "Do you know, I think you're right."

Callie gave her a wry look. "You knew damn well he was a man and you didn't tell me."

Earlier that morning, when Callie had complained about how useless the three temps they'd already sent her had been, Neve had told her, "Don't worry, the agency's sending someone called Jean. Apparently the best they've got. Came in early this morning after a long vacation, looking for a new post." It was only now that Callie realized her friend had carefully avoided using pronouns.

She glared at Neve. "You told me they said 'Efficient, organized, and *hot as* office skills.'"

"And?"

"Hot piece of ass is what you meant. Deny it."

"I'm standing right here," Gene said.

Callie ignored him. Since she'd broken up with Jamie, her friends had tried to fix her up on no fewer than three occasions with someone new. Callie had refused each time, but she was certain this appointment was another of Neve's attempts to pair her up. "This morning, you've brought me a sixteen-year-old whose only experience was working in a DVD rental shop on a Saturday afternoon, another girl who spelled the word lingerie with a 'j', and a woman whose typing speed was twenty words a minute."

"I can type faster than that with my feet," Gene commented.

She glanced over at him. He raised his eyebrows. She was tempted to laugh, but she wasn't about to give in yet.

"Did you pick the other three on purpose?" she asked Neve suspiciously.

"Not at all." Neve looked affronted. "When you leave it to the last minute, these are the kind of people left on the shelf."

"Gee, thanks," Gene said.

"I didn't mean you." Now Neve was laughing. "Come on, Callie. Give the guy an interview at least. He comes with great references, and he can do shorthand."

Callie blew out a breath. It may have been old-fashioned, but she enjoyed dictating letters and reports while she paced her office looking out at the view. She'd been doubtful that she'd find anyone these days who could still do shorthand. That at least worked in his favor.

"You really can type?" she asked him.

"I can."

"What's your speed?"

"Ninety words a minute."

That wasn't bad at all. "Shorthand speed?" she queried.

"A hundred and thirty words a minute."

Maybe not as fast as Becky, but still pretty good. She tried not to look impressed. "Anything else?"

"I can use old-fashioned Dictaphones and the new digital ones. I'm proficient in all the major word processing, spreadsheet, and presentational packages. I can book flights, organize meetings, make coffee, charm customers, and unjam printers. And I know my alphabet and can tie my shoelaces on my own."

Neve burst out laughing. Seeing Callie's glare, she turned and walked out of the office, still chuckling.

Callie turned her glare on Gene, whose eyes danced with humor. "Do you really think I'm looking for a smart-mouthed *man* to be my PA?" she demanded.

Pursing his lips, he looked at his shoes, giving her a moment to admire him. He had boyish good looks, but there was a touch of toughness to his hardened features, as if he were a guy she'd known since childhood that had been away to war and seen terrible things, returning a changed man. His face was grave and serious, and she had the feeling he didn't smile much—and yet the corners of his eyes were creased with laughter lines, suggesting his seriousness hadn't been there since birth, but had crept upon him as life took its toll. It was difficult to see what kind of physique he had beneath the suit, but he had wide shoulders and a broad chest, suggesting he worked out. His short hair stuck up at the front, although it was unclear whether it was natural or if he'd styled it like that.

He cleared his throat before looking back at her. This time, his amusement had faded. "I apologize. I assure you, I'm usually very respectful and good at my job. I'm organized and efficient, quiet and hardworking, and I promise I'll make your life easier."

Callie highly doubted that. The man had trouble written all over him. It could have been the steely glint in his eye, or the way he was standing, still and watchful, like a coiled spring… She couldn't put her finger on it, but there was definitely something dangerous about him.

How the hell was she supposed to work with Mr. License-to-Kill at her side all the time providing the ultimate distraction?

"Ma'am?" He looked concerned. "Can we start over again?"

She picked up a pen and notepad, walked over to the armchairs on one side of the room, and indicated for him to take one. She sat opposite him, taking care to keep her knees together so he didn't get an eyeful. "Let's start by you calling me Callie," she said.

"Yes, ma'am," he replied.

Her lips twitched. And then suddenly it struck her. The metaphor of a childhood friend who'd been away to war hadn't been so far from the truth. "You're ex-military," she observed.

He leaned back in the chair, resting an ankle on the opposite knee, and nodded slowly, either amused or surprised she'd guessed. "Yes. What gave it away?"

"The way you stood with your hands behind your back. The deferential manner. And the MAG 58 machine gun I'm sure you've got rammed up your backside."

To his credit, he gave a short laugh. "Don't tell me you're into guns."

"Dad was in the Army." She chewed her lip while she surveyed him properly for the first time.

He bore her perusal calmly, and to his credit his gaze stayed firmly on her face. She let hers slide down him, though, knowing she was being rude but too interested not to pay further attention. He'd fashioned his tie in a complicated Windsor knot, if she wasn't mistaken. His shoes bore a shine, also reflecting his military background. As he'd sat, he'd unbuttoned his jacket, and it hung open now to reveal a dark gray matching waistcoat over his white shirt. She could count the number of men who wore a three-piece suit to work on the fingers of one hand. Suave, a little old-fashioned, and incredibly sexy at the same time. What a combination.

His Army training was no doubt what she'd picked up on when she'd thought he looked dangerous. "How many ways can you kill a man?" she asked, admitting that it gave her a tingle to think he was a trained soldier.

"How many do I need?"

She grinned. He had a great poker face, and it was difficult to tell what he was thinking, but as she continued to study him, the corner of his mouth curved up.

"Do I meet with your approval?" he asked.

"You're a puzzle," she admitted, trying not to think about how low and sultry his voice was.

"A puzzle?" he queried.

"Yes. A soldier with a ninety words per minute typing speed?"

"When I left school, I trained as a journalist and photographer."

"Ah." That made more sense. "What did you do then?"

"I was hired by a national TV news program as a trainee war correspondent. I shadowed an older guy and went with him to Egypt, Iraq, and Afghanistan. Spent a lot of time around Army guys and loved it so much I signed up."

"So what happened? Why did you leave? I'm guessing because you were wounded—in the leg, yes?" She'd detected a slight limp when he'd walked in.

His eyes met hers for a moment. Hesitant, wary, guarded. He'd meant to keep that a secret, but now she'd asked him, he didn't have a choice unless he intended to lie outright. He didn't like that she was so observant, and had guessed things he'd wanted to keep to himself.

He shifted in the seat. On the surface, it looked as if he was making himself more comfortable, but she sensed unease in his posture. He didn't like talking about it. She waited for him to change the subject, but instead he said, "I was out on a scouting mission. We stumbled across a hidden base and they opened fire on us. I took a bullet in the thigh, crawled off into a hole somewhere, and passed out. They didn't find me for three days, and by then it was infected. They operated, and it healed, but it's not good enough for active duty." He shrugged. "I didn't want an Army desk job. Didn't seem much point in staying in."

"Is it still painful?"

"Sometimes."

In the other office, she could hear Neve answering the phone, the whirr of the photocopier, the clang of a spoon in a cup as someone—probably Bridget—made a coffee. Outside the office, she heard the sound of traffic in the busy streets, and somewhere in the far distance the whine of a police car. Inside, though, the comforting tick of the clock on the wall filled the room.

Gene sat patiently, his gaze fixed on hers, calm, a tad challenging. There was something he wasn't telling her, but she couldn't work out what it was.

Callie uncrossed her legs and re-crossed them. His gaze stayed on her face, which she found interesting—no sexy slide down her body, no suggestive looks or comments. Either he didn't fancy her, or he was determined not to bring sex into the office, for whatever reason. Of course, he could be married, or at least have a partner, in which case kudos to him for not straying.

Suddenly, it became quintessentially important that she discover if he was single.

She shook her head a little, hoping it would dislodge the issue from her brain. His professionalism ranked him high on her list. However, working with him would be a nightmare, surely, whether he was married or not. Wasn't it weird that a once-soldier wanted to be a PA? Or was she being sexist? The thought made her uncomfortable, as she was a great advocate of women being able to do any job they chose. And if she believed in equality, it had to work both ways.

She frowned. "So instead of taking an Army desk job, you decided to go into secretarial work? What's the difference?"

He shrugged again. "Freedom. I'd had enough of being told how to live my life."

"Why not go back into journalism?"

"I've seen enough of the world, and I'm not getting any younger. I just want to settle down."

"How old are you?"

"I'll be thirty-two on Valentine's Day." His eyes dared her to find that funny.

She bit her lip. "Married?"

"No."

"Living with anyone?" *Oops.* That wasn't relevant to the job, but it had slipped out.

"No."

"Children?"

"No."

"Girlfriend?" She was taunting him now, wondering how far she could push him.

His gaze remained steady. "No."

"You don't like talking about yourself," she observed, curious about this guy, whose impassive expression held a multitude of secrets, she was sure.

"I've just told you more about my injury than I've told anyone in a long time." He looked slightly puzzled at that.

Callie studied him, intrigued. He fascinated her. But that didn't mean him being her PA would work. She had to think of her customers, the majority of whom were women. Okay, most of them would probably think it fun to chat to a male PA, but she had to bear in mind that it might make some of them feel awkward. And what about him?

"You know what business I run here, right?"

He nodded. "Yes, ma'am."

"I ask because working with lingerie all day can make some men twitchy. Does it make you uncomfortable?"

"No, ma'am." He remained straight-faced. It didn't surprise her. Somehow, she couldn't imagine this man getting flustered over lacy underwear. He looked like the kind of guy who could open a bra catch with one flick of his fingers.

His cool gaze egged her on. "You think you can remain professional when dealing with customers enquiring about extra-large cup sizes? Or when they ask you to describe the different styles of panties we supply?"

He brushed at a speck of dust on his trousers. "Yes, ma'am." He met her gaze, and then finally gave in to a smile, showing her why he had all those laughter lines at the edges of his eyes, and baring a row of neat white teeth. "And I'm happy to work late to catch up on any knowledge I may be missing."

Ah, so there was a man beneath the soldier, then. Wickedly, she raised her eyebrows as if to say, *Oh, really?* He dropped his gaze back to his hands, pursing his lips as if cursing himself for his comment. He'd tried so hard to be professional, and he'd only caved when she'd provoked him. She couldn't blame him for that.

She gave a short, silent laugh. If he could do the job—and it appeared he had the necessary skills to do so, more than any of the other applicants, anyway—then there wasn't a relevant reason why she shouldn't hire him.

He looked back up after he'd composed himself. "Please give me a chance," he said. "I swear I'll be professional. We'll work together really well. I'll look after you."

She blinked. What a strange thing to say. It made her feel slightly uncomfortable. "I don't need looking after."

"I meant in the office. A good PA makes sure he knows what his boss wants before she does," he added. The twinkle in his eye told her he'd been aware of the double meaning behind it, and again he hadn't been able to help himself.

It would be fun teasing him. But she still wasn't sure it was a good idea.

"It's a busy job," she said. "Lots of travelling."

"That's fine."

"But you said you wanted to settle down."

"Staying in swish hotels with air conditioning and minibars is not the same as camping with a dozen guys in the desert, believe me."

She was not going to think about him showering with a dozen other sweaty guys. "I'm going on a tour of the country over the next few weeks," she said. "I need my PA to come with me."

"That's no problem."

"It's a long way. Lots of flying and car journeys."

"I like flying. And driving. I'm happy to double as your chauffeur. It'll be fun," he said. "Trust me."

She met his gaze. His eyes were gray, like a sky heavy with rain, late on a summer's evening.

"Trust me," he said again, gently. A strange phrase, but one that reached inside her and warmed her all the way through.

SERENITY WOODS

She pushed herself to her feet. "You can have a one-day trial. Work with Neve, let her show you the ropes. If she gives you the green light, I'll trust her judgment." He had to be able to do the job. And she knew Neve wouldn't let him through just because she was trying to fix her up.

He stood—a little awkwardly, she noticed. That leg did still give him trouble. "That's great. Thank you for the chance, ma'am, you won't regret it."

She walked out, her lips curving at the feel of his eyes burning into her butt like lasers.

Chapter Two

Gene let Callie walk a few paces ahead of him before following her out. It gave him time to admire the way her high heels lent her hips an enticing swing as she walked across the room.

He hadn't expected her to be such a cracker. Phoebe Hawke—who went by her maiden name—had painted a picture of her daughter as plump and mulish, and had somehow managed to suggest she was a little stupid. At the time, he'd thought it didn't marry with the fact that Callie was also apparently the very successful CEO of a thriving company she'd built from scratch, and it certainly didn't fit now he'd met her.

When he'd stood in the doorway and his gaze had fallen on the girl standing by the window, his first thought had been, *Oh no.* Surely this wasn't the woman he was expected to lie to for the next three months.

Although not model-thin like her mother, she wasn't fat by any means. Rounded, maybe. Curvaceous, with a full bust and a tiny waist that flared out to generous hips—a true hourglass figure like an old-fashioned Hollywood starlet—Gina Lollobrigida, maybe, or Sophia Loren. She wore a sleeveless cream blouse and a fawn-colored pencil skirt, and sexy high heels with painted toenails peeking out of the cutaway toes. Shiny strawberry-blonde hair bounced around her shoulders. She had an English-rose complexion with dark pink lips pursed in thought. She was much younger and far sexier than he'd been led to believe. Her expression had looked a little sad, though, and instead of announcing his arrival, he'd found himself taking the opportunity to study her while wondering what she was thinking about.

She certainly wasn't stupid, either. He'd read an article that a prestigious New Zealand fashion magazine had done on her company. Callie had left Victoria University with a top-class Management degree and had started up the business with her three friends at the age of twenty-two. The magazine had said she worked sixty-hour weeks, although after speaking to her he suspected that was a low estimate. It had also reported her as having "a perceptive mind astute enough to challenge Sherlock Holmes," and that seemed to be the case from the way she'd spotted his military background and his wounded hip, which he tried hard to hide.

He was going to have to be on his guard all the time if he intended to see this through to the end.

"We're going to give him a trial," Callie announced to Neve. She walked over to a spare chair and rolled it across the floor to the desk. Looking at him expectantly, she gestured to it. "Sit."

"Yes, ma'am."

She gave an odd little shiver. "Please don't call me ma'am."

"We used surnames in the Army. I'm happy to call you Summer, if you like." The name fit her perfectly. Everything about her was like a piece of summer captured and brought inside.

She gave him a wry look. "Callie will be fine."

He took the seat next to Neve, who smiled and indicated the drawers to the right of her desk.

"Okay, so these are the main forms you'll need when a new customer calls." She opened the drawer. "Yellow for the South Island, blue for the North Island." She looked up at Callie, who hovered with folded arms. "Can I help you?"

Callie ran her tongue over her teeth, glanced at him, then turned on her heel and walked back to her office, where the door swung slowly shut.

Neve blew out a long, relieved breath, bent forward, and rested her forehead on the table.

"Are you all right?" he asked with concern.

She sat up again and rolled her eyes. "I thought she'd never leave." She gave him an exasperated look. "And I thought you'd blown it in there, being cheeky to her. She was already flustered because you have a... well, you know." She gestured at his crotch.

Gene opened his mouth to give a sarcastic retort, then stared at her. *Wait a minute.* He frowned. "What do you mean, 'blown it in there'? You need a replacement that much?"

"Well, yes, but I meant the secret mission." Neve's voice dropped to an amusing stage whisper. "Phoebe told me everything."

"Really?" That surprised him. Callie's mother had been very clear that he was to keep his ulterior motive for being there from her daughter.

"Phoebe needed my help," Neve admitted. "It wasn't too much of a stretch to convince Callie that Becky needed to finish work early. But we knew she wouldn't go for a male PA unless there was no alternative."

"So you made sure the other candidates were bad on purpose?"

Neve just grinned. Striking rather than pretty, with brown hair cut in a long bob, boyish clothes, and a 'don't fuck with me' attitude, she obviously cared enough about her friend to go through with this elaborate charade.

She leaned back in the chair and gave him a curious look. "Can you really type ninety words a minute?"

"Damn straight. And I do know how to tie my own shoelaces."

She chuckled. "You may mock, but it's a pretty good speed for a soldier. And by the way, I thought you weren't supposed to tell her you were ex-Army."

"I wasn't, but she guessed. I don't want to lie unless I really have to."

Neve nodded. "She's very astute."

"So I gather."

She cocked her head at him. "You're really the director of Safe & Secure?"

"Yep."

"So you're, like, a real bodyguard?"

"Yep. Except we call them PPOs, personal protection officers."

"Phoebe told me she'd asked for you personally."

"Yes. That was… unexpected. But she wants to keep her daughter safe—I can understand it."

"Callie doesn't want a bodyguard," Neve said.

"I know. Hence the undercover act."

"She threw a fit when Phoebe suggested it."

"I bet. Why didn't she want one?"

"She doesn't like being told what to do—especially by her mother."

"Fair enough."

Phoebe was a Crown prosecutor at one of the biggest law firms in Wellington. A gangster she'd put away six years ago and who had recently come out of prison had sent her a death threat that had also mentioned her daughter, prompting her to seek protection until he was caught.

Gene had known her for a long time, and he suspected he was one of the few people she didn't boss around. He could only imagine the kind of pressure she'd put on Callie to accept security. He was amazed Callie had managed to resist. Clearly, it hadn't done her any good. Phoebe had just changed to underhanded measures to get what she wanted. He couldn't blame her, though, when the safety of her daughter was at stake.

"So what are the rest of your company doing while you're up here?" Neve asked.

"They're doing stuff I can't do while I'm not in the office, mainly with Phoebe, as she's the main target. Callie was mentioned in the letter, but it was Phoebe's life that was threatened directly. I am still surprised that Callie's going on this tour, though."

"You'll learn that she's very trusting and thinks the best of everyone. She doesn't really understand there might be someone out there who wants to kill her." Neve's lips twisted. "She's a great believer in the underlying goodness of the human race."

"Sucker," Gene said.

She laughed. "Yeah."

"She knows about the death threats, though?"

"Yeah, but she believes her mother's using it to scare her, to force her to stay put. She thinks her mother resents her success, so it's a natural conclusion."

Was Callie wrong there? Phoebe might not have painted her daughter in a wonderful light, but the whole reason for her setting up the protection was because she obviously loved Callie dearly, and she'd seemed proud of her achievements.

Neve's gaze slid to his chest. "Do you wear a bulletproof vest?"

"Not at the moment. I will do, though, when we're out on the road."

"Won't she be able to see it?"

"The company that supplies our equipment makes what's called an executive vest—it looks like a waistcoat. That's why I'm wearing one now, so she gets used to seeing me in them."

"I thought a three-piece was a bit over the top."

"I don't know, I quite like it." He straightened the waistcoat. He hadn't missed the way Callie's gaze had slid down him, soft and sensual as a warm hand on bare skin. "My new one's bullet resistant and protects against hypodermic needles and edged weapons." He spoke with some pride.

Neve's smile faded, and her face paled. "Jeez."

Shit, he'd said too much. "Don't worry. We'll do everything we can to make sure she stays safe."

Neve's gaze appraised him. "You'd really jump in front of a bullet for her?"

"That's my job."

"You don't know her. She can be really grumpy sometimes. Especially early in the morning."

He could imagine Callie early in the morning. With her blonde hair ruffled, wearing nothing but his shirt, nipples showing through the cotton like buttons. Seducing Summer. Now that was a fantasy that would carry him through any sleepless nights.

Neve raised an eyebrow, and he blinked, realizing his eyes must have glazed over. "Sorry, what were you saying?"

"Don't even think about it," she said.

"Think about what?"

Her previously warm expression turned cool. "Maybe this wasn't such a good idea."

"I don't know what you're suggesting, but I can assure you I'm excellent at my job, and I'll do everything in my power to keep her safe."

Neve leaned back in her chair, tapping her pen on the table as she surveyed him. "And her heart?"

He frowned. "What about it?"

"This is important, Gene. I'm serious. You need to stay focused. Callie's love life is important to us, and we're determined to fix her up with someone soon, but her safety is even more important than that. I'll be in touch with her on a regular basis, and if she gives me any kind of hint that there's something developing between the two of you, I'll be straight on to Phoebe, and before you know it you'll be off the job."

"And I won't be able to show my face around Wellington again?" He glared at her. "Come on, give me some credit. I have no intention of getting involved with her."

"You don't know her." Neve's face softened. "Her IQ is bigger than yours and mine added together, she works harder than anyone else I've ever known, she's very perceptive, and she has this weird knack of knowing what you're thinking. Men find her fascinating, and it always leads to disaster. Because although she's generous and funny, and has a heart of gold, her astuteness doesn't extend to her personal relationships."

"What do you mean?"

Neve hesitated. "You mustn't tell her I told you. But I think it's best you know. Four months ago, she walked in on her ex in bed with his secretary."

"Christ." That was why she'd looked so sad.

"We all knew he was bad news, but she couldn't see it. She trusted him completely, and it nearly destroyed her. She's just climbing out of the black hole she'd fallen into, so the last thing she needs is for someone like you making a move on her."

"I don't know what you mean."

"Come on, Gene. You're gorgeous, smart, and there's something dangerous about you. Don't roll your eyes. You know perfectly well what I mean. You're the kind of guy who goes after the woman he wants and doesn't let anything get in his way. Well you can't afford to do that with Callie. If you let her, she'll fall for you, so you've got to make sure that doesn't happen."

Gene felt as if he'd walked into some kind of teen movie. He should have known better than to take on a job in a lingerie business. "I have no idea what you're talking about," he said sharply. "This is a professional working relationship and it's going to stay that way." Callie might not have been what he was expecting, but that didn't mean he'd jeopardize his job to play with her, and it was insulting to him that anyone would think otherwise.

"I hope so," Neve continued, ignoring his glare. "Because you can't tell her that you're actually her bodyguard, and that means lying to her, and she won't take it well when she finds out—because she will, eventually. She's too smart not to. Life's thrown a lot at her, including a cheating boyfriend, a mother who's determined to control her, and a father who's an arrogant ass but absolutely adores her, so much so that she can't see his bad points. I don't know how much more she can take." She frowned. "I don't understand why Phoebe didn't ask for a female bodyguard. Why did she insist on you?"

"We go back a long way," he said. He didn't elaborate, even though Neve's expression glimmered with curiosity.

"You're one for secrets, aren't you?" She shrugged. "Whatever. I just want you to know that when you say you're out to protect her, that means all of her, heart included. Do you swear?"

"Want to find me a Bible?"

"Look at my face. Do I look like I'm laughing?"

His lips finally curved up. "I'm glad you care for her so much. Please don't worry. I'll make sure she stays safe, in every way."

"Okay." She gave a heavy sigh. "We might as well get started, then. Open your notebook."

Gene did so, trying not to look up at the Sword of Damocles he was sure was hanging over his head.

Come on, dude, he scolded himself. He only had to do this until the NZ Special Tactics Group had tracked down the man sending the death threats, which would hopefully be only days, a week at most, and should definitely be well before Becky came back from her maternity leave in May. Gene liked sex as much as the next guy, and it was true that he hadn't had any for a while, but in spite of Neve's predictions, he'd never been a man to give in to his desires. He was sure he could remain aloof, even if it took three months to catch the bastard.

Ninety days of being practically glued to the curvy blonde's side. He stifled a groan, gave himself a mental image of stapling her blouse shut, and concentrated on his notepad.

Chapter Three

"Coffee," Gene said, placing the cup on her table. "Small amount of milk, quarter of a teaspoon of sugar. Stirred anticlockwise."

It was mid-afternoon. He'd already brought her lunch to her desk and had also managed then to give her a look that implied her tastes were particular, just because she liked her salad from a certain place with a particular dressing. She normally bought it herself—she had no idea why Neve had sent him out for it.

"I don't know how you manage to make me sound fussy," she complained. "It's not a word I'd ever call myself."

"Becky left detailed instructions on par with planning D-Day." He stood in front of her desk, hands behind his back as usual.

She reached for the cup. "I suppose we all have our quirks. And at ease, soldier."

"I like standing like this. It's not cool for a man to put his hands in the pockets of his suit trousers." His eyes held enough steel to warn her that she wasn't going to be able to boss him around.

"Fair enough." She leaned back in her chair and sipped her coffee. She still hadn't made up her mind about him yet. He'd been right in that a good PA's job was to anticipate her—or his—boss's needs before she knew them herself, and Becky had been very good at doing that, without the additional judgmental looks and rolls of the eyes. He was hardly perfect PA material. And yet he fascinated her.

"Do I get a biscuit?" she asked. "Becky normally puts a chocolate Hobnob on the side of the saucer. Was that not on the list?"

He raised an eyebrow as if to say, *Seriously?* She sipped her coffee. He pursed his lips, turned, and walked out, then came back a minute later with a Hobnob on a plate, which he placed in front of her.

"Thank you." She took a bite of the biscuit and chewed it. "Mmm," she said with great enthusiasm.

That made him laugh, which pleased her in turn. Knowing she could encourage his smile out gave her more pleasure than it probably should have.

She'd expected him to return to his desk, but he began to walk slowly around her office, looking at the pictures on the walls. All but one were shots of women in Four Seasons lingerie, tasteful photos with clever lighting that made all the models—most of whom had generous body shapes—look sensual and sexy.

"Do you like?" She rose and walked over to him, carrying her coffee and biscuit, wondering if he'd give her some comment about being mad not to like photos of women in their underwear.

"They're excellent." He gestured at the one in front of him. "Superb lighting."

"It makes them look quite beautiful, doesn't it?"

"All women are beautiful regardless of lighting." He tipped his head, studying the model in the photo.

"That's a nice thing to say."

He turned his gaze to her. "I would imagine you have to think that to work in a place like this."

"It helps, for sure. We believe that everyone should be proud of their body no matter what shape or size you are. Everyone's different, and that should be celebrated. Nobody should have to change themselves to fit society's version of the perfect person."

He studied her for a long time. He didn't say anything, and his gaze didn't move from hers, but she couldn't shake the feeling that he was thinking about her naked.

Finally, though, he just said, "You have a biscuit crumb on your lip."

Sticking out her tongue, she searched along her top lip, then along the bottom one, until she found it, and sucked it into her mouth. "Waste not, want not."

His gaze had dropped to her lips, but now it rose back to meet hers. She couldn't tell what he was thinking, though. Probably what an idiot she was with biscuit all around her mouth.

Without saying anything else, he continued walking around the room before stopping at the largest photo on the wall. It was of Callie, Rowan, Neve, and Bridget, taken on the day of Willow's wedding. They stood in a line, backed by cherry trees and purple, pink, and white wisteria. The photographer had taken the shot at the moment a brisk summer breeze whipped across the green, and all four of them were laughing, fighting the way their dresses were lifting in the wind.

"The Four Seasons," Callie said.

"That's Neve, isn't it?" He gestured to the girl in the light blue dress.

"Yes. That's Rowan—she designs our lingerie. And you must have seen Bridget downstairs, too—she runs the shop."

"You met at university, right?"

"Yes." She gave him an appraising look. He'd done research on the business? Another point in his favor.

"I like that your lingerie caters for all sizes," he said.

"Everyone deserves to feel pretty in what they wear, and it's not only thin women who want to look sexy. I can personally vouch for that." She smiled.

"Not every man wants a stick insect," he said. "Some of us like a woman to have curves."

Was he saying that *he* liked curvy women? He didn't elaborate, and again, she couldn't read anything else in his expression. He certainly wasn't flirting overtly. Which was appropriate, of course. It would make her life much easier over the next few months if there was no spark between them.

Would be a bit dull, though.

She shrugged. "Well there are plenty of curves to go around at Four Seasons. None of us is keen on dieting."

Laughing, she walked over to the architect's desk that stood against the wall. If he was going to be her PA, he'd need to know the business, so she might as well try to forget he was a guy and talk to him the way she would have talked to Becky. "Come and look at these."

Two huge catalogues sat on the desk. Finishing off her biscuit, she placed the coffee cup to one side and opened the first catalogue. The pages were made of board and slotted into clear plastic sleeves that clipped into the folder so she could add or replace items as necessary. Each page featured a large picture by the same photographer who'd taken the shots on the wall.

Gene stood shoulder to shoulder with her, a few inches taller than her in her heels. As they leaned forward, his aftershave wound around her like a ribbon—something with sandalwood and a touch of citrus, making her mouth water.

"This is the Four Seasons swimwear." Trying to concentrate, she began to leaf through the photos of models in bikinis and costumes, taken on the quay by the Te Papa museum. "Rowan's aim was to design swimwear that women with more generous body shapes can feel comfortable in while still feeling sexy. For example, our bikini tops have more material in the cups so the wearer doesn't have to worry that she'll turn to the side and pop out."

"Very thoughtful."

"We think so. We do offer the traditional tiny bottoms, but we concentrate on the hip- or waist-high bottoms, often matched with tankini tops, as well as one-pieces. Rowan's very clever at designing patterns that draw the eye away from the bits we don't want to be seen. Many women don't mind having a larger bust, but they're uncomfortable about showing their midriffs, so our designs are based around disguising that area by having fancy tucks or folds of the material between the boobs, dark-colored panels down the sides or across the tummy, and bright colors in strategic places."

He lifted a hand, and for a brief moment she thought he was going to cup her cheek. He just touched her earlobe, though, and to her surprise, produced a two-dollar coin as if he'd pulled it from the shell of her ear.

She laughed. "Magic tricks?"

"The theory of misdirection. It's what the swimwear does." He smiled and pocketed the coin.

Her earlobe tingled where he'd brushed it, sending a ripple through her entire body. He'd obviously shaved that morning, she thought. An image flashed through her mind of him standing in front of a bathroom mirror wearing only a towel, tipping his head back as he ran a razor across his cheek.

Ooh.

Blinking away the haze of lust that threatened to overwhelm her, she pushed the swimwear to one side and opened the lingerie catalogue. "Yes, you're right. Misdirection is the key for swimwear. Underwear is slightly different, as generally it's not made for others to see. It serves two basic purposes—to support the figure and make one's outer clothes look good, and to make the woman feel sexy, both for herself and her partner. Quite often, she'll buy two separate sets of lingerie—comfortable, well-fitting bras and panties to wear every day, and prettier lingerie to wear for special occasions. Rowan wanted to design a range that fulfilled both purposes—that was both practical and sexy." She gestured at the model on the page, who wore an underwired bra with full cups, a wide back, and generous straps, that was nevertheless pretty with its intricate lace and embroidery.

Callie had shown the catalogues to various men over the past few years, from the occasional salesman to partners of women who visited the office. Nearly all of them had cracked jokes to cover their discomfort, while the gazes of a few had lingered longer than was necessary as they ogled the models.

Gene turned the pages at the right pace, though, without making lewd remarks or suggestive comments. "How is the range priced? Compared to other brands?"

Wow, this guy was pure class. Callie wanted to hug him, but just managed to restrain herself. "High-end rather than cheap, but competitive compared to some of the more well-known brands. A price that says quality without being expensive. We did a lot of surveying of women and discovered that underwear—especially bras—is something most are willing to spend money on, if it's comfortable and makes them feel good. They may buy cheap T-shirts and two pairs of shoes for the price of one, but they won't skimp on their underwear."

"Glad to hear it," he said.

She glanced at him, but he was examining the last page that showed the same model in all the different styles of panties they produced, and Callie couldn't tell how wry he'd meant his comment to be. Was his humor just exceptionally dry, or had he merely been commenting on the penny-saving abilities of her customers?

Finally, he moved back and closed the book. "I'm impressed. So why are you touring the country?"

She wandered back to her desk. "I'll be approaching high street stores to ask whether they'd consider stocking the Four Seasons brand."

"Couldn't you do that by phone or email?"

"I'm better in person," she said, sitting down. "You can't appreciate my sparkling personality and lively wit until you talk to me face to face."

He stood before her desk, hands behind his back again. "I see." He kept a straight face, obviously trying hard to be polite. For whatever strange reason, he wanted the job, and it was clear he'd be professional behind the desk.

Mischievousness surged through her. "Plus, I do a fashion show and model all the underwear personally. It works especially well when the managers are men."

His eyebrows rose. "Really?"

"No!" She rolled her eyes. "Come on, Gene. If we're going to work together, you're going to have to let that sense of humor loose. It's difficult to take life seriously when you spend your days discussing things like whether the fabric of a bra is going to be too scratchy on the nipples."

He looked at his shoes for a long moment. Callie bit back a laugh. She really shouldn't tease him.

"If it's any help," she said, "I'm amazed you've lasted this long without any sexual innuendo."

He raised his gaze to hers. "I wouldn't dream of it," he said. But his eyes warmed with amusement.

She sat back in her chair. "Just so you know, although I don't like it when people make fun of my job or treat women as sexual objects, I do have a sense of humor, and you're allowed to have one too."

"That's good to know."

"Would you like to work here?"

"It's a dream come true." He gave an impish smile that warmed her right through. *At last.*

"In that case, you're hired, Mr. Bond—and I hope you're prepared for endless 007 jokes."

"I'm sure I've heard them all."

"I'll do my best to come up with some new ones. In return, you may ask me a question. Anything you like, and I promise to answer it truthfully." Now she'd given him free rein, she waited for him to enquire about her cup size, or what style of panties she preferred.

He surveyed her for a long moment. Then he picked up her empty cup. "What's Callie short for?"

"Oh." She sucked her bottom lip. Talking with this man was like being blindfolded and then turned around and around, leaving her disoriented and reeling. "Um, Calinda. It means summer."

"So your name's Summer Summer?"

"I prefer to think of it as Sunny Summer."

He picked up the saucer containing a few leftover biscuit crumbs. "It suits you." He lifted his eyes to meet hers. Once again, they held enough heat to suggest he was thinking something sexy.

The ability to think of a witty retort deserted her, and all she could come up with was, "Thank you."

"And thank you for hiring me. I'm sure we'll work well together."

Something in his expression made her think of the two of them naked, in bed. Working together beneath the sheets. Her cheeks heated, and she was certain he noted that before he turned and left the room, his lips curving in a slight smile.

Chapter Four

The rest of Gene's day passed swiftly. Neve went through the rest of the diligent Becky's notes with him, most of which seemed to imply that although Callie was a wonderful saleswoman who had no trouble putting people at their ease, she couldn't organize a piss-up in a brewery. Becky made it quite clear that he couldn't expect Callie to do anything unless he wrote it on a Post-It Note and stuck it to her phone or her laptop screen, and even then, if it was an important task, it was best he did it himself.

Neve gave him a rundown of the running of the business, in between pestering him with questions about his real job.

"So what do you know about the guy who's made the death threats?" she asked in a hushed voice when she knew Callie was on a long call. "Phoebe said he was someone she put away a few years ago."

"Yeah. He's a nasty piece of work—a rich gangster who thought he was untouchable. Like Al Capone, they got him on taxes, and she put together a watertight case he couldn't wriggle out of. He got ten years and was out in six. Two days after he was released, he shot his lawyer and then vanished. A week later, Phoebe got the first death threat. He's a nutcase, hell bent on revenge against all those who had a hand in his incarceration, intent on making them suffer."

"You think they'll be able to catch him?"

"Oh, they'll get him eventually. This time, though, they'll be able to put him away for murder. He's not some top-level mastermind— he's just a rich bully, and money can only get you so far. He's threatened some pretty important people. We're working with the Special Tactics Group—what used to be the Anti-Terrorist Squad— and they'll track him down. But until they do, we have to protect those he's threatened. Like I said, he didn't threaten Callie directly, but she was mentioned in the letter, so we're not taking any chances."

"Do you think he's hiding in the bushes with a rifle, or do you think he's hired a hitman?"

"I think he's probably high on drugs and alcohol somewhere worrying about picking up the soap in the shower when he's back in prison. I doubt he'll ever carry out the threats. But we'll take them seriously, of course, until he's caught."

Neve seemed happy with that, and continued briefing him on deliveries and stock takes.

"What do you do when you're not filling in here?" he asked when she'd finished.

"I'm in charge of marketing and promotion. I design our catalogues and promotional material. I've been scouting out suitable shops for Callie to approach to stock our brand. And I run lingerie parties." Her eyes gleamed.

"Parties?"

"Yeah. It's turned into quite a thing. We're having one next weekend, Saturday the thirteenth. Rowan's twin sister's having a baby shower."

"The one whose wedding you all went to dressed as the four seasons?"

"Yeah. She's hired us for the evening. She's the focus, of course, but she knows getting all her friends together is a great opportunity for us to tout our wares."

"So you bring a selection of lingerie to these parties?"

"Yeah. And other… bits and bobs."

He realized she was talking about sex toys. "Hmm, I see."

Neve's eyes widened. "Of course you'll have to come to keep an eye on Callie. You can be a waiter! We always need someone to serve the drinks."

"I'm not sure being the only man at a baby shower-come-lingerie party is my idea of a good night out. I'll be eaten alive."

"Only if you're very lucky."

They both laughed.

"There's too much fun going on out here," Callie announced, walking out of her office.

"Sorry, miss," Neve said. "Won't happen again." She leaned toward Gene and spoke in a mock whisper. "Watch out—she can be very strict when the mood takes her."

Gene knew she hadn't meant that to be as suggestive as it sounded, but it was difficult to stop his mind from straying to sex when Callie stood in front of him. He had no intention of carrying out his daydreams, but that didn't mean he couldn't let his mind wander when the mood took him. It did so now, tempting him with thoughts of her giving instructions in the bedroom. Maybe she liked tying her partners up—or being tied up. Either way sounded fun.

There were worse things than dating the CEO of a lingerie firm, he was certain. He could imagine Callie Summer modelling her range of underwear for him. He wasn't sure what would be his favorite of those he'd spotted in the catalogue—the virginal white bra and panties, the saucy red teddy, or the sexy black lace set with sheer black thigh highs. She'd look pretty damn good in any of those.

He blinked. Callie's cheeks had turned red. He'd been staring too long and, judging by the blush, she'd read something of what he was thinking in his eyes. Luckily, Neve was chattering on about something and hadn't noticed.

He raised an eyebrow.

Callie blinked rapidly and lowered her gaze. He hid a smile. She wasn't sure what to make of him. He wasn't being obvious enough that she could be sure he liked her. That was good. He was happy to keep her in the dark for a while.

In the dark. Chained to a bed. Totally at his mercy.

Suppressing the urge to roll his eyes at himself, he tidied the items on the desk into a neat pile and followed Neve's suit as she got to her feet.

"Five o'clock," Neve said. "I'm done."

Gene looked at Callie. "When do you finish?"

"I've got a few phone calls to make."

He sat back at the desk. "No worries."

"You can go," she said. "I don't expect my PA to stay on after five."

"I go when you go."

"Well I don't." Neve picked up her bag and headed off. "See ya."

"Saturday the thirteenth?" Callie called after her.

Neve stopped and turned. "Are you going to make it?"

"Yeah, of course, I wouldn't miss it for the world. Next week, we'll do the South Island, stop in Wellington for Willow's baby shower, then carry on to the North Island the following week."

"Cool. I'll see you then." Neve disappeared.

"Neve's invited me, by the way," Gene told Callie, leaning back in his chair and twirling a pen in his fingers. "To the party."

SERENITY WOODS

She perched on the edge of his desk. "Really?" A flicker of doubt crossed her face—she wasn't sure that Neve hadn't been cheeky enough to do that.

"I understand some interesting things are for sale."

"Mmm," she said, surprisingly cool. "Neve has connections with a Wellington-based company, and they supply a range of examples for her parties. Plus, she gets freebie gift packs that come in handy. It would be a nice pre-birthday treat for you." Her eyes gleamed—she'd remembered his birthday was on Valentine's Day.

She'd called his bluff, and he couldn't stop his lips curving up. She had bright blue eyes the color of a summer sky—surprise, surprise—and they lit with amusement now. This woman fascinated him. She blushed when she thought he might be thinking about sex with her, but she ran a lingerie company, and she was obviously quite open where bedroom matters were concerned.

"Sounds like fun," he said, smiling.

She chuckled. "They are. Experimentation with lingerie and... other items can be about availability. Women are often too afraid to go into sex shops and even lingerie shops because they're easily embarrassed. The idea of parties like the one next week is that they can go into a bathroom or bedroom on their own to try on the lingerie, and maybe purchase something fun they wouldn't ordinarily have the courage to if they were on their own. If your best friend's treating herself to a vibrator, you don't feel like such a floozy having a look yourself. Unless you're Rowan, who blushes scarlet at the mere mention of anything to do with sex."

Loving her open manner, he studied the way her blonde hair slid over her shoulder like melted butter poured from a jug. "You enjoy enabling women, don't you?"

"I do. It makes me feel good."

"Do you consider yourself a feminist?"

She studied him, her expression curious. "Depends what you mean by that. It's come to mean someone who thinks women are better than men, and who seeks to punish them for having a penis. In its true sense, it means someone who believes in equality for women. Culturally, economically, politically, socially... So yes. I consider myself a feminist in that way." Her eyes appraised him. "What was her name?"

"Whose name?"

"Your ex. The one who didn't like men."

He'd never felt like this before—as if he were made of glass and all his thoughts were visible whirling around in his head. Over the past few years, he'd erected a barrier around himself that very few were allowed to see behind, and it was bizarre to find it suddenly transparent.

Should he answer her? He decided to sidestep. "What makes you think I had an ex who didn't like men?"

She considered the question seriously. "Something in your eyes. Wariness, hurt. I make up stories about people in my head—it's a habit."

"So what would my story be?"

She sucked her bottom lip for a moment. "Her strength and independence attracted you in the first place. You appreciate the difficulties that women can have gaining equality, and you were proud to have a girlfriend who stood up for her sex, maybe even campaigned for women's rights. But over time, you came to resent the way she made you feel privileged, as if you should constantly apologize for being male. That's because... you come from a poor background. You've worked hard for everything you've achieved, and you've been given nothing, so you didn't appreciate being made to feel that you'd gotten to the top because you're a man. What once attracted you to her began to annoy you, and that made you feel bad because you believe in equality yourself, and yet you felt resentful that she'd gotten where she was by being a woman. It shouldn't matter. It should be irrelevant. That's true equality—everyone being on the same playing field and being judged by their talents, not their gender, color, or religion. She's the one who broke it off, but you were relieved when it happened."

He stared at her. It was so close to the truth that it gave him the shivers. But he wasn't about to admit that to her. "So how did you come up with this piece of fiction?" he asked, linking his fingers and trying to appear relaxed, even though his heart banged away against his ribs.

She laughed. "Just like your coin trick, it's not magic. You're working as a PA—clearly you believe in equality. You're respectful to women. But when someone asks a question, it can be as revealing as the answer to it. Your query about whether I consider myself a feminist and the wariness in your eyes told me you were worried I'd say yes, which means you'd met someone who'd made you uneasy about feminism. It could have been a sister, but the fact that you're a good-looking, decent guy who's still single at thirty-one suggests it was an ex."

"And the poor background?"

"That was a guess, but resentment toward her makes more sense if that was the case."

"And the fact that the ex broke up with me?"

Callie tipped her head to the side. "You seem sad, but not angry. Maybe in time, you would have left her, but she obviously sensed what was coming and took the leap first, and ultimately you were relieved she did. Although..." Her expression softened. "The sadness is deep. You used to smile a lot, but you don't so much now. Something happened to you that made you look at life differently. You have more scars inside than outside. Was that your ex? I think maybe not. It was something—or someone—else."

Her blue eyes held him captive. Neve had been right—there was something exceptional about this woman. He'd never met anyone like her. Her insightfulness stunned him, and made him uneasy in equal measure. He relied on his barriers and his aloofness—they were an exoskeleton that kept him standing upright, and if she took them away, he was sure he'd collapse to the ground in a heap.

Callie smiled, obviously aware he wasn't going to reply. "Maybe I should write detective stories."

"Maybe you should."

Chuckling, she looked down, turning his notepad toward her. He always wrote in shorthand, and the page was covered with neat lines and loops. She ran her finger across the lines. "It's so strange—it's like another language, like Arabic or Japanese, with all these symbols. What system is it?"

"Teeline."

"I think Becky uses Pitman."

"Pitman is one of the oldest systems. In the US, they tend to use Gregg. New Zealand journalists are taught Teeline, though, and it's the recommended system for the National Council for the Training of Journalists, which is why I use it."

"Write my name for me."

He picked up a pen and did so, a small 'c' with a long 'l' and a little line for the 'ee' sound at the end. Then a tiny circle for the 's', followed by a long arc for the 'mer' sound. "Callie Summer," he said.

She ran her finger across it. "Nice."

While she studied it, his gaze caressed her face, then moved down her neck to the top of her blouse. All the buttons were done up and there was no sign of her bra, but even so, the triangle of pale skin revealed by the V at the top sent his heart racing again.

"I'll finish my calls," she said, getting up. "Then we can go home."

"Yes, ma'am."

She gave him a wry look and disappeared into her office.

Gene watched her go, conscious that his lips were curving in a smile. *Men find her fascinating*, Neve had said, and he could understand why now. She was warm, funny, clever, and sexy, and in any other circumstances, he might have considered asking her out.

But that wasn't appropriate here. He dropped his gaze to his notepad. Picking up his pen, in shorthand he wrote, *Stay focused*. Neve was right—he couldn't afford to become embroiled with Callie. His job was to protect the CEO of the Four Seasons, and he had to concentrate on that and push all other thoughts to the back of his mind.

Chapter Five

Gene spent half an hour typing up the notes he'd taken from Neve during the day. By five thirty, Callie had finished her phone calls and announced she was going home.

"I'll walk you to your car," Gene said. He stood and slipped on his jacket.

She locked her office door. "That's not necessary."

"I know. But I'm a gentleman." He put the computer to sleep and made sure the desk was tidy, then slid his notepad into his pocket. "Come on."

"By the way," she said as they walked down the stairs, "you don't have to wear a suit to work every day. We don't get a lot of visitors, and as you know, we're all about comfort. And of course we'll be travelling next week."

"Thanks," he said, although he would continue to wear the suit so he wouldn't look odd in his bulletproof waistcoat.

Bridget had just closed the shop and was in the process of tallying up. "Great day," she said as they entered the back door of the shop. "Having that Valentine's Day promotion in the window has brought loads of guys in."

"Excellent!" Callie beamed.

"That's Neve for you," Bridget said. "She has all the best ideas."

"Yes, but you put the display together, Birdie." Callie gestured at the window. "It's amazing."

Gene had noticed it when he'd arrived for his interview. "I have to agree," he said. Letters pasted across the top of the window read, *Buy the lady in your life a present you'll both appreciate*. Bridget—blonde, pretty, curvy, and bubbly—had arranged one completely bare male mannequin standing behind a female one, her head turned a fraction as if she were watching his hand as it slipped the ribbon strap of her lacy nightie off her shoulder. It was such a simple pose, but a suggestive, sexy one, and customers had obviously thought so too.

"We've sold heaps of that red lacy nightie," Bridget said. "Twice as many as the black one, which surprised me, and hardly any white. I guess men don't think the virginal look is in vogue at the moment."

They both glanced at him expectantly, as if asking his opinion. He gave a lazy shrug. *I like them all.* He couldn't deny to himself, though, that the thought of Callie in a white lacy bra and panties didn't turn him on.

Callie laughed. "We're off. See you tomorrow."

"Have a good evening." Bridget waved them goodnight.

They stepped out into the warm February sunshine and walked around the corner of the block to the car park.

"Which is yours?" Gene asked, although he knew it was the red Mazda parked against the fence.

She pointed it out, and he walked her over to it. "Thank you," she said, with a little wryness to her voice as if to say, *I could have done that perfectly well on my own, thank you.*

"You're welcome." He remembered that he wasn't supposed to know that her boyfriend had cheated on her not that long ago. "Busy evening planned?"

She unlocked the car door and paused. "Not really. I have a bit of work to finish, then I'll have dinner. Maybe go out for a walk before watching *Game of Thrones*." She smiled.

He fought the urge to ask her to stay indoors. "What time will your husband be home?"

Lifting a hand, she waggled her ring finger at him. "Not married."

"Partner?"

"Nope."

"Kids?"

"Nope."

"Boyfriend?"

She smiled, and he realized he was copying the questions she'd asked him in the office. "No," she said softly. "No boyfriend. And quite happy being single, thank you very much."

"Fair enough."

"What are you up to?" she asked. "Going out?"

"Maybe to the gym. Then a quiet evening. See you tomorrow?"

"Eight thirty sharp."

"Yes, ma'am."

She rolled her eyes and got in the car.

Gene walked over to his Holden and got in. He watched her exit the car park, and saw Ian's car pull out a few seconds later to follow her home. Ian would shadow her when she went out for her walk, and would sit outside the house she shared with Rowan while she ate dinner, watched TV, and slept.

Gene's hands tightened on the steering wheel. He hadn't been completely honest with Neve when he'd described the guy who'd sent the letters to Phoebe. He hadn't wanted Neve to worry, so he'd played down the danger, but the truth was that Darren Kirk wasn't the emptyheaded, unfocused maniac Gene had said he was. He was a cool, calm psychopath who'd had the connections and the money to escape the life sentence he should have gotten. The worst part of it was that the man he'd killed just days after being released was the lawyer who hadn't been able to prevent Kirk from going to prison, and his wife—who'd been with him—had been seriously injured.

After that, the Special Tactics Group had taken the death threats very seriously. They'd wanted to take Phoebe and her daughter somewhere safe until they tracked Kirk down, but Callie had refused—why, Gene wasn't quite sure, possibly because Phoebe had downplayed the threat so as not to alarm her too much and so therefore she hadn't taken it seriously. Phoebe had defended her daughter's right not to have security, but had agreed privately with the STG to hire Gene's firm and have a permanent watch on both herself and Callie.

Gene had read the dossier on Kirk, and the thought of the cold killer coming after the soft and sensual Callie Summer made him feel ill. Almost certainly, it had been an empty threat meant to frighten the prosecutor who'd put Kirk away, but Gene wanted to drive to Callie's house and sit outside there himself. To stay by her side and protect her until the man was caught.

But that was impractical, and besides, she was just another customer. She was nothing special, not a friend or family member, and certainly not a love interest. He had a job to do, and he had to concentrate on that and keep his emotions out of it.

With that in mind, he had things to do before he was able to call it a day. First, he drove to his house on Massey Road, high on a hill overlooking the harbor. The wind was getting up and had whipped the blue-gray water into choppy waves that made the outgoing ferry bob about like a piece of polystyrene. No wonder it was nicknamed the Vomit Comet, he thought, feeling a little queasy just looking at it.

He went inside and changed out of his suit into a T-shirt and sweatpants, then drove to the gym. He'd only planned to have a quick workout, but while he moved through the various pieces of equipment, his mind began to wander. Unfortunately, it seemed to want to conjure up images of a certain strawberry blonde in various pieces of lingerie, and, cross with himself, he pushed his body harder and longer until he was limp as a beaten chicken breast and dripping with sweat.

He showered and changed again, annoyed with himself for getting carried away. Although he liked to stretch the muscles around his damaged hip and keep it flexible, he'd pushed it too hard, and it ached now, a dull throb deep inside. He popped two Panadol, drove home, fought the urge to pick up takeout on the way, and made himself pasta with a large salad, which he ate sitting at the table as he checked his emails.

He scrolled through the daily report the office had sent him of comings and goings around Callie's office—nothing suspicious, from the looks of it—then checked the report from Phoebe's security team. One operative had recorded that she'd seen a dark-haired, bearded man out in front of Phoebe's home in Wellington not once but twice, several hours apart. He'd only stayed thirty seconds the first time and twenty seconds the next, but she'd highlighted it as a yellow alert, and Gene copied the photo she'd taken of him from her parked car and sent it to all his teams and their contact at the STG so they could watch out for possible sightings of the guy.

Still eating his pasta, he took out the notepad he'd used during the day and flipped to the pages where he'd made notes during lunch about Callie's office and her general routine. He typed them up, mentally running through possible problems in his head, planning out the best route to take if an incident occurred, thinking about ways he might be able to improve security there without her noticing.

Then he started up a new file called "Security on Tour." After staring at the title for a while, he pushed away from the table, took a beer out of the fridge, and went outside onto the deck. Easing into his favorite deckchair with his sore hip, he took a long swig of the beer and stared out to sea.

Working as a personal protection officer often involved lots of tedious, dull work—from surveillance to intelligence gathering to threat recognition and assessment. Facts and data were important, and as it was easy to miss little details in a sea of information, it required a keen eye and constant concentration to make sure nothing important was overlooked.

But it also involved a large percentage of instinct. In his days in the Army, and then in security, Gene had learned to rely on his gut feelings, and now they were telling him that the real threat to Callie—if there were to be one—would come when they were out on the road. It would be harder for whoever was following them to keep track of them, but it would be a lot easier for a hitman to get close to her. Unless Gene revealed his mission, and possibly even if he did, he couldn't stop her shopping, eating at restaurants, or going out for walks late at night. All he could do was remain as vigilant as possible, and do his best to protect her when they were together.

In the pocket of his jeans, his phone rang. He pulled it out and checked the screen, expecting it to be someone from his office, then smiled when he saw the name of his best mate.

"Hey, Felix." He lay back in the deckchair, one arm tucked under his head. "How's things?"

"Hey, Gene. Yeah, all good here, thanks."

"Finally got back to work?" Gene liked to tease his lawyer friend about his extra-long summer break. Felix worked at the biggest law firm in Wellington, and, like many firms in New Zealand, they closed for several weeks over Christmas and January.

"Only just. Apparently some companies make you go back to work before February. It's shocking."

Gene laughed. "What's up?"

"Thought I'd share some news with you. Coco's pregnant."

"Ah, mate." Gene was genuinely pleased for his friend. Felix had married the head secretary of his law firm the previous year, and he'd mentioned that they'd decided to try for a family straight away. "That's wonderful news."

"Yeah, we're pleased. It took a while, and there's always that niggling thought in the back of your mind that you're not going to be able to have kids, you know? So it's a relief."

"When's it due?"

"She's just three months, so July."

"Great. I bet she's happy."

"A mixture of nervous and excited, yeah." Felix chuckled. "Anyway, how did it go today?" Gene had told him about his undercover mission.

"Well, she agreed to take me on, so that's the first step done. She's touring the country starting Monday, so I'll be away for a couple of weeks."

"What's she like? As bad as her mother made out?"

Gene watched a ferry heading toward the harbor, the sea behind it glinting in the evening sunshine, the color of Callie's eyes. "Ah, no. Not really. She's nice. Young. Smart. Funny."

Felix said nothing for a moment. Then he said, "I see." Gene could almost hear the smirk behind the words.

"Don't start," he said wryly.

"And she works for a lingerie firm? Does she get to try out some free samples?"

Gene decided not to tell him about Neve's parties. "Honestly, I don't know what I'm going to do. I'm her personal protection officer—that means I have to be glued to her side for the next three months. It's going to be torture."

"Oh..." Felix drew the word out. "You really do like her. I was teasing before."

"There's nothing not to like. She's gorgeous. It's going to be like the Temptation of St. Anthony. Except my name's not Anthony. And I'm no saint."

"Now ain't that the truth."

"Felix..."

"I don't see the problem."

"The problem is that I have a job to do. I can't afford to get distracted."

"Surely it'll be easier to protect her if you're... you know, sleeping in the same bed?"

"Jeez."

"Look, I can't remember the last time I heard you talk about a girl with a smile in your voice. Why not have a bit of fun over the summer?"

Gene couldn't stop himself smiling at that. "That happens to be her surname."

"Summer?"

"Yeah."

"Well there you go. It's a sign. You're heading north next week, aren't you?"

"Yeah, south first, then north after my birthday."

"It's fucking hot in the Northland. Toby says it's been hot and sultry for weeks. Sounds like a bit of *Summer* seduction is on the cards."

"I can't."

"Yeah." Felix snorted. "That sounded real convincing." Someone called in the background, and Felix said, "Coco's ready and we're going out. Got to go. Speak later. Let me know how you get on."

"I don't..." But it was too late. Felix had hung up.

Gene blew out a breath and slipped the phone back into his pocket. He'd only known Callie for an afternoon. She might be completely different when he got to know her properly, when he was with her day in, day out. She might irritate him by talking all the time. Perhaps she was untidy, or hated the music he liked, or refused to eat unusual food. There were a million reasons why he might not find her attractive.

He thought about the V of her blouse, and the pale skin that had tempted his gaze to search out what he was certain would be a lacy bra beneath her top. Closing his eyes, he groaned. This whole mission had disaster written all over it.

But that was just it—disaster wasn't just a broken heart or hurt feelings. In his line of work, disaster meant injury or even death. Darren Kirk was a menace in the shadows, a man out for vengeance, who didn't care if innocents got hurt along the way. He was a real threat, and Gene had to stay sharp. He couldn't afford to think with his dick for the next few weeks.

Seducing Summer was definitely off the cards.

Chapter Six

"Coffee, ma'am?"

Callie smiled at the flight attendant. "Yes, please. With milk and sugar, thanks."

She glanced at Gene, sitting in the seat next to her, daring him with her eyes to say something about how pernickety she was with her coffee, but although he raised his eyebrows at her, he didn't say anything.

It was Monday morning, and they were on a flight to Dunedin, at the bottom of the South Island of New Zealand, about to start their tour of the country.

Friday had been busy, filled with finalizing their plans, as well as tying up any loose ends with the business before she left. To be fair, Gene had been invaluable. As he'd promised, he was efficient and organized, and he'd dealt with a couple of last-minute emergencies calmly, a perfect PA.

She still found him a little unnerving, though. In some ways, he was easy to read, and his reaction to her Holmesian deductions had told her she hadn't been far from the mark. He seemed to respect her business and her role in it. But on a more personal level, she wasn't sure what he thought of her. Occasionally, a look glimmered in his eyes like the flash of a coin on a riverbed—quite what it was, she couldn't be sure. Admiration? Desire? And for a brief moment, she'd think maybe he liked her.

But then his seriousness would wash it away, and his eyes would appraise her coolly, the shutters coming down to shelter him from her searching gaze. When he was like that, he had a way of looking at her that made her think he found her foolish. He was only thirty-one—okay, nearly thirty-two—and she was twenty-six, so hardly a kid, but sometimes she felt the way Emma must have felt when Mr. Knightley scolded her for being rude to Miss Bates.

He was doing it now, because she'd accepted the cup of coffee, lowered it onto her tray, and then promptly knocked it as she opened the stick of sugar, spilling a quarter of the liquid.

"Give me your serviette," she said crossly.

"Would you like a bib, too?"

"Because you never make a mistake, Mr. Perfect."

He chuckled and handed her his serviette, and, adding it to her own, she mopped up the mess.

"Don't look at me like that." She cleaned the last few drips, conscious of his gaze on her.

"Like what?"

"Like I'm your brother's toddler you're supposed to look after who's embarrassing you in public. I'm a grown woman who runs a business, thank you very much. I'm not hopeless."

"Hmm."

She decided to ignore that. "Well, now we're finally alone, you'll have to tell me some more about yourself."

"Will I?"

"Yes. We can't go the whole trip without talking."

"That's a shame."

"Gene…"

He sighed. "What do you want to know?"

"Tell me about your family."

"Parents still alive, one brother."

She waited for more. When more obviously wasn't coming, she nudged him with her elbow. "Come on."

"What?"

"Jeez. It's like getting blood out of a stone. Where do your parents live?"

"In Wellington."

"Brother younger or older than you?"

"Younger."

"What's his name?"

"Freddie."

"As in Mercury?"

"As in Fred Astaire and Gene Kelly. Mum's a big fan of old Hollywood musicals."

At last, she was getting somewhere. "What does he do? Did he go into the Army too?"

Immediately, the shutters came down again, his smile fading and his tone turning clipped. "No. He's an accountant."

Hmm, he didn't like talking about the Army. Was it because of his injury, or something else that happened there?

She couldn't ask him yet—he'd just clam up. Instead, she'd have to steer the conversation to other things if she wanted to get him to talk. "You never did answer me when I asked you what her name was. The ex who was a strident feminist."

"No, I didn't." He sipped his coffee. Clearly, he didn't want to talk about her, either.

His reticence was frustrating, but it also told her more about him. People had reasons for not wanting to divulge details about themselves. Opening up, even a little, made people vulnerable. It exposed them to criticism and comment, to being judged, and to being hurt. Something had happened to Gene in the past. He'd been terribly hurt, maybe more than once, and because of that he'd sealed himself in a concrete shell that he was determined not to let anyone breach.

He pulled his iPad out of the pocket in front of him, apparently determined to shut her out.

She turned toward him in her seat. There was something so intimate about plane journeys. His upper arm and thigh pressed against hers. She could smell his aftershave, and see how neat his sideburns were up close, carefully shaved into a small rectangle to the base of his ear. His jaw was clean shaven. He had a small mole on his neck just below his earlobe. She wished she was brave enough to lean forward and kiss it.

"I've just thought," she said, "I forgot to arrange a car in Dunedin."

"I did it. Don't worry."

"Oh. Thanks." She watched him for a moment. "What are you reading?" she asked.

"A thriller."

"By whom?"

He sighed. "John Grisham."

"I love Grisham. I read *The Runaway Jury* and got hooked after that."

"Yeah, I liked the theme of that one, stitching up the tobacco firm."

"Do you mainly read thrillers?"

"Mostly, but I'll read anything."

"I like psychological thrillers, mainly." She watched him lower the iPad to his lap, but didn't comment. "And detective stories. Things I have to puzzle out."

"That makes sense. I bet you love Sherlock Holmes." He smiled.

"I do! Conan Doyle rules. And I love Cumberbatch's portrayal of him. Have you seen the *Sherlock* series?"

"I have. All of them. And the movies." He tucked his iPad back into the pocket of the seat.

So, he was comfortable talking about some of his interests. "I'd die without my TV," she admitted. "I don't sit in front of it all the time, but I do love movies and series especially. I've been watching *Game of Thrones*, and *Mad Men*, and a Danish thriller called *The Bridge*."

"I've seen it. Thought it was brilliant."

They continued to talk for a while about movies and series, then moved on to music. He didn't volunteer much about himself and she had to pry most of it out of him, but it was a start, anyway.

They stopped while the flight attendant topped up their coffee cups, and they each accepted a cookie in a packet.

"So why are you single?" Gene asked out of the blue. He opened his packet and took a bite out of the cookie.

"Oh, so you won't tell me anything about yourself, but I'm supposed to tell you my life story?"

He grinned, apparently having warmed up a little after their conversation. "Fair enough."

"Ah, well, the difference between us is that I don't mind revealing a little of myself."

His eyebrows rose.

"I meant I don't mind revealing some details about my life. I'm not about to strip for you on the plane."

"I didn't say a word."

"You didn't have to." She suppressed an inner shiver at the mischievous smile that curved his lips for a moment. Beneath the somber exterior was a rather naughty man, she was beginning to suspect. What fun. It would be interesting to see if he made more of an appearance over the next few weeks.

She nibbled at her cookie. "I was living with a guy up until about four months ago."

"Oh?"

"His name's Jamie. He works at Te Papa—he's a historian, and he acquires artifacts for the museum."

"Sounds like a good job."

"Yeah. We dated for a few years, then finally decided to move in together at the beginning of last year. I thought it was going well, and then..."

Suddenly, the cookie stuck in her throat, and she had trouble swallowing. Why was she telling Gene about this? She didn't like talking about Jamie to anyone, not even Neve and the others, although maybe that was worse because they'd known him. Their comments when she'd broken up with him had told her that they had seen right through him in a way she'd been blind to while she was living with him.

She'd finished her coffee, and so she accepted Gene's cup gratefully when he held it out to her, and drank until she'd dislodged the lump in her throat.

"Sorry." She handed him back the cup. "I keep thinking I'm over him, and then I realize I'm not quite there yet."

She waited for him to say, *You don't have to talk about it if you don't want to*, or something similar to put her off showing emotion, because he didn't seem like the kind of guy who'd be comfortable with a blubbering girl.

"What happened?" he asked. He frowned, concerned, and his eyes were gentle. He wouldn't make fun of her.

"I came home early from work one day and found him in bed with his secretary."

"Fuck."

"Yeah. It would have been shocking even if we hadn't been getting on, but I hadn't suspected anything at all. I thought we were doing well, that he loved me. I was half-expecting him to propose." Shame filled her, and she concentrated on lifting her tray and fixing it with the latch to the seat in front. "I felt such an idiot. Still do."

Tears pricked her eyes, and her throat tightened again. She clenched her jaw. She wasn't going to cry, not on the plane, not in front of Gene, not ever again about Jamie.

They fell quiet for a moment while she struggled with her emotion. Music was playing in the plane, mixed with the hum of conversation, but she felt as if the two of them were in a bubble, isolated from everyone else. Gene's quiet manner was oddly soothing, like Aloe vera for her soul.

After a while, he shifted in his seat. "Angela," he said.

"What?"

"That was her name. My ex."

Callie held her breath for a moment. She sensed this was very unusual for him, to talk about himself. "Oh."

"I met her about a year after I came out of the Army. We lived together for a few years. But... it didn't work out."

"Why not?" she prodded gently.

He swirled what was left of his coffee in his cup. "She felt I wasn't fully committed to the relationship."

"Did you cheat on her?"

He looked startled. "No! Of course not." He blinked a few times, the hard look in his eyes disappearing, as if he'd realized that although the accusation might have sounded insulting, Callie's experience had led her to jump to that conclusion. "I wouldn't do that," he said.

She was certain that this upright, honorable soldier wouldn't, but then she'd been wrong before, and no longer felt she could trust her own judgement where men were concerned. "So why did she think you weren't fully committed?"

"Women like to talk," he said, and smiled. "And I was worse than I am now."

"Wow."

"Yeah. She felt I was hiding something."

"Were you?"

He hesitated. "I wasn't keeping terrible, dark secrets from her. But I didn't see why I had to explain every thought that passed through my head. Some memories, or feelings, are private, upsetting, or traumatic. Why should I want to share those?"

"If you didn't want to, it's a shame she pushed you. Everyone is entitled to their privacy. But it's a natural fear that if your partner's keeping quiet, he or she is hiding something."

"I guess."

"So you broke up?"

"I could feel the relationship crumbling around me like a Roman wall. I didn't want to break up with her, but I couldn't seem to do anything about it. I couldn't be what she wanted. Eventually, she said it was over and moved out." He sipped his coffee.

"Do you see a therapist?" Callie asked.

His eyebrows lifted. "About Angela?"

"About the war. About what happened to you." She gestured at his hip. Most of the time, his limp was unnoticeable, but occasionally he moved stiffly, as though it pained him.

"No," he said. "And I don't want to."

"Fair enough. But sometimes shining a light in those deep recesses of the mind can banish the shadows. Fears are like mushrooms— they only grow in the dark."

His lips curved up. They studied each other for a moment.

"I'm sorry your ex cheated on you," he said. "I don't even know the guy and I want to smash his face in."

"Aw. Thanks." She liked his protective streak. Kind of like a big brother.

Except she was certain that if he was her brother, she wouldn't be thinking about kissing him all the time. The more she was with this guy, the more she liked him. How was she going to cope spending two weeks with him glued to her side?

The flight attendant was coming toward them to collect their rubbish, so she gathered her cup and serviettes and sugar packets together, then promptly dropped them, scattering grains of sugar across her skirt.

"Jeez." She scrambled to pick them up.

"Are you normally this clumsy?" he asked, amused, before raising his coffee cup to his lips to drain it.

"It's probably orgasm deprivation," she said with exasperation. "It's making me jittery."

Gene coughed into his coffee cup, spilling some of it over his hand.

"Want a bib?" she said.

He wiped his bottom lip and then his hand, checked that the person sitting beside him was still wearing his earphones, and glanced at her. "Do you always say what's on your mind?"

"Do you ever say what's on yours?"

He grinned, his eyes crinkling at the edges, and Callie melted a little. He was opening up to her, a bit, revealing a glimmer of the man inside, like cracking open a chest at the bottom of the ocean and seeing the glint of gold doubloons in the dark. She couldn't wait to see what other treasure lay within.

Chapter Seven

Dunedin was cooler than Wellington, although the cloud-free sky shone a brilliant blue. After arriving at the airport, they collected their bags and picked up the hire car, a blue Toyota Corolla that Gene was relieved was comfortable to drive, as they wouldn't be giving it back until they reached Wellington, nearly four hundred miles away. He'd booked it on Friday, because Becky had made a note that Callie would forget, which indeed she had.

They were going to spend a night in Dunedin, then drive up the coast via Oamaru, Timaru, and Ashburton to Christchurch, checking out the high street stores on the way. At Christchurch, they would stay two nights because Callie had hopes that a few shops would stock their brand there. After that, they were going to drive through Kaikoura, where people went to see the whales and dolphins, to Blenheim, center of the South Island's wine country, and then the sunny town of Nelson, before returning to Wellington for Willow's baby shower. The following week, they would head north and tour the major cities of the North Island until they reached Kerikeri in the Bay of Islands, where they'd fly back down.

"I feel knackered already." Gene glanced at the map of New Zealand on Callie's knees as he took State Highway One to Dunedin town center, noting the marked route across the country and all the circled towns, presumably organized by Becky.

"Don't worry, I have plenty of stamina. I can keep going for hours."

He raised his gaze to her face, but she was concentrating on the map. Had she meant that to sound as suggestive as it had sounded? Or was it just his sex-starved brain trying desperately to join the dots?

He looked back at the road, stifling a sigh. He should have insisted to Phoebe that one of his operatives take his place. The next few weeks were going to be torture, and not only because every time he looked at Callie, he wanted to kiss her. There was something about her that managed to cajole details out of him, like wheedling a whelk out of its shell. Normally, he never revealed details about himself to a client, but it seemed rude not to answer her questions. And she had an uncanny ability to analyze everything that came out of his mouth. How he said things, and even what he didn't say, seemed to tell her as much about him as the actual words, which was rather unnerving. But the main problem was definitely going to be the fact that he found her attractive.

Okay, so that was a massive understatement. Callie Summer was like a cool glass of lager on a hot day, or a fillet steak when a guy was really, really hungry. It was all he could do not to salivate when he looked at her. From her shiny blonde hair that always looked just-washed, to her generous breasts he was desperate to weigh in his palms, to her wide blue eyes that gave him the shivers, to the plump lips he wanted to kiss to see whether they were as soft as they looked… He'd not met a woman for a long time that he hungered for so badly, and that he couldn't have.

It was the story of his life. He felt as if everything he'd ever wanted had been placed on too high a shelf, just out of reach.

The therapist he'd seen when he first came out of the Army had told him he set his sights too high, which was why he was always disappointed. *Am I asking for the moon?* he'd snapped at her. What did he want that was so incredibly ambitious? Some would say that a father's approval, a mother to love him, a supportive brother, a partner who loved him the way he was, a career that didn't end in near death, and friends who managed to reach the age of forty wasn't particularly ambitious.

Or maybe it was. Many people weren't lucky enough to have all those things, he was sure. But he couldn't stop wanting them, even if he was shooting for the stars.

He gripped hold of the steering wheel and glared at the road. He wasn't going to think about the past now, about all the things he'd lost. And he wasn't going to let a surge of hormones deter him from his task. He was a grown man, not a teenage boy. Desire was all in the mind, and God knew he'd learned to deal with not thinking about certain things for a while now. He'd trained his brain to sidestep memories and triggers that evoked emotions he no longer wished to feel. He could damned well add lust to the list and put thoughts of Callie Summer to the attic of his mind in a dusty old chest where they belonged.

"Have you been to Dunedin before?" Callie's gentle voice stirred him from his dark thoughts.

He glanced at her. She was watching him, and something in her eyes told him she was perfectly aware of the gloomy path he'd been heading toward, and she was attempting to distract him away from it.

Half of him resented her for being so astute—it was intrusive, and he didn't like being so transparent. But the other half felt a surprising lift of heart at the fact that she'd noticed but had been nice enough not to ask him directly about what was bothering him, because she knew he didn't like to talk about himself.

Forcing himself to loosen his grip on the wheel, he took a deep breath and released it slowly before answering. "Yes, a few years ago, though." He'd done the training course to become a protection officer there. "You?"

"Once, although the same as you, many years ago. I'm looking forward to it. I mean, I know we won't get to see much of the city in one day, but even the road in is gorgeous."

Her eyes were alight with excitement, and warmth spread through him at her enthusiasm. She had such a ready smile. It had upset him when she'd talked about her ex and had gotten all emotional. He hadn't found out as much as he'd hoped because he'd distracted her by talking about himself. Did she still see the guy? Did she still have feelings for him? He wanted to know, but now wasn't the time to bring it up.

He also found it strange that she seemed so unaffected by the fact that she'd had death threats. Clearly, she hadn't taken them seriously, and that wasn't good, because it meant she might take unnecessary risks and put herself in danger. He would have to work hard to ensure that didn't happen.

"So what's the plan?" Callie asked.

Becky had stated on her instructions that he would have to arrange their itinerary, because otherwise Callie wouldn't allow them enough time to get from one appointment to another, and she'd forget about lunch, and then suddenly realize they didn't have a hotel room booked for the night.

He glanced at the clock on the dashboard. "It's nearly eleven thirty. We'll head straight to the first appointment with Hollywell's at twelve. You said each one will probably take around thirty minutes, but I've allowed plenty of time so you don't get stressed if one runs over. After Hollywell's, we'll probably catch some lunch, then go to Fernz for appointment number two at two thirty. We can check in at the hotel and leave our bags there afterward, and head off for Lingerie Plus at three thirty. Onto JimJam's at four thirty. Then we're done, so we can return to the hotel for the evening."

"Wow. I'm impressed."

"Army life," he said. "Forces you to get organized."

"Forces. Nice pun." She grinned.

He smiled. They were in the city center now. Following the GPS, he took the road to the first high street store, turned off the State Highway into Stuart Street, and headed for the Octagon. "Well, I hope I've planned it all okay."

"Gene, whatever happens, you'll have done a hundred times better than I would have done."

"Why are you so disorganized?"

"I've worked very hard to maintain this level of incompetence, I'll have you know."

"It makes things much easier when everything's in order."

"Sir, yes sir." She saluted him.

He rolled his eyes. "Whatever."

She turned her gaze out of the window. "I don't like having my life planned out. Where's the fun in that?"

"So what would you have done if we'd landed here and you'd forgotten to book a car?"

"One of the firms would have had a spare one somewhere."

"And if they hadn't?"

"I'd have gotten a taxi. Or hitched. Come on, don't you think there's some excitement in not knowing what's going to happen?" She turned her bright gaze back to him.

"I don't know. There's not a lot of room for impulsiveness in my world." That was an understatement, to say the least. Being in the Army and then working in security meant that his life had revolved around timetables and structure for longer than he cared to remember. In his world, trains always ran on time, meetings occurred dead on the hour, and he was never, ever late. And he liked it that way. Not knowing what was going to happen made him uneasy and edgy.

"How dull." Her lips twitched.

"I am dull. Very boring and predictable." He turned into Princes Street and began looking for the store.

"Hmm. We'll have to see what we can do to loosen you up."

He glanced across at her. The look in her eyes sent a shiver running down his back as if she'd dropped an ice cube there.

"Don't even think about it," he warned before he could think better of it. As soon as the words were out of his mouth, he realized he'd opened a can of very wriggly worms.

Her smile widened. "Is that a challenge?"

"Fuck, no. I meant..." What had he meant? His brain scrambled like cooked eggs at the suggestive look in her eyes. He was only barely keeping this together by repeatedly telling himself it was a bad idea to get involved with her, and that if he kept his cool, she would never be aware of his interest. What the fuck was he going to do if she started coming on to him?

Her smile faded. "There's no need to look so alarmed. I'm not a bunny boiler. I'm teasing you, that's all."

But he could see the hurt in her eyes. She thought he didn't find her attractive.

Jeez.

"Callie..." His words trailed off as he saw the sign for Hollywell's clothing store ahead. He concentrated on the road for a moment, turning the car into a car park and finding a spot. He switched off the engine, then turned to face her.

"You don't have to say anything. I was teasing," she said, a little flatly.

Hating that he'd unerringly knocked her confidence after her recent rejection by her ex, Gene met her eyes, and their gazes locked. Heat rushed through him. There was something so intimate about being in a car with someone. Her right knee in the cherry-colored skirt was only an inch from his left, and her light, flowery perfume filled the car. Every time he inhaled, he was breathing her in, until she was part of his system, rushing around his body with his hot, hungry blood.

I was teasing, she'd stated.

"Were you?" he said before he could stop himself.

Her gaze remained locked on his, and she must have seen the desire there, because her lips lifted up, and she gave a tiny, sexy shrug of her shoulders. *Maybe.*

He wanted to kiss her... God, he wanted to kiss her. She moistened her lips with the tip of her tongue, and his erection sprang to life. It would be the easiest thing in the world to slip a hand behind her head, lean forward, and press his lips to hers. He wanted to wrap his arm around her and pull her to him, lift her onto his lap, and feel her soft body against his. Cup her breast in the thin blouse she was wearing and feel the heat and weight in his palm. Her arms would slip around him, her hands searching beneath his shirt to find his warm skin. He wanted to get naked with this woman, and find out if she was as fun in bed as he suspected.

At that moment, Neve's warning rang in his head, and he swallowed hard. "Callie, we can't get involved. I have to stay professional." Once again, though, as soon as he'd spoken, he knew she'd read between the lines and deduce that he wanted her.

Her gaze rested on his lips—she was thinking about kissing him too. Her eyelids lowered to half-mast, her expression turning hot and sultry. "I don't see why the agency has to find out."

The agency? He realized she was talking about his role as PA. For a brief moment, he'd forgotten about his cover story.

Cold sluiced through him, dampening his ardor. What was he doing? Phoebe Hawke had placed her daughter's life in his hands. What the hell was wrong with him? Why couldn't he focus on the job?

"That's not the point," he said. He tore his gaze away and yanked the keys out of the ignition. "It's about integrity—it's nothing to do with the agency, although I can't imagine they would approve of their staff performing personal services for their employers."

He'd meant the comment to insinuate that if anything happened between them while she was employing him, it would verge on her paying him for sex. He'd meant it to be insulting, half hoping and half dreading the way the sparkle in her eyes would fade and her lips would straighten and thin.

They didn't, though. Instead, she just laughed. "Personal services? I'm going to have to put that in my employees' contracts."

"Callie..."

"Oh, relax," she scolded, collecting her handbag. "You're far too uptight. Someone needs to loosen your laces." She turned and got out of the car.

Gene grumbled beneath his breath. He couldn't imagine anything more delightful than his laces being loosened at that moment. But it wasn't going to happen anytime soon, and when it did, Callie Summer certainly wouldn't be the one to do it.

Chapter Eight

The meeting at Hollywell's didn't go as well as Callie had hoped.

After she'd walked out of the store manager's office, she stopped at the ladies', went to the loo, then stared at herself in the mirror as she washed her hands.

"You only have yourself to blame." Her too-loud voice rang through the small bathroom. Thankfully, the other cubicles were empty.

She lowered her gaze to the basin, seeing her knuckles white where she'd clutched hold of the ceramic edge, and she forced herself to relax her grip. It wasn't the end of the world. She was long past blaming herself for every little thing that went wrong in her life. It wasn't her fault that she'd been distracted by Gene's brooding blue eyes and his deep, sexy voice.

I was teasing.

Were you?

His words bloomed in her head like beautiful roses. It wasn't even a sentence, and yet just that fraction of a phrase told her he found her attractive.

She was flattered, and couldn't stop a glow spreading through her, but that didn't mean anything would happen. Clearly, he was determined to remain aloof, and although she was sure it would be fun to keep teasing him, she didn't want to make a fool of herself.

She slid her hands beneath the dryer and turned them in the hot air. She'd be an idiot if she let a glint of sexual attraction ruin the tour she'd planned all year. The success of Four Seasons depended almost singlehandedly on her. That wasn't an egotistical way of looking at things—it was fact. Rowan was an exceptional designer, but she had zero business sense and, if she'd been left to her own devices, would still have been designing dresses for her dolls. Bridget was great at running the shop, but had no vision in terms of expanding the business. Neve had some brilliant promotional ideas, but they tended to be just that—ideas rather than practical applications.

It was Callie who had the business degree, the personal skills, and the ambition to make the business more than the one shop making a profit just large enough to keep them all above the breadline. She wasn't expecting to surpass Victoria's Secret or Triumph or Berlei, but she didn't see why Four Seasons couldn't become one of the best brands in New Zealand and possibly Australia, and she knew Rowan's designs were pretty enough to expand even beyond that.

Besides, life would be dull if she saw the limits of their shop as the outskirts of Wellington. She might open shops in a dozen New Zealand towns and half of them might fail, but so what? Better to have tried and failed than never to have tried at all.

The same could be said about her personal life, she thought as she opened her handbag, took out her lipstick, and applied a new coat. She didn't wish she'd never met Jamie. She did wish she'd noticed the signs that he was cheating on her before she'd walked in on him in bed, because the image of the skinny brunette sitting astride him, her hair tumbling down her back as his hips thrust up into her, had seared itself onto Callie's brain and refused to come off, even though she'd done the mental equivalent of scrubbing the inside of her skull with a scouring pad. But although he'd hurt her terribly, she couldn't wish they'd never gotten together. She'd tried a long-term relationship and she'd failed, but that was okay. It didn't mean the next one wouldn't work.

When she was a child, her mother had shown her how to color a page with wax crayons, in any patterns, using every color in the box. Then she'd told Callie to go over the whole page with thick black paint. Puzzled, Callie had done so, even more confused when her mother had given her a cocktail stick and told her to draw something on the black page. She'd carefully drawn a star, and had then stared in delight at the rainbow colors that had appeared through the black paint.

Being with Gene was kind of like that, his desire showing occasionally through his reservation, giving her the same feeling she'd had the day she'd seen the rainbow star through the black. If she scratched the surface, she knew she would find a passionate man beneath his tight control. He wanted her—she could see it in his eyes, and part of her was tempted to see if she could indeed loosen his laces and find out what he was like when he relaxed.

But it was a stupid idea, because she'd get distracted, and she wouldn't forgive herself if she blew the whole tour because she wanted to get her leg over. She'd only have the one chance to approach these shops, and she had to concentrate when she had these appointments and stop thinking about Gene Bond and his license to thrill.

Leaving the bathroom, she walked along the corridor and paused in the doorway to the reception area. He sat in one of the comfy chairs, reading a magazine. She'd told him to go and find a coffee shop, but he'd insisted on waiting for her. She'd been lucky he'd not demanded to go into the ladies' room with her. The guy seemed determined that being a good PA meant gluing himself to her side.

As she watched, he shifted in the chair, his brow creasing for a moment, suggesting his hip was bothering him. He'd been the same on the plane—although most of the time it didn't seem to affect his walking, sitting for any length of time apparently gave him trouble.

Her gaze lingered on him for a moment. She'd informed him that he didn't have to wear a suit, but he'd insisted, saying he preferred to maintain a professional appearance as they were on business. He looked rakishly handsome in his three-piece suit and smart blue tie, but then most men looked good in a suit, especially a well-cut one like his. What would he look like in jeans or shorts and a T-shirt? Would he just look normal, like a guy-next-door, with his ruffled brown hair?

Somehow, she doubted it. Even though he'd not even rolled up his shirt sleeves yet, she had the impression the hard edge to his features continued to his physique, both remnants of his Army life. When she'd enquired about the hotel he'd booked, the first thing he'd said was, "It has a gym and a swimming pool." So she knew he worked out, because she'd have said, "It has a five-star restaurant, room service, and a spa bath." He'd be muscular and lean beneath his shirt, his body tanned and hard. And although he'd said his ex had broken up with him because he hadn't been able to communicate with her the way she'd wanted—which didn't surprise Callie at all—she was certain that Angela whatever-her-name-was wouldn't have criticized him in the sack.

I was teasing.
Were you?

The words haunted her. His gray eyes had sparked with desire when he'd said those words, like a stormy sky lit with lightning. In spite of her promise to herself, Callie was suddenly desperate for him to look at her like that again.

He glanced up and saw her standing there, and his eyebrows rose. "That was quick." He put down the magazine—a gossip mag, she noted with interest—got to his feet, a little stiffly, and came over to her. "How did it go?"

She smiled at the receptionist and led the way down the stairs. "Not great," she said when they were out of earshot.

"Oh? Any idea why?"

"Not really. I didn't perform at my best."

"What's up? Are you tired?"

No. I was imagining you taking off your waistcoat and shirt, then unbuttoning your trousers.

"A bit," she said. "But it's okay, I'll perk up after I've had my coffee."

"Come on, then. Let's fill you up with latte and see if that makes a difference."

Let's fill you up… She stifled a groan. She definitely had sex on the brain. There was no way that should sound as erotic as it did.

There was a coffee shop opposite the store, so they ordered lattes and cake and found a seat by the window so they could watch the world go by.

"Anything I can do to help get your mind in gear?" Gene asked after they'd made themselves comfortable.

Callie looked out of the window. Dunedin was an attractive city, busy and thriving, its distinctive Edwardian architecture pulling in many tourists. It was also a university town, so the coffee shops were filled with students, and the city had a young, fresh air to it.

She could smell Gene's aftershave. It wound around her, gentle and subtle as a silk ribbon, drawing her toward him. She really hadn't thought this through. Sitting on the plane squashed into a seat next to him, travelling in the false intimacy of a car, eating in cafés—she wasn't sure she'd spent that much time being so close with Jamie.

But she was a professional, and jeez, it was only a couple of weeks. She might not have had sex for a while, but it wasn't as if she were going to jump on the first guy who came along.

She looked back at Gene. Probably not. What was the chance of the first guy being so sexy he made her mouth water every time she looked at him?

His cool eyes observed her. He unnerved her somewhat. He always seemed so in control. Callie knew she had a tendency to flap, usually when she'd forgotten to organize something, but Gene didn't appear to panic at anything. She supposed that after you'd been shot and wounded, forgetting to book a car or discovering you'd left the perfect pair of shoes for an outfit at home didn't seem worth worrying about.

Anything I can do? he'd asked. She was tempted to say, *Help me out with an orgasm,* but couldn't quite pluck up the courage. What would his reply be if she did? Would his eyebrows rise and a look of disapproval cross his features? Or would his eyes take on that sultry look of desire, his lips curving up as his gaze slid down her body to heat her right through?

"Um..." she said, "not really." She leaned back as the waitress brought their lattes and cake over. "Thanks." She picked up a spoon and stirred the foam, breaking up the picture of a fern that had been drawn on the top. "I'll be okay when I get going. I'm a bit rusty, that's all." She rested her elbows on the table and sipped her latte, then realized he was staring at her. "What?"

He blinked and raised his own coffee. "Nothing."

"No, go on. What did I say?"

"It doesn't matter, really."

"Gene. Tell me."

He huffed what sounded like an irritated sigh, although humor sparked in his eyes. "I can't make my mind up whether your words keep sounding suggestive on purpose or whether it's pure accident." He blew on the coffee.

Callie thought back over what she'd said. *I'll be okay when I get going. I'm a bit rusty, that's all.* "In that case, it was pure accident. I think it says more about your state of mind than mine at the moment." *Liar,* she thought.

"Oh, okay."

Their gazes met, and they both started laughing.

"Sorry." He put down his cup and pulled his piece of chocolate brownie toward him. "I've been single for a while. I think it's having an effect on my brain."

"I know what you mean." She reached out her fork and removed the corner of his brownie. "I'm having trouble thinking about anything but sex at the moment."

He stared at his brownie. "Callie…"

"What?" She wondered if he was going to react to her comment.

He blew out a long breath, and she had the feeling he'd been going to remark on it but had changed his mind. "Do you normally help yourself to other people's food?"

She paused with the forkful of brownie halfway to her mouth. "All the time. Sorry, is that a problem?"

He looked up at her, and his expression softened. "No," he said. "Not at all. Help yourself."

For a brief moment, she imagined he was referring to himself. She had to fight not to lean over and unbutton his waistcoat.

Instead, she ate the forkful of brownie, then her own carrot cake, making sure to offer him a piece. Not everything was about sex, she told herself sternly. She had to try to control herself, or she was going to get into serious trouble.

Chapter Nine

After lunch, Gene drove them to Fernz, and this time Callie came out smiling, and announced the meeting had gone very well.

"They loved Rowan's designs," she said as they got into the car. "They were keen to stock a full range of lingerie, as well as some swimwear."

"That's great." Gene was genuinely pleased for her. She'd come out of the first meeting very flat, and he'd hoped it hadn't boded ill for the rest of the tour. Luckily, that didn't seem to have been the case. This time, her eyes sparkled, and she even did a little dance in her seat to a tune in her head.

"Where next?" she said.

"The hotel. We can check in and leave our bags in our rooms, then head out to the last appointment."

"Cool." She looked out of the window, watching the houses and shops speed by. "Where is it?"

"By the sea. It's a bit out of town, in St. Clair, on the Esplanade, but it's close to Lingerie Plus."

"Great." She beamed at him. "I'm so glad you came along. I'd be lost without you."

"I'm sure you would. You'd probably be halfway to Australia by now."

"I mean it, Gene. Becky's great, and we always have fun when we go away, and I was really worried when I knew she wouldn't be able to go, but you're a terrific substitute."

"Thank you." His gaze slid across to her. Her cherry-colored skirt reached to just above her knees, and she wore a white sleeveless top with cherry and pink flowers that gathered beneath her breasts to flow down to her hips. She looked fresh and summery, like a sorbet, and she made his mouth water like one. Her bare legs were tanned and smooth, and he could imagine sliding his hand up her calf to her knee, then even higher, to the soft silkiness of her inner thigh.

He turned his gaze back to the road. Best stop there, unless he wanted to sport an erection when they arrived at the other end.

"Was it hot in Afghanistan?" Callie asked.

He blinked at the randomness of the question. "Where did that come from?"

"I was thinking about how hot it is here in summer, and that you seem very cool considering you're wearing a waistcoat, and that made me wonder if you coped this well in uniform in the heat."

He said nothing for a moment, returning in his mind to the dusty land, the discomfort he'd had to fight as he sweated into his thick uniform. The three days he'd spent in the blistering heat, in pain, thinking he'd never be found. The bodies lying around him.

His heart raced, and he swallowed hard. "It was hot a lot of the time. There's nothing like a cool shower after days out in the desert."

"Mmm. Did you all shower together?"

That made him laugh, and he loosened his tight grip on the wheel. "You have a one-track mind."

"You started it. I was asking a perfectly standard question about the climate and you had to bring naked soldiers into it. Were there women in the Army?"

Her changes of direction threw him every time. He glanced across at her. Her bright eyes told him that somehow she'd seen through him again.

"Yes," he said. "Some."

"Was there a woman in your scouting party?"

"Yes." How had Callie known?

"What happened to her?"

"She died," he said.

They fell quiet. He concentrated on finding the road to St. Clair, sliding on his sunglasses as the bright sun bounced off cars and windows.

He waited for the consolatory phrases, the *I'm sorry* and *Oh, Gene, how terrible.*

"Do you disagree with having women in the Army?" she said instead.

He shook his head. She should have been a psychologist. "No, absolutely not."

"You're saying what you think a woman would want to hear."

"It's what men do."

"It's what you've trained yourself to do because of your ex. I'm not Angela. Tell me what you really think."

He slowed at a roundabout and took the road south toward the coast. "I think women should have all the opportunities men have. If they want to fight, they should be able to. And I mean that."

"But you'd rather they didn't?"

Now he felt irritated. He didn't want to discuss this. It was like she kept poking him with a cattle prod until all his carefully restrained emotions and feelings came tumbling out. Maybe if he answered her, she'd stop asking questions. "When the scouting party was fired on and I was shot, four of the party died instantly. I lay there for three days with them dead beside me. If you're asking whether I have more nightmares about Lisa's blank eyes staring up at me than I do the three guys who were shot with her, yes, I do. She was tough and brave and fearless, and I respected her as a soldier, but she was a woman, and I don't care how many times I'm told we're all the same, I don't feel that way."

Callie studied him calmly, apparently unconcerned about his outburst. "You think of us as the fairer sex?"

"If by that you mean am I glad that you'll never be on the front line with a rifle in your hand, yes. Am I relieved that all you have to think about is making yourself and other women look gorgeous without their clothes? The answer is a resounding yes. I know it's sexist, but you know what? I don't care. I think it's great that women have every opportunity to excel, and I admire and support those who do, but I have an urge inside me to protect you, and that's never going away, no matter how many times I'm told it's sexist."

He stopped, his heart pounding. He'd said too much. She was going to roll her eyes and tell him to shove his opinions where the sun didn't shine.

But when he glanced at her, he saw her lips curving up, and warmth in her eyes before she slid her sunglasses on.

"We must be nearly there," she said, tapping on the window. "There's the sea."

"Callie, I…"

"It's okay." She laid her hand on his briefly on the steering wheel, her fingers cool against his skin.

So he let it lie, and instead studied the view of the waves running up the beach, the Pacific Ocean sparkling in the afternoon sun, and lowered his window to let the fresh sea air calm him.

It was so odd how Callie made him feel. When he'd been with Angela, he'd often felt as if he were a dog she enjoyed brushing the wrong way, against the growth of hair. He'd felt constantly on edge as she picked apart and analyzed every little detail of their conversation. She hadn't understood him at all, hadn't had a clue what made him tick, and even though it hadn't all been hell and they'd had some good times, ultimately it had been a relief when they'd broken up.

Callie was so different that it was like trying to compare apples and oranges. It was as if she already knew the answer to her questions, but she asked them anyway because the way he answered gave her even more insight into him. He thought he didn't like to talk about himself, and yet she was able to coax details out of him right to the point where he couldn't bear to talk anymore, which she appeared to understand. It puzzled him, irritated him, and warmed him through all at once.

"Here it is." He spotted the hotel sign and signaled to take the turning into the car park. At that moment, his phone started ringing in his jacket pocket on his back seat.

"Want me to get it for you?" Callie half turned in her seat to retrieve it.

"No, it's okay, it'll go to voicemail." It was probably someone from his office, and he didn't want Callie talking to them.

He parked, and they retrieved their cases and made their way to the front desk. He fought against the urge to carry Callie's case for her. Women didn't like men offering to help them nowadays. He'd already made an idiot of himself by saying he had an urge to protect them—he didn't need to compound it by doing the modern equivalent of laying his cloak over a puddle and offering to duel for her.

The hotel was all white walls, glass, and brightly painted pictures, fresh and cheerful. They checked in and took their cases up to their rooms on the first floor. Gene heard Callie exclaim as she walked into her room, and he left his suitcase propping open the door and followed her in, smiling as he saw her hands cupping her face in wonder as she looked out at the sea.

"How gorgeous," she said.

"Mmm." He let his gaze slip down her from behind, following the dip of her waist, the swell of her bottom, the shapeliness of her legs. Her ex must have been a Class A idiot, he mused. Callie was sexy, funny, and intelligent, and the prat had cheated on her. On second thoughts, he wished duels still existed, because he would have been happy to call Jamie whatever-his-name-was out on one.

She looked over her shoulder and caught him admiring her. "Enjoying the view?"

He gave her a wry look. "I'm going to my room. Thirty minutes and then I'll be knocking on your door, okay?"

"Can't wait." She flared her eyes at him. He loved how expressive they were, and how much they reflected her mood.

"Stop it," he scolded, returning to pick up his suitcase. "You're incorrigible."

"It's my middle name," she called out just before the door closed.

Smiling, he let himself into his own room and went inside.

Like Callie's, it had a beautiful view of the ocean, and he spent a few moments just looking at it, letting his emotions settle like a pile of feathers that fluttered slowly to the ground. Talking about his time in the Army, especially about Lisa and the others who had died, always stirred him up, so much so that he rarely spoke of them to anyone now. He remembered the cool touch of Callie's fingers on his, her gentle words, *It's okay*. How did she read him so well?

His phone rang again, making him jump in the quietness of the room. He took it out of his jacket pocket and answered it, still looking at the sea. "Hello?"

"Gene? It's Kev." Kev was in charge of Safe & Secure when Gene was absent.

"Hey," Gene replied. "How's it going?"

"Depends on your point of view. You okay to talk?"

He turned from the window and crossed to sit on the bed. "Yeah, I'm alone. What's up?"

"Ms. Hawke has had another death threat."

Gene felt as if he'd swallowed an ice cube. "Shit. What did it say?"

"The usual horrific stuff. But it also goes into great detail about what she did that day—what time she left the house, where she visited, how long she stayed."

Gene leaned forward and sank his fingers into his hair. It was the first time they'd been certain that Phoebe was definitely being watched. "Did the letter mention Callie?"

"Only in passing, the same as before. 'I promise I'll take away the lives of those you love,' blah blah."

Gene's hand curled into a fist. Over the past few hours, he'd almost forgotten about his real reason for being with Callie. She made him feel as if nothing bad would ever happen, her bright smile washing away all the darkness in the world. But when the sun went down, the darkness was still there, and he had to remember why he was with her. It wasn't an idle threat. Her life was in danger, real danger, and he was the only one standing between her and the madman who was hunting her down.

"Do you think he's watching you both now?" Kev asked.

Standing again, Gene forced himself to stay calm and think it through as he paced the room. "I'm betting not. None of us has spotted anyone shadowing Callie, and he's not yet related her day-to-day steps, so I think he's concentrating on Phoebe. If all he wanted was to take them both out, he would have done it by now. He wants to scare them, to make them live in fear for a while. But ultimately I think he'll come after them. And we have to be ready when that happens." He spoke to himself more than Kev. He had to remain focused.

"Saffie spotted that guy again outside her house," Kev advised. "She's taken more photos and distributed them around the team, and we've sent them to the STG. Don't worry, boss. They'll catch him."

"Yeah. Okay, thanks. Keep me informed on any developments, okay?"

"Sure thing. See ya."

Gene hung up and tossed his phone onto the bed. Of course, he had to know all the details about what was happening back at the office. But part of him wished that for once he could leave it all to someone else and just concentrate on being with Callie.

He leaned his forehead on the cool glass and closed his eyes.

Chapter Ten

Callie's next two appointments went even better than the previous one. Lingerie Plus were thrilled to discover a new line of generously proportioned underwear, and their manager—a young woman around the same age as Callie—loved Rowan's designs and bought some items for herself on the spot. The best thing was that the store had branches in all the major cities, and the manager promised to bring the Four Seasons brand up at the next head office meeting and spread the word.

JimJam's was similarly as successful. Primarily a sleepwear shop, they fell in love with Rowan's large collection of nightwear and pajamas, and agreed to stock all of her designs, as well as a few pieces of lingerie.

By the end of the day, a buzz of excitement had begun to grow in Callie's stomach. She hadn't imagined it all. Four Seasons really was going to be as successful as she'd hoped. She couldn't wait to tell the others.

"What now?" she asked Gene as they got in the car. "Snazzy restaurant and a nightclub?"

"I'm far too old for that," he said wryly. "Plus, you need your rest—we have a long drive tomorrow. Back to the hotel, dinner, and bed for you, young lady."

She stuck out her tongue. The corner of his mouth curved up, but he didn't say anything. He'd been quiet since they'd arrived at the hotel. She suspected it had been something to do with the phone call he'd ignored in the car and presumably taken in his room. He seemed preoccupied, solemn. And that wouldn't do at all.

"I might go on my own," she said. "I feel like dancing."

His eyes widened with alarm. "Please don't. Because then I'll have to go with you, and I don't dance."

"You don't dance?"

"Nope. And don't think I don't read in your eyes how much you'd enjoy torturing me by making me do it. I beg you, dinner, then bed."

"If you insist," she said.

His gaze slid from the road to her. "Alone," he clarified after meeting her eyes.

"I'm to be alone at dinner, or alone in bed?"

He sighed. "I'm happy to accompany you to dinner."

"Aw, Gene. You're such a spoilsport."

"And you're a terrible tease."

"Well, you look so serious. In fact, I shall call you Mr. Serious from now on."

"I've been called worse." He pulled into the car park. "What time do you want dinner?"

"I'm starving. Let's eat early."

"Okay, five thirty?"

"Great. It'll give me time to get changed."

They returned to their rooms, and Callie took a shower, then chose a pretty summer dress to wear to dinner. Rowan had made it for her in a stunning, silky fabric covered with orange and red flowers. Callie felt that it complemented the summer weather, which seemed to be turning hotter by the hour. As she listened to the TV while she got ready, she heard the weatherman say that almost the whole country was experiencing a heatwave that showed no signs of moving at the moment. Thank God the hotels and the car had air conditioning, she thought, knowing that it would only get warmer and more humid the further north they went. She'd be a puddle by the time they reached the subtropical Bay of Islands.

At five thirty, a knock sounded on the door, so she picked up her bag and opened it to find Gene waiting for her.

She rolled her eyes as she shut the door behind her. "Don't you ever relax?" She gestured to his outfit. He'd changed, but only into another three-piece suit.

"Is that a complaint?" he asked as they walked along the corridor. "I thought women liked guys in suits."

"We do. I feel guilty, though."

"Why? This is a business trip."

"I know. But you are allowed to relax."

"I don't do relaxing." He held the door open for her to precede him down the stairs.

"You don't dance, you don't relax… How do you let off steam, Mr. Serious?"

"I work out. I'll go to the gym later."

"How dull."

He smiled. "Don't you keep fit?"

"I walk a lot, and I go to a dance aerobics class at home twice a week. But I don't like gyms."

"I can't imagine you sitting still long enough to use a piece of equipment," he said. "You're quite a fidget."

"Mum used to say I had ants in my pants when I was a kid."

"That's a fair description."

They walked into the busy restaurant, where Callie discovered that Gene had booked a table for them, which was a relief because if left up to her they'd have been forced to eat in a burger joint.

"Shame it's not outside," she said as they took their seats in the center of the restaurant. "It would have been lovely in the evening sun."

"Unfortunately, there wasn't anything else available," he said.

"Never mind, this is lovely."

The waiter gave them a menu, and they perused it for a while before ordering an oven-baked salmon fillet filled with oysters in Gene's case, and pan-seared scallops in avocado and coriander cream and bacon aioli for Callie.

"I'll have a glass of Sauvignon, please," Callie said when the waiter asked what she'd like to drink.

"A Diet Coke for me," Gene advised him.

The waiter nodded and left.

"Don't you drink?" Callie asked.

"Not while I'm on duty." He smiled.

"Please have a beer or something. I feel bad drinking on my own."

"No you don't."

"No, I don't, but I feel as if I should."

"I'm good, thanks."

She relented. Clearly, he wanted to remain clearheaded. Better that, she thought, than be the sort of man who always had a drink in his hand. Looking out of the window, she gave a silent sigh. She wasn't going to think about her father now.

*

"Tell me about your parents," Gene said.

Callie's eyes widened, and she frowned at him. "Don't do that."

"What?"

"Read my mind."

"I apologize. I was just following your example."

Her lips curved up again. He realized that was their default position—they were nearly always set in a smile. He liked that about her.

"What do you want to know?" she asked.

Obviously, he was going to have to pretend he hadn't met her mother and father. He shifted in his chair, uncomfortable with lying to her, half wishing he hadn't started the conversation, but he was interested to hear her side of the story. "Are they both alive?"

She considered him for a moment, and he could almost see her rifling through the filing cupboards of her mind, deciding which files to extract and what information to tell him. "Yes. My father's also ex-Army—a major. He lives in Napier now with his second wife."

"Do you get on well with him?"

"I do. Most people find him grouchy and pompous, but I'm an only child, and he's always spoilt me, so we get on fine." She smiled.

He wondered whether she'd mention Peter Summer's alcoholism, but she said nothing, and he couldn't think how to raise the subject, so he changed tack. "What about your mother?"

Callie leaned back in her chair and looked out of the window. He followed her gaze. The sun wouldn't set until nearly nine o'clock this far south, and the beach was still busy, filled with holidaymakers enjoying the summer heat. Kids splashed around in the shallows, throwing beach balls and making sandcastles, while parents read books and took the opportunity to relax while their children were entertained for a while.

Gene didn't really look at them, though. He was too busy scanning the area and noting any suspicious activity—single, watchful men, or people hanging around parked cars. His phone call to Kev had filled him with renewed enthusiasm to protect Callie and help track down the madman hunting her.

Finding nothing, he glanced around the restaurant. He'd deliberately asked for a table indoors as he felt too exposed outside. It was busy, but so far there were no signs of anything to worry about. He'd remain alert, though. He wouldn't drink alcohol again until the tour was over and hopefully Kirk had been caught.

Suddenly aware that Callie still hadn't said anything, he looked back at her. For once, her smile had faded, and her eyes were distant. "Callie?"

She brought her gaze back to him and cleared her throat. "My mother and I have a... complicated relationship."

"In what way?"

"She's a Crown Prosecutor in the Wellington Crown Solicitors. She's very highly regarded, and extremely good at what she does. She's a strong woman—the strongest I know. Competent, courageous, determined. She's a great role model for young women."

"But..."

"But I think her ambition caused her marriage to fail, and I don't know that I'll ever forgive her for that."

Gene sipped his drink. Obviously, Phoebe had never told her the truth about why their marriage had ended. Well, it wasn't his place to tell her. Even so, he hated having all these secrets from her. "That's a shame," he said, the most noncommittal comment he could think of.

"I think I'm a disappointment to her," Callie added.

He softened inside. It was true that Phoebe had put Callie down a little when describing her. Why was it that parents had such power over the rest of one's life? "I can't imagine that's the case," he said, knowing nevertheless that she probably spoke the truth.

Callie sighed. "When I was young, she gave me frequent speeches about aiming high and how I could achieve anything I put my mind to. She expected me to follow in her footsteps. Maybe not be a lawyer, exactly, but she assumed I'd run the police force or invent a cure for cancer, or something. Running a lingerie business wasn't quite what she had in mind."

"She's told you that?"

Callie tipped her head from side to side. "Not in so many words, but she's very good at being disapproving without actually saying anything. She thinks I'm decadent and self-indulgent. She thinks we should all aim to improve the lives of our fellow men and women, and any career that focuses on beauty or clothes or the arts is pointless." She turned her wine glass around in her fingers. "What do you think?"

"Does it matter?"

"I wouldn't ask if it didn't. You don't like to share your opinions, and that interests me."

He scratched an eyebrow. "Some would call that being nosey."

"Don't evade the question. Do you think what I do is pointless?"

"Designing and selling beautiful undergarments so women can make themselves look gorgeous when they take off their clothes? Yeah. That's a real of waste of time."

"Be serious," she scolded.

"I am. That's my name, isn't it?"

"I suppose so."

He wanted to make her feel better, to lift the shadow of sadness that had fallen over her eyes. "My opinion—as you seem so keen to know it—is that everyone is given a gift, and life is about discovering that gift and using it the best way you can. Not everyone is made to be a top surgeon or to run the country. Life can be harsh and cruel, and it's the arts—paintings, music, beautiful things—that make it worthwhile. I can't paint to save my life, but I certainly wouldn't have told Monet that he should have gotten himself a job as a lawyer."

"When you put it like that…"

"You and Rowan and Neve and Bridget make and sell garments that make women feel better about themselves. It's a very rewarding career, in my mind."

She smiled at him. "That's a lovely thing to say, even if you don't mean it."

"I don't say things I don't mean, Callie. Life isn't all about momentous decisions and world-scale events. It's the little things that make it special. A smile from someone when you're having a bad day. Treating yourself to an ice-cold lager or a bar of chocolate. Sharing a meal with a beautiful woman. Those are the things that make it all worthwhile."

She raised her glass to her lips and sipped from it, her lashes downcast. To his surprise, a touch of color appeared in her cheeks. He'd made her blush. *Aw.*

"Tell me about your parents," she said before raising her gaze to his.

He'd wondered whether she'd tell him about the death threats she and Phoebe had received, but she obviously didn't feel able to confide in him yet.

He sighed and leaned back in his chair. "Much the same as you, I'm afraid to say. My father hated me going into the Army. He thought I should have been a writer. I think he wanted me to be Ernest Hemingway. Freddie's his favorite."

"Because he's an accountant! That's so dull."

"It's respectable, and he makes a great deal of money."

She blew a raspberry. "Boring."

He chuckled. "You don't like that word, do you?"

"I don't. What about your mother?"

The question whipped the rug out from under him. His smile faded. "She died when I was eleven."

"You still miss her." It was a statement, not a question.

"Yes."

"Were you close?"

"I don't know. No more than any other eleven-year-old boy and his mum, I guess. She was... in my corner, I suppose. She often stood up for me and defended me when my father picked on me, and I've missed that as I've grown up." He blinked, only realizing how true the words were when they'd fallen out of his mouth. He leaned forward, resting his forearms on the table, closing the distance between them. "I don't know what it is about you that makes me say things I wouldn't normally say to people."

"I have that kind of face." She sipped her wine, her gaze remaining fixed to his. "You called me beautiful."

"Are you fishing for compliments? You are beautiful, you must know that."

She leaned forward too, and suddenly they were only a foot apart. He could smell her perfume, and the sweet wine she'd drunk. She had long eyelashes, and now he could see she'd applied a sparkly eyeshadow that was probably what was making her eyes look so blue tonight. "You really think so?"

His gaze slipped to her mouth, resting on the soft pink velvet of her lips. Every cell in his body urged him to lean forward and touch his lips to hers. "I really think so," he whispered. "Now behave, or I'll do something I'll regret."

Chapter Eleven

Callie had difficulty concentrating during the meal on anything other than Gene's mouth and her desire to kiss him. Maybe it was the wine, although two glasses wasn't usually enough to make her throw herself at the first guy who was nice to her. His compliment had warmed her to him, but again, just the fact that he'd been nice wasn't enough to turn her lust dial up to eleven.

It didn't help when he slid off his jacket, asked her to help him remove his cufflinks, then proceeded to roll up his shirt sleeves, exposing his forearms to the elbow. She felt like a Victorian gentleman who'd seen a lady's ankle. His arms were tanned and sinewy, and he looked as if he lifted weights on a regular basis. Everything about this guy was hard, from his eyes to the set of his jaw to his masculine body.

He'd be hard down below, too, she knew it—she'd unzip his trousers and his erection would spring into her hand, stiff as a lamppost. When she stroked it, the velvety layer of skin would glide over the concrete shaft. She could almost imagine the way he'd close his eyes and tip back his head as she massaged him, until he shuddered and groaned as he came…

Callie blinked. Gene was sliding a forkful of salmon and oyster into his mouth, but his lips were curving up, and he smiled now as he chewed. The muscles of his throat constricted as he swallowed. "Penny for them," he said.

"Sorry." Callie fished out the last scallop from her meal. "Far too lewd to relay."

He laughed and shook his head. "You say exactly what's on your mind, don't you?"

"Don't see much point in being coy." She chewed the scallop. "We're both single, aren't we? Where's the harm in a little lighthearted flirting?"

"Why are you single?" He wiped his mouth on his serviette and sat back. "I know you broke up with Jamie, but that doesn't explain why some other man hasn't snapped you up."

She shrugged. "Actually, offers haven't come flooding in. I think it's about signals—when a person's actively looking for a date, he or she transmits some kind of vibe that announces they're free. I don't think I'm ready to put out that vibe yet. Apart from to you, obviously."

"Callie… you are an outrageous flirt."

"I know. I'm sorry. It's fun. And you're… safe."

He raised an eyebrow. "What do you mean?"

"I know it can't come to anything. I'm just teasing, that's all."

"You realize that if it was the other way around, you'd probably be accusing me of sexual harassment?"

Her smile fell. She hadn't thought of it like that, but he was right, of course. An office manager who made constant sexual suggestions to his PA would be rapped on the knuckles in no time. Her face filled with heat. "Oh, of course. I thought it was funny—I hadn't considered that it might make you uncomfortable."

Immediately, concern filled his features. "It doesn't. I'm sorry, I didn't mean to make you feel bad. I'm flattered. It was just a passing comment."

"Even so…" Now she felt embarrassed and angry with herself. Equality was a two-way street. She couldn't take offence at a man making unwelcome lewd suggestions to her when she was doing exactly the same to him! No wonder men got so confused nowadays. "I apologize."

"Callie…" His expression softened. "Don't get me wrong. I don't want you to think I'm not interested, because I am, very much so. But until I stop working for you, I can't do anything about it. I just can't. It wouldn't feel right."

He really liked her. Tears pricked Callie's eyes and she sucked her bottom lip. "You have principles," she said. "I like that."

"I like to think I'm a gentleman, if nothing else. I hope you understand."

"I do," she said softly.

They studied each other for a moment. His eyes were clear and honest.

"So," she whispered, "the day when Becky comes back and you stop working for me…"

"I'll be knocking on your door asking for a date the day that happens."

"Seriously?"

"Seriously."

Three months. She could wait that long, surely?

"You want me to stop flirting?" she asked playfully.

His lips curved up. "Not necessarily. As long as we understand each other."

She nodded. "I think so."

"Okay, then." He accepted the menu from the waiter who'd come up to clear their plates. "I reckon it's dessert time."

They both chose a Belgian chocolate pot and ate it slowly, dipping the biscotti into the velvety chocolate cream, and Callie knew she'd forever associate the taste of dark chocolate with that moment—the sun falling across the table and turning Gene's hair from brown to golden, the jazz music playing in the background, the smell of the sea drifting in through the windows, and the look in his eyes that said what his lips couldn't yet—that he liked her, and that he wanted to get to know her better. The air held the promise of something beautiful, like the russet-and-orange sky outside, promising it would be a gorgeous day tomorrow.

They talked about this and that while they ate, about music, books, movies, and whatever else came into their heads. Then, eventually, it was time to go.

As they walked through the restaurant, Callie felt the touch of Gene's hand in the center of her back. Ostensibly, it was to guide her through the busy tables, she was sure, but it felt like a brand, as if he was telling her, telling the men seated around them, that they had to keep their hands off. It should have annoyed her. How long had she known him, four, five days? And all he'd said was that in three months' time he might ask her out on a date.

But as they passed the mirrors behind the bar, Callie saw that she was smiling.

They walked up the stairs to the first floor—it wasn't really far enough to take the elevator—and along the corridor to their rooms. There they stopped and turned to face each other.

"I'm glad most of your appointments went well today," he said.

"Yes, the day ended better than it began." She smiled up at him. Gosh, he was tall, probably because she wore flat sandals. His jacket hung over his arm and he still looked crisp and fresh in his white shirt. If she leaned close, she'd be able to smell his aftershave. Instinctively, she knew he was a man who showered often, and who cared about his appearance, without staring into the mirror every five minutes to check his hair.

"You're very yummy," she said.

He gave a short laugh. "Thank you, I think."

"Oh, it's definitely a compliment."

"I see. This is what I'm to expect over the next few months, is it?"

"Yes. As long as it won't be misconstrued as sexual harassment."

His gaze caressed her face. "I promise it won't."

"Good." She held her breath. He stood only a few inches away from her, and the look in his eyes had turned sultry, as if he was thinking about kissing her. God, she wanted him to kiss her. She didn't care that he worked for her, she didn't care about anything at that moment but the yearning to feel his lips on hers. They'd be firm, and warm, and his tongue would slip between her lips into her mouth, and she'd lean against him, and her whole body would ache with desire.

"Goodnight, Callie," he said, his voice husky but filled with humor.

"'Night." She swallowed hard and backed away to her door.

"Sleep well." He let himself in, and his door closed.

Callie went into her room and sat on the bed. It was only seven thirty, far too early to go to bed yet. She'd only been joking when she'd mentioned going to a nightclub, although she did enjoy dancing, but she wished they could have gone for a walk. She'd go later, she decided, once the sun had started to set and it was a little cooler.

So she typed up the notes from her meetings, studied a little from the portfolio she'd prepared for the businesses in Oamaru, Timaru, and then Christchurch, and watched some TV.

At around eight, her mobile rang. She picked it up and groaned when she saw her mother's name on the screen. It was tempting to switch it off and pretend she hadn't heard it, but she sighed, swiped the screen, and answered it.

"Hello?"

"Callie? It's your mother."

"Hi, Mum."

"Where are you, darling?"

"In a hotel in Dunedin."

"Oh, of course, you're doing that tour. How's it going?"

Callie sat back against the pillows and stretched out her legs. "Good. I had a couple of successful meetings. Three shops have agreed to stock the Four Seasons brand."

"That's wonderful, darling, well done."

Callie tried not to sigh. At least she's trying, she thought. It was difficult not to hear insincerity in her mother's voice, though.

"How about you?" she asked Phoebe. "How are things going?"

"Busy," Phoebe said. "I'm still at work."

"Jeez, Mum. Aren't you supposed to start easing off when you get higher up the ladder?"

"Doesn't seem to work that way."

"How's... everything else?"

Phoebe cleared her throat. "That's just it. I've had another threat."

Callie looked out of the window. The color was fading from the sea and the street lights were flicking on, casting yellow circles onto the pavement. Two seagulls squabbled over a bag of chips left on a bench. "Oh?"

"Yes. He wrote down everything I did today, times I went out, places I'd been. It appears he—or someone—is watching me."

Callie shivered. "Oh, that's awful."

"He seems very determined to scare us, darling."

"Well, we're not going to let him, are we?" Callie spoke with determination.

"No... But he mentioned you again. We have to assume he's serious."

"I think he's serious about wanting to frighten us. I still can't believe he's really bothered about causing me harm. What's the point in that? I had nothing to do with the case." It was an old argument, and Callie had to fight not to throw the phone across the room.

"Okay." For once, Phoebe didn't argue back. Maybe she was as tired of it all as her daughter was. "I just wanted you to know. Be careful, won't you?"

"Of course. You too."

"How's your new PA doing?"

"Fine," Callie said. "He's very efficient. He's getting me organized." *And hot under the collar.*

"That's good. I'm glad he's there to keep an eye on you."

Callie rolled her eyes. "I have to go now."

"All right, darling. See you soon. Take care."

They said goodbye, and Callie hung up.

She stood and walked over to the window and looked down at the ocean, which had turned a rusty color in the setting sun. For most of Callie's childhood, Phoebe's career had dominated Callie's every waking moment. She'd walked in her mother's shadow while Phoebe gained accolade after accolade for her work, blazing a trail through the southern hemisphere like some kind of superhero as she put away criminals, gangsters, and villains, condemning them all to years behind bars without a second thought.

It wasn't that Callie thought the people her mother had sent to prison were innocent, but she couldn't shake the feeling that the arrogance with which she'd done it meant that somehow her pigeons were coming home not only to roost but to move in and set up camp. Phoebe saw herself as an avenging angel, as some kind of symbol of goodness, and yet all Callie could remember of her youth was being unhappy—first being dragged from post to post across the world when she was young, and then after her parents divorced, sitting alone outside courtrooms, or alone at home, waiting for her mother to grant her some snippet of her precious time. And it had come so rarely. Phoebe had treated her daughter like a nuisance, like a dog she had to go home to feed.

Callie didn't wish her mother ill, and of course she hoped Kirk would be caught soon and the threat of danger lifted. But she wanted no part of the drama. At eighteen, when she'd gone to uni, she'd stepped out of the center of the hurricane where she'd made her home for so many years, put up with the buffeting winds as she fought her way out, and had emerged in a more peaceful place of her own, where the world didn't revolve around her mother, where life suddenly had promise. The last thing she wanted was to go back to that maelstrom.

Crossing to the bed, she pulled the strap of her bag over her shoulder, slipped on her sandals, and left the room.

Most of the holidaymakers had left the beaches now, and the tide was coming in, the sea sending white fingers up toward the esplanade. Callie walked slowly along the sea front, letting the warm evening breeze lift her hair around her shoulders, thinking about the business, the appointments she'd had that day, and about Gene.

It wasn't as if, after breaking up with Jamie, she'd decided she wasn't going to date again. He'd broken her heart, but Callie had no intention of remaining a spinster for the rest of her life. But she'd thought it would take a while before she felt interested in another man. And then Gene had walked into her office, with his cufflinks and his firm jaw, and it felt as if someone had thrown a handful of fairy dust over her.

His declaration that he couldn't date her while he was working for her sucked, but she admired his principles. Would he still be interested in dating in three months' time when Becky returned? Only time would tell. Ninety days felt like an awfully long time. How was she supposed to keep her hands off him until then?

Her lips curving, she daydreamed about his wry smile and the heat in his eyes as the evening breeze played with her hair and the seagulls cried around her.

It was only as she reached the end of the esplanade and turned to make her way back that she began to have the feeling she was being followed. She couldn't have explained why. She glanced over her shoulder and saw nobody out of the ordinary, no suspicious men with binoculars, no one who turned away hurriedly as they saw her look around. *It appears someone's watching me.* Phoebe's words rang in her head. Her skin crawled, and her heart rate picked up and began to race.

Dammit, why hadn't she told Gene she was going for a walk? No doubt he would have insisted he go with her.

Then she scolded herself for being a wuss. She wasn't going to let a few stupid idle threats force her to live like a hermit, or make her too afraid to go out on her own.

Still, she walked back more quickly than she'd walked out, and when she finally entered the hotel, she couldn't suppress a wave of relief that she'd made it back safely.

After running up the stairs to her room, she paused outside Gene's. Part of her wanted to knock on his door and tell him what she'd felt, hoping for his reassurance.

But she didn't. Instead, she went into her room, locked the door, undressed, climbed under the covers, and pulled them up to her chin, even though it was a warm night.

It took a long time for her to fall asleep, though.

Chapter Twelve

The next day, they'd checked out and were on the road by ten o'clock. It was about four to five hours' drive to Christchurch. They could have flown, but Callie wanted to call at some shops on the way, and Gene had to admit to himself he had no problem spending several hours in the car with her.

Callie offered to drive, but Gene told her he wanted to earn his money as her assistant, and she seemed to accept it, and slid into the passenger side without any argument. He got into the driver's seat, started the engine, and pulled away, relieved she hadn't insisted. He needed to remain in control, just in case a threat came. He'd taken several advanced driving courses over the years, so he knew what to do if they were chased or attacked on the road.

At first, he sat stiffly behind the wheel, determined to keep his wits about him. As the hours passed, though, and the road became almost empty, he began to relax and enjoy the drive and being with Callie.

She plugged her phone into the car and played music as they drove. He teased her about some of the songs from boy bands, but sang along with her to those he knew—some older alternative rock and, surprising him, some really old bluegrass.

"My father," she said when he enquired why she had those songs on her phone. "He likes all that. He used to play it in the car whenever we were alone, and I guess I picked up a love of it over the years."

Gene said nothing, concentrating on the road.

After about an hour and a half, they arrived at Oamaru, and Callie stopped there to visit a boutique lingerie shop, the manager of which appeared more than happy to stock some of the gorgeous underwear that Callie showed her. Another hour's drive took them to Timaru, and she did the same there, visiting a smaller lingerie shop to tout her wares. Gene was impressed that she wasn't focusing only on the large department stores. She seemed keen to reach out to even the tiniest corners of the country, and he could only admire her for that.

They continued north along the quiet road through wide-open fields filled with sheep and cows and, in the distance to their left, the white-topped mountains of Mount Cook National Park, right out of *The Lord of the Rings*. For a while, they were the only car on the road, and it became easy to think they were the survivors of some kind of natural disaster, the only two people left in the world.

They'd have to repopulate the Earth, of course, Gene thought as they crossed the long bridge over the Rakaia River. That would be fun.

"Penny for them," Callie said, breaking into his daydreams.

"Too lewd to say." He glanced at her and grinned.

She giggled and looked out the window. Smiling, he returned his gaze to the road. It was good to see her enjoying herself. He'd seen her face the night before, when she'd become afraid, out on her walk along the sea front, and it had chilled him.

When he'd arrived at the hotel, he'd slipped the receptionist fifty bucks and asked her to let him know if Callie left the hotel at any point, and in the evening the receptionist had found him in the gym to tell him Callie appeared to be going for a walk. Cursing, he'd left hurriedly, still in his sweats. Luckily, she hadn't gone far, and he'd followed her discreetly until she turned and began to walk back to the hotel. He'd seen her stop and glance over her shoulder, had seen the fear on her face. Had she sensed him following her, or someone else? Either way, part of him had been glad she'd quickened her pace and returned to the hotel. He didn't want her to be scared, but equally he'd rather she wasn't blasé about her safety, either.

As they passed through Ashburton and headed east toward Christchurch, the roads became busier, and before long they were caught up in typical city traffic. The city had suffered heavily in the earthquake four years before, but it was gradually clawing its way back to normality, rebuilding itself like a person whose relationship had crumbled and failed, and who had to learn how to exist again on their own. Much of the city had been rebuilt, but he tried not to look at the cathedral as they passed it, finding the partially demolished ruins of the once-beautiful building just too sad.

They threaded their way through the streets, heading up past the museum and following the line of the Avon River to the hotel. In the end, it was nearly five o'clock by the time they finally parked, got out, and stretched.

"Jeez, that was a long day." Callie retrieved her bag from the back of the car. "We should have flown."

"Now you tell me." He didn't really mean it, though. "Come on. Let's check in and get some dinner."

They ate together again, enjoying the view across Hagley Park and the river. Willows wept over the quiet water, and oak and beech trees framed the grassy park where people were walking their dogs and enjoying the summer evening.

Callie went through her itinerary for the next day, which promised to be a busy one, with several appointments at large department stores as well as visits to a few boutique lingerie shops. Gene listened to her talking about her plans, unable to hide a smile at her enthusiasm. She might not have been the most organized person in the world, but she was knowledgeable about her business, and she'd done her research on the shops she was going to visit.

All day, in the car, she'd been bright and chirpy, and she certainly seemed excited about the next day. As the evening wore on, though, she gradually grew quieter and more preoccupied, and it wasn't long after they finished their dessert before she said she was going up to her room.

Gene walked with her, hiding his disappointment. He'd hoped she might agree to stay for drinks in the bar, as he'd been enjoying talking to her and getting to know her better. Had she taken his request to wait as a brush-off? Maybe she didn't believe him when he said he was interested in her.

When the elevator doors closed, he turned to her with concern. "Are you okay?"

She leaned against the wall, her shoulders sagging a little. "Fine, thank you. Just very tired."

"You're sure? Not worried about anything?" He was still hoping she'd confide in him about Phoebe's predicament and the threats, but she just shook her head and gave him a small smile. Maybe she really was just tired. "Anything I can do for you?" he asked. "Order up for you?"

"No, really, I'm good, thanks." The elevator dinged and the doors opened. They walked in silence along to their rooms, and she swiped her card.

"Callie…" He reached out and caught her hand. Her fingers lay cool in his. Her hand seemed small. She'd feel small in his arms, he knew, even though she was taller than average.

She squeezed his hand and released it. "I'm fine, Gene, please, don't worry. My mind's on other things, that's all. I'll see you in the morning for breakfast at eight again?"

"Sure." He watched her go, feeling helpless. It occurred to him that maybe her mother had told her about the new death threat. Maybe the reinforcement of someone being after her had shaken her up.

Anyway, her mental status was irrelevant. His only concern was that she was safe.

Yeah, he thought as he let himself into his room. *Keep telling yourself that, and you might begin to believe it.*

*

In his dream, a T-rex was pounding on his hotel door, trying to get in.

Trained to transition from sleep to being awake in seconds, it nevertheless took Gene a moment to understand it wasn't actually a dinosaur, as the door shook on its hinges and the whole hotel groaned. It was another earthquake, a big one, by the feel of it.

Within seconds of him leaping out of bed, the fire alarms went off across the hotel. He'd left the curtains open, and watery light from the half-moon filtered into the room, which was useful because when he flicked on the light switch, he discovered the quake had knocked out the power.

Currently naked, he tugged a pair of pajama bottoms up his legs and pulled a sweatshirt over his head. Shoving his feet into a pair of Converses, he grabbed his phone and opened the door. Callie opened hers at the same moment and appeared next to him, a ghost in the semi-darkness.

"Jesus." She was white-faced, dressed only in a thin nightie. "It's another fucking earthquake." He could hardly hear her above the alarms.

"Yeah." The tremors had stopped, although it was possible there might be aftershocks. "Come on," he yelled.

Taking her hand, he led her across the corridor to the fire exit and they ran down the stairs, joining other guests in various stages of undress, lit by emergency lighting and the glow from people's phones. Luckily, they were only two floors up, and it was less than a minute before they found themselves on the bank of the Avon, which the moon had cast in an eerie light. All the color had been bleached out of the scene, leaving them in a black-and-white movie, a mixture of highlights and shadows.

He hadn't even checked what the time was yet, so he swiped his phone. 1:35 a.m. "It felt like a big one," he said, bringing up Twitter. Tweets were just starting to appear, reflecting the shock—physical and emotional—across the city, although nothing yet about the magnitude or effects. He glanced up at the hotel. There didn't appear to be any visible damage, but that didn't mean the city had escaped untouched.

"Close one," he said. He looked back at her, and his heart almost stuttered to a stop. Her bottom lip trembled, and she shook visibly, her arms wrapped around her waist. Like him, she'd brought only her phone, obviously not even taking the time to fetch a jacket, and her feet were bare. Her nightie was one of Rowan's designs, made of a thin, silky fabric gathered under the bust and falling to just above her knees, with thin ribbon straps. It was a pale color with darker butterflies that sparkled in the moonlight, beautiful but hardly warm, and even on a summer night, the cool breeze was obviously enough to make her shiver.

"Jesus, Callie." Without asking, he tugged his sweatshirt over his head and started to put it on her.

She let him do so automatically, like a child. He dragged his gaze away from her breasts, cupped in the silky fabric, maneuvered her arms through, and pulled the sweatshirt down her body. It fell past her hips, the sleeves hanging over her hands.

"Makes me feel like I'm a gorilla," he said, trying to make her laugh, but she seemed in shock, and just turned wide eyes up to him, still shaking. "Hey." He lifted her hair out of the neck of the shirt, then put his hands on her upper arms and rubbed them, once again thinking how small she felt in his hands. "Are you okay? Callie?"

Chapter Thirteen

Callie blinked a few times. Her heart was racing at a million miles an hour. "I'm... I'm all right. Sorry. I can't believe it, that's all."

"Don't worry, it's normal to—" He was interrupted by her ringtone; someone was calling her, at this hour.

She lifted her hand to see who it was. "It's Rowan." She held the phone to her ear. "Hello?"

"Callie? It's Rowan."

"Hi. What are you doing up?"

"Just reading, but I have the TV on in the background and it says there's been another earthquake. Are you still in Christchurch?"

In front of her, Gene gestured toward the river, presumably asking her whether she would prefer it if he walked away. She shook her head. The last thing she wanted at that moment was to be left alone. He nodded and stood with his hands behind his back, military-style.

She didn't know whether to laugh, cry, or drool over him. Now he'd taken off his shirt, he was bare-chested, and all that expanse of tanned skin would have been enough to send her senses spinning, even if she hadn't already felt as if she were on a carousel. As she'd suspected, he was muscular and toned, with a definite six-pack of abs and pecs that made her want to run her tongue over them. He had a manly scattering of body hair, a distinctive happy trail drawing her gaze to where his pajamas hung on his hips. Quite clearly, he wasn't wearing any underwear beneath them.

"Callie?" Rowan's voice echoed in her ear.

She blinked, remembering she was on the phone and there had just been an earthquake. "Sorry. Yes, I'm in Christchurch. I'm standing on the bank of the Avon right now."

"Are you... You're not hurt?"

"No, I'm okay. It was loud and the hotel shook, but I don't think there's any damage, although the quake's knocked the electricity out."

"Are you on your own?"

She looked up at Gene again, who continued to stand as still as if he were on duty. "No," she said. "Gene's here."

"Oh, that's good. Does he know about last time?"

"No, I'll tell him now."

He raised an eyebrow. She held out a hand to ask him to wait. "Thanks for ringing," she said.

"Okay. You know where I am if you need me."

"Thanks."

They hung up. She folded her arms, huddling into Gene's sweatshirt, which still held some of his body warmth.

They stood in silence for a moment, half listening to the hotel staff explaining that they had to have the all clear from the fire service before they could return to their rooms. People were milling around, talking excitedly about the earthquake. Callie knew the phone lines would probably be jammed by now, even though it was the middle of the night, with everyone trying to contact friends and family to let them know they were okay.

A fire engine roared into the car park, lights flashing, and firefighters spilled out of it. They'd have to go floor to floor to check there was no damage before anyone else could go inside. It would be a while before she'd be under the warmth and safety of the duvet.

She turned and walked away from the hustle and bustle toward the river, and Gene followed.

"Sorry about that," she said.

"It's okay."

"Rowan was just checking I was all right. We were here when the big earthquake struck."

His eyes widened. "You were here in 2011?"

"Yeah. The four of us—Rowan, Bridget, Neve, and me—had come here for a fashion show. We were having lunch when the earthquake hit."

He stared at her. "You were in the middle of the city?"

"Yes. The ground cracked right under our feet. We ran down the road and were nearly hit when a supermarket crumbled in front of us. Actually, Neve *was* hit—she hurt her shoulder quite badly. She had to go to hospital. The rest of us were okay, but it was horrible."

She started shaking as she thought of it, and couldn't stop. "There were people crying all around us. Entire buildings crumbled into dust before our eyes. People's homes were destroyed in seconds, the walls just wrenched apart. Roads rippled and buckled as if they were made of plastic. A guy nearby us was crushed by the wall that hurt Neve. I watched his wife trying to get him to talk, but I knew he was dead." His sightless eyes would haunt her for the rest of her life, she was certain.

"Callie…"

"I can't believe it's happened again. I'm like a fucking jinx for this city!"

"Callie. Jesus." Gene pulled her into his arms. "It's okay."

She rested her forehead on his chest, rigid as a poker as she fought to control the wave of emotions sweeping over her. "It's not okay."

"No, it's not. I'm sorry." He kissed the top of her head.

That tender gesture was enough to tip her over the edge, and she started crying.

As the tears trickled down her cheeks and her chest heaved with uncontrollable sobs, she wondered whether he'd pat her arm awkwardly, or maybe even move away, embarrassed by her emotion.

He didn't, though. His arms tightened around her, warm and comforting, and he rubbed her back with a hand, murmuring, "Shh, shh, don't worry, I'm here."

Callie rested her cheek on his chest, the tension draining out of her, leaving her limp, like an old piece of celery. Gene felt solid, though, like a tree trunk warmed by the summer sun, his chest and arms hard, smelling of body wash and cotton sheets and hot, sexy male.

She'd tucked her arms against her chest, but as her tears subsided, she splayed a hand on his ribs, unable to restrain herself from touching him. He went still, and she thought that he might actually be holding his breath, too. Around them, the hubbub continued— firefighters coming and going in the building, people talking, phoning, the hotel staff trying to relay information. But for a brief moment, it faded, and her whole world became his warm breath on her temple, his strong arms, and his skin under her fingers.

His chest was wet from her tears, and she brushed her thumb through the wetness, spreading it a couple of inches across his skin, his light brown hairs moving and then springing back beneath her touch. When she exhaled, he shivered, although she wasn't sure if it was from the cool air or her breath on his wet skin.

She knew hardly anything about this man, but she liked him so much. When he'd said he might ask her out in three months, did he mean he wouldn't date anyone else until then? She didn't like the thought of him going out with another woman, holding her like this, kissing her.

"She's okay," Gene said suddenly over her shoulder, and she realized someone had asked him if she was all right. "Just a bit shaken up. Memories of 2011."

"Yes, there are quite a few people around here saying the same. Let us know if you need anything. It shouldn't be long now until you can return to your room." The man walked away, his footsteps crunching on the gravel.

Room, singular. He thought they were a couple. She supposed that made sense considering Gene was semi-naked and had his arms wrapped around her.

She should move back now, wipe her face, and thank him for comforting her. Put some distance between them.

But he didn't lower his arms, so she stayed put, and they remained like that for a while, saying nothing, until the firefighters declared the hotel was safe and everyone could return.

Gene finally loosened his arms, and Callie stepped back. She wiped her face and turned to go, then felt Gene's hand grasp hers firmly. She didn't complain.

"It was a six-point-five," the hotel manager explained as everyone returned, "but deep, and way out to sea. There doesn't appear to have been too much damage across the city, and so far nobody's been hurt."

"Thank God." Relief washed over her, and she sagged, exhausted.

Gene put one arm around her shoulders, pulling her against him as they walked back up the stairs, not wanting to wait with the crowds for the elevator. "Not far now," he said soothingly.

She was so tired she could hardly keep her eyes open. She dragged herself up the steps, exclaiming when she stumbled, her feet refusing to lift. Gene bent and slid an arm under her knees, and lifted her easily into his arms to climb the last few stairs. Callie held on while he carried her along the corridor to their rooms. His hair was prickly at the nape of his neck where it was so short, a little longer as she moved her hand up. If he was surprised by her sliding her fingers through his hair, he didn't say anything.

He bent to swipe her card, then opened the door. Carefully, he carried her through the doorway, into the room, and over to the bed. After pulling back the duvet, he lowered her onto the mattress. Then he covered her back over.

He cupped her face, his thumb brushing her cheekbone, wiping away the last of the wetness. "I'm just next door if you need me."

Callie felt overwhelmed with tiredness and emotion, and suddenly the last thing she wanted was to be alone. "Don't go," she whispered.

He hesitated, and she bit her lip. What a stupid thing to say, after they'd had that discussion about waiting until the time was right. Of course he wouldn't stay.

But to her surprise, he nodded and walked around the bed to the other side. He climbed on to lay beside her, on top of the duvet, and moved close to her. Then he lifted his arm.

Callie met his eyes for a moment, then shifted flush with him and rested her head on his shoulder. He lowered his arm around her, tight and warm even through the duvet, and held her close. He traced a finger around her face, lifting a strand of hair that had stuck to her wet cheek, and tucked it behind her ear.

"Don't be scared," he murmured. "I'll keep you safe."

"I know." She closed her eyes, and within seconds the world faded to darkness.

Chapter Fourteen

The next morning, Gene was on his second cup of coffee when Callie finally appeared at the breakfast table at eight.

"Afternoon," he said, turning off his phone and sliding it into his pocket.

She stuck her tongue out at him and took the seat opposite. "It's hardly late. Anyway, I forgot to set my alarm."

"You slept well, then?"

"Yes. Thank you." Her eyes met his. He was glad to see the emotion of the night before had vanished, and she seemed relaxed, if a little cautious. "Um... about last night..."

He waved a hand. "Just another of my PA duties. Nothing needs to be said."

She sucked her bottom lip for a moment. Then she said, "Okay," and turned to smile up at the waiter.

Gene surveyed her while she listened to the waiter relay the breakfast options. She wore a smart pantsuit today, in a light gray, with a sleeveless cream top, and she'd clipped up her hair, which made her look fresh, cool, and classy.

The night before, he'd lain there for an hour while she slept in his arms, enjoying the warmth and softness of her body against him, and just the feel of being close to someone. It was eight months since he'd broken up with Angela, and although he didn't miss her as much as he felt he should, he did miss the human contact. And the sex, of course. He missed the sex very much.

That was the main reason he'd risen from Callie's bed and left her sleeping, because he'd known that if he'd continued to lay there, eventually he wouldn't have been able to fight the temptation any longer. His hand would have stroked higher, brushing her ribcage, then finding its way to her breast, which would have felt uncaged and soft in his hand, and then it would only have been seconds before he would've rolled her onto her back and kissed her senseless.

"I'll have the full breakfast," she said. "With coffee, please."

Gene grinned. "I'll have the same," he told the waiter, who left to place their order.

"What are you smirking at?" She glared at him.

"Every other woman I know would have chosen toast or grapefruit."

"Boring," she said. "Besides, I need to keep my strength up. We've got a busy day today."

That was true on several accounts. They had visits planned to six stores throughout the day, and Gene knew it was going to be up to him to make sure Callie didn't run late.

Not only that, but he was expecting Kev to keep in touch during the day with any updates. When Gene had returned to his hotel room, with Callie's scent lingering on his skin and her tearstained face imprinted on his memory, he'd opened up his laptop and sat there for a while staring at the screen, wondering how he could help. He ran a security firm, not a detective agency, and the Special Tactics Group would have the hunt for Darren Kirk well in hand. But that didn't mean he couldn't try to think for himself.

After the same dark-haired man had been spotted on two separate days near Phoebe's house, Gene had instructed Kev to submit the photo to the STG and ask them to run it through their Australasian database to see what it threw up. The STG had sent the death threat to their labs to see if they could discover anything about its origin. They were keeping tabs on Kirk's family and friends that they knew of, and everyone involved in the trial had some form of security.

But Gene now had a personal, emotional investment in Callie's safety, and it wasn't enough for him to just sit around and wait to save Callie's life. He needed to do something. So he'd requested that his team leaders email in detailed hourly reports that Kev would scan, summarize, and then forward to him, rather than relying on an end-of-day report. They were to take photos of every person Phoebe interacted with, and these would be emailed to him, too, so he could compare them day to day. Any recurring faces he would immediately forward on to the STG.

He was sure the STG would find Kirk and arrest him before any danger was done, but Kirk probably wouldn't have made any personal attempts on the lives of those he hated. He would have hired a hitman or gotten one of his own crowd to do it, so it wasn't as simple just keeping an eye out for his face.

"You're quiet this morning," Callie said. "Did you sleep okay? How long did you stay in my room for?"

"Just an hour. You were sound asleep."

She accepted a cup of coffee from the waiter and dipped her spoon into the foam on the top. "I thought I would dream about the earthquake all night, but I didn't, thank God. I probably snored, though." She sipped the coffee.

"You did, very loudly. And dribbled all over my chest."

"I did not." She nudged his knee under the table.

He had to resist the urge to lean across and kiss away her pout. "Have you heard from Jamie again?"

She put down her cup. "No, and I doubt I will. We're not in regular contact, and he was just concerned because of the quake. I have no desire to get in touch with him again."

"So it's definitely over?"

She studied him. "Yes, it's over. I could never date him again. Once the trust is gone, you can't regain it, can you? It's like baking a cake. You can't get the eggs and flour back once it's been in the oven. The act of baking it changes it, and it can't be undone."

Gene looked out across the river, shifting in his chair. Trust was obviously an important factor for her, as it should be in all relationships. He hated that he was lying to her about his true identity. Would she understand when he finally told her, when Kirk was found? Or would she be angry?

It was a thought that would trouble him for the rest of the day, as he drove Callie from appointment to appointment, keeping a close eye on the time so she wouldn't be late. As he waited in another coffee shop for her to finish a visit, he wondered whether he should in fact tell her he was doubling as her bodyguard. But what would happen if she sacked him? He couldn't force her to have him as a personal protection officer. Shadowing her when she went out for a walk was one thing—doing it full time was another, and he wouldn't be able to protect her properly from a distance.

For now, he had to put his growing feelings for her to one side and concentrate on keeping her safe. The best way to do that would be to continue working as her PA, which meant he could practically glue himself to her side without her noticing. Everything else would have to wait.

And if, when he eventually told her who he really was, she became angry, he'd have to deal with that when it happened. Hopefully, she'd come to see both he and her mother were acting in her best interests. If she refused to accept that, well, there would be little he could do about it, and he'd just have to deal with the fact that she would be the one that got away.

The notion of that made him a little depressed, but his time in the Army had taught him it was pointless to worry about things that hadn't happened yet, and to live for today. So he drank his coffee, ate his brownie, and read through Kev's latest report while he waited for Callie to finish her appointment.

Halfway through the day, he made sure she stopped for some lunch. It was difficult, because she was on a high, super excited because two of the three morning appointments had brought definite agreements to stock the brand, and the other was open to discussion once the manager had spoken to his head office.

"I really think this might work," she announced as they tucked into pasta salads in a food mall conveniently placed between two stores she would be visiting.

"Of course it's going to work," he said. "You're so enthusiastic—how can anyone fail to be won over?"

Her brow furrowed. "Am I overdoing it?"

He chuckled and speared some pasta on his fork. "Of course not. It's nice to see you so happy. Especially after last night."

"I'm just glad the earthquake didn't do any lasting damage. I couldn't believe what the 2011 one did. It really makes you realize how small and insignificant you are compared to the wrath of nature. It was as if an enormous monster had taken both sides of the city in its hands and torn it apart. Whole houses destroyed, roads cracked and buckled. I've never seen anything like it. It was terrifying."

"Well, it seems as if this one was too deep and too far out to sea to have done much damage," he said.

She chewed on her pasta, her lips curving up. "You're good for me," she said. "I'm too airy-fairy and prone to panic. You're very calm and practical. Were you like that before you went in the Army?"

"Yes, although the Army taught me a lot about patience, and waiting. And that running around screaming doesn't get the job done. We're taught to work through our fear, and the chain of command means you have faith in your superiors and trust them to lead you through any dark times."

"I think you would have made a good leader yourself. I'm surprised you're not running your own company." Her eyes were cool, appraising. What was she thinking? Had she guessed he was hiding something?

Afraid she might look into his eyes and see the truth, he lowered his gaze and scraped up the last of the pasta. "I might do, in the future. I'm quite happy where I am at the moment, though."

"That's good." She pushed her plate away. "So, where are we off to now?"

He finished off with a swallow of soda. "Lacey's first. Then Prim & Proper."

"Come on, then."

So they set off for their second round of appointments. It was a busy afternoon, racing across the city. Thank God for GPS, Gene thought as he navigated his way to the last store. It made things a whole lot easier.

The afternoon turned out to be even more successful than the morning, with all three stores interested in stocking the Four Seasons brand. Callie was on an absolute high. She talked all through dinner about her plans for the business, a completely different girl to the one who'd shaken in his arms the night before.

She asked him his opinion of some of her ideas, and Gene was happy to talk, but mostly he just listened, captivated by her enthusiasm and the sheer force of her sparkling personality. He felt as if she were casting a spell on him, gradually encasing him in invisible threads that drew him slowly closer to her, binding him. What was wrong with him? He hadn't drunk anything, and he wasn't sick, and yet he felt feverish, his heart rate up, the blood racing through his veins.

"Oh my God, I've talked far too much this evening," she said when they eventually left the restaurant. "My voice is almost hoarse. I'm so sorry."

"Don't worry. I've had a great time. I like to see you so enthusiastic. I'm glad the day went well." He pressed the button for the elevator, and the doors opened immediately. They went in, and the doors slid shut. He could smell her body wash, something fresh and fruity, winding around him like ribbons.

"Me too. It's such a relief." She leaned against the wall. Her cheeks were a little flushed, her eyes sparkling.

"And I'm glad you feel better after last night." Their words were polite and courteous, but seemed disconnected from their bodies, which were having another conversation all of their own. This girl fitted her name perfectly—Sunny Summer. From her eyes to her dazzling smile to her curvy figure that made him think of bikinis and tanned skin damp with sweat, she was like a strawberry warmed by the sun, sweet and mouthwatering, filling his dull life with bright color and flavor.

"I do." Her gaze fixed on his, impish, challenging. "I think it was because I slept well."

Was she talking about him lying beside her? Gene couldn't think what to reply to that. It was as if all his social niceties were fading away and his prehistoric caveman tendencies were coming to the fore. He'd had enough of talking. The memory of being with her the night before had haunted him all day, and now it rose to overwhelm him.

He wanted her, so badly it made him ache. He wanted to crush his lips to hers and wrap his arms around her until he could feel her soft body against him. He wanted to rip off her cream top, then her trousers, and cover her warm skin with kisses. Peel off her flimsy lingerie with all its straps and lace and sexy satin. Take her then and there on the elevator floor.

"Oh, Gene," she said, scolding, mischievous. "There's only one thing I can do when you look at me like that."

She pushed off the wall. Not sure what she was going to do, Gene just stared at her, eyes widening, heart pounding, as she strode across the floor of the elevator. He inhaled sharply as she walked right up to him and cupped his cheek with a hand. Before he could say or do or think anything, she lifted up onto her tiptoes and pressed her lips to his.

Because he hadn't initiated it, and because he knew it was wrong, he didn't move. He didn't return the kiss, and didn't wrap his arms around her, pressing his hands against the wall of the elevator so he wasn't tempted to touch where he shouldn't.

But neither did he move away. Instead, he closed his eyes and breathed in the sweet, fruity scent of her body wash, tasting cherries on her lips. They were as soft as he'd dreamed, and he couldn't stop a small groan of pleasure rising within him as she pressed her lips to his a few times, sedate and gentle, but sexy as hell.

The elevator dinged, and the doors opened. Callie moved back. Her eyes danced with laughter.

"I wasn't going to do that," she said, walking out. "Your eyes led me on."

He followed her, heart hammering, head spinning. "I'm sorry." He had to remain professional. "I didn't mean to—"

"Oh, relax," she scolded, taking out her card as they reached her door. "No harm done. I'm not going to ravish you on the carpet or anything." She stopped and turned to him. "One thing last night did remind me of is how much we have to live for today. Life's short, Gene. It can be hard and harsh and filled with all kinds of trials and tribulations. So when something nice comes along, I'm not going to walk away. I'm going to follow my instincts and grab pleasure where I can."

Her eyes were bright, daring, rebellious, refusing to apologize for her act. And a teensy, tiny bit nervous, as if maybe she was worried he might quit on the spot and walk away.

"Fair enough," he said. "See you for breakfast at eight?"

He held her gaze. Her lips curved up slowly, and she gave a little nod.

Gene turned, let himself into his own room, and closed the door behind him. Then he finally blew out a long breath. Waiting for three months before dating Callie was a trial he knew he was going to struggle with. And if she was going to do things like that, he would need willpower of iron to survive.

He crossed to the bed and flopped onto it, face down, with a long, heartfelt groan.

Chapter Fifteen

The drive to the wine district of Marlborough was long and, for Callie at least, rather blissful—five uninterrupted hours in the car with Gene, broken only by a short stop in Kaikoura for a visit to a small lingerie store, following which they took a detour to drive out to the peninsula for lunch, eating it while watching the seals sunbathing on the rocks.

Apart from that, they hardly saw a soul on the winding road that shadowed the coast on their right, the land on their left consisting of tilled fields, hills and valleys stocked with the iconic New Zealand sheep, and, in the distance, white mountains, their icy tops lost in the clouds. Any settlements they passed through were small and quiet, with little more than the standard 'dairy' or general store selling not only dairy products but also newspapers, tinned goods for campers who might be passing and in need of stocking up on emergency supplies, cold drinks, and the traditional Kiwi staple—meat pies, usually containing cheese. Sometimes, a camper van meandered past, and occasionally they passed a parked car with a family having a picnic, but most of the time it was just her and Gene and the long stretch of road disappearing into the distance.

Conscious that she'd waffled on for most of the previous evening, Callie was worried Gene might be bored, but he certainly didn't seem it. They talked about everything under the sun, music, movies, even religion, something she didn't usually enjoy because it tended to bring out the worst in people, but Gene listened to her point of view, offered some of his own, and didn't try to browbeat her to think like himself, which she appreciated.

The night before, she'd lain awake for hours thinking about the way she'd reached up to kiss him, and cursing herself for being so forward. Her mother would have been horrified, not because she was old-fashioned and didn't believe in the girl expressing her thoughts, but because Gene had made it quite clear that he couldn't—or wouldn't—get involved until Becky came back. He worked for her, and he was a gentleman, and she knew she'd put him in a situation where it would have been very difficult for him to say no. No doubt he would have been concerned that, if he'd refused to return the kiss, she would have sacked him.

He hadn't actively kissed her back—he'd frozen, and he hadn't wrapped his arms around her, or done anything in fact but stand there and let her kiss him. He had closed his eyes, though, and he hadn't jerked his head away or exclaimed his disgust. Instead, a low, satisfied groan had rumbled in his chest, almost a moan, and when she'd finally pulled back, his eyes had been half-lidded with desire.

But that wasn't the point. The earthquake might have renewed her feelings that life was short and it was important to grab the bull by the pointy things, but she had to let this proceed at its own pace. When Gene was ready, he'd make a move on her, she was sure. Until then, she had to restrain herself and behave in a ladylike fashion.

She sighed. *Boring.*

"We're nearly there," Gene said. "Are you tired?"

Oops. She'd sighed too loudly. "No, nothing like that. It is a long way, but it's been a beautiful journey."

"This is a fantastic part of the world. I love Blenheim. I could live here." He spoke with enthusiasm.

"What do you like about it?"

He took the turnoff for the town center. "It's a thriving town. It's always been sunny whenever I've visited, and it seems to have everything—coastal activities, bush walks, and of course the vineyards."

Callie could see some of them stretching away to the hills surrounding the Wairau Plain, and she knew the vines would be heavy with ripe fruit. "I've got an idea," she announced. "After the appointment today, why don't we go for a wine tasting at a local vineyard?"

Gene glanced across at her. "I don't drink, you know that."

"Rubbish. You were just telling me about how you prefer Merlot to Shiraz."

"I don't drink at the moment. Not while I'm working."

"Please. I don't come here very often, and it seems a shame to travel all this way and not make the most of the local produce."

"You talk as if they sell cabbages. It's not as simple as tasting the local coleslaw."

"I'm not saying we have to get out of our heads. Have you seen how much wine they put in your glass when you do a tasting? It's, like, a fraction of an inch."

"I'll think about it," he said, in a voice that told her he was still going to say no, but he was fed up with her badgering him about it.

She stuck out her bottom lip. "You're thirty-one—that's only five years older than me."

"Thirty-two on Sunday."

"Well, that's still only six years. You're hardly old enough to be my father, so I really wish you didn't talk like him." There was enough genuine exasperation there to make her turn her head away and glare out the window.

Gene said nothing, concentrating on navigating the roads. He drove straight through the town, and didn't turn off until they were heading toward the fields of vines.

Callie soon forgot her grump as she looked out and saw a range of long, low, whitewashed buildings with terracotta roofs. She looked at Gene in delight. "We're staying at a vineyard?"

His lips curved up, and he steered the car into a space. "Don't get any ideas."

"Oh, how lovely." She leapt out of the car and ran up to the gate. Cobbled paths surrounded the central wooden reception building. To its left were the buildings she assumed incorporated the wine cellar. To the right, a large courtyard backed onto the restaurant. All its doors stood open, and she could see through it to the vineyards beyond. Vines were everywhere, curled around posts and across the latticework over the courtyard. Everything was rich, green, and fertile. She felt as if she were visiting the home of Mother Earth herself.

"I'm glad you like it." Gene held out his hand to her. "Come on, let's check in."

She took it, surprised, thinking that his offering it must have been a reflexive gesture, because he hadn't done it before. He held it until they reached the reception desk, then gave her fingers a squeeze before releasing it. Her skin tingled from his warmth and the delight of touching him. She wanted more! But she reminded herself of her promise in the car. *Practice restraint, Callie.*

They checked in and were shown to their rooms, which both faced the vineyards. Callie unpacked a few things and hung up her dress for the evening and her clothes for the next day, then opened the sliding doors to the small patio and stepped outside. It was heading toward four o'clock, and the sun had begun its descent to the west. The vineyards were bright in the sun, bunches of grapes hanging below the leaves, ripe and sweet.

"Beautiful," she whispered, tipping her face up to the sun and closing her eyes.

"I'll second that."

She opened her eyes in surprise and turned to see Gene leaning against the post between their rooms, watching her.

"Oh." She shielded her eyes. "I was talking about the view."

He just smiled. "Are you ready to get going? You're supposed to be at the store at four."

Something about his steady gaze unnerved her and sent her heart hammering. "Yes, of course. I'll meet you out by the car."

He nodded, but made no sign of moving. What was he thinking? Was he remembering the way she'd kissed him in the elevator? Because Callie was. His lips had been firm, warm, and dry. They'd parted a little when he'd gasped in surprise, but she hadn't taken advantage of that. Instead, she'd pressed her lips to his a few times, enjoying the sensation of his bristles against the pads of her fingers, and the deep, spicy tones of his aftershave, sensations masculine enough to send tingles through her lady bits that made her want to pin him to the wall and strip him naked.

He raised an eyebrow. Callie turned on her heel and went back into her room.

*

She was nearly an hour at the store. The manager loved the Four Seasons brand and wanted to go through every piece of lingerie and swimwear. The two of them lost themselves in talking about designs and the clothing business, and both of them were surprised when they heard the store announcement that it would be closing in five minutes.

Callie shook the manager's hand and left the store, crossing the high street to where she'd agreed to meet Gene in the bookshop opposite. He came out as she neared, looking—to her surprise—a little flustered.

"What's up?" she asked, puzzled at his demeanor. He stood before her with his hands behind his back, shuffling from foot to foot, not meeting her gaze.

"How did it go?" he asked.

"Great. Sorry I was such a long time, but we got talking. Is everything all right?"

"Yes, yes." He brought one hand up to scratch his nose. "You were gone a while, so I had a look in the shops. I found something, and I thought of you, so I bought it, and then I realized it was inappropriate." He looked pained.

"What is it?" she asked, intrigued. "A vibrator?"

His expression turned wry. "No, not quite." He hesitated, then brought his other hand from behind his back. He was holding a red rose, a perfect bud, with a piece of silvery ribbon around the stem. "Sorry," he said.

Callie reached out and took it, automatically bringing it to her nose to sniff its scent. "Don't apologize."

"It's not appropriate at all, and I do apologize for that. I didn't mean to suggest—"

"Gene," she said softly, "it's okay. It's beautiful, and I like beautiful things. Thank you."

He paused, then nodded. "Let's go back to the car."

Callie said nothing more, but inside, she had filled with warmth. He was right—it wasn't an appropriate gesture from an employee to his employer. But it said everything that words couldn't right now. He liked her. He wanted to get to know her better. And just knowing that would be enough to keep her going.

Chapter Sixteen

One of the reasons Gene had bought the rose was because while he'd waited for Callie in the coffee shop, he'd chatted to Kev, who'd told him there had been no more suspicious activity around Phoebe, no more death threats, and things appeared to have quietened down. Kev had also spoken to their contact at the STG, who'd informed him that they had a lead on Darren Kirk and were hoping to have him in custody within a day or two.

Gene had felt a rush of relief at the knowledge that it wouldn't be long before Callie's life was free from danger. It also meant that he wouldn't have to act as her personal protection officer anymore. And that meant they would be free to date.

He'd seen the rose with its light red velvety petals—the same color Callie's cheeks turned when she blushed—and he'd bought it on impulse, disappointed that up until now he'd not been able to express his true feelings for her. Straight afterward, as he'd walked out of the shop, he'd felt stupid and wished he hadn't bought it. Kirk wasn't yet in custody, and a hundred things could go wrong between now and that coming to pass. He had to remember that Callie wouldn't be safe until Kirk was caught and his men stood down, and until then, Gene had to keep himself emotionally removed from her and remain on guard at all times.

He'd taken the rose to a rubbish bin and held it there for a long while before cursing himself and walking away.

Now, he had mixed feelings about his decision to give it to Callie. She hadn't made a fuss, and didn't appear to have taken it as a declaration of love, which of course it wasn't, because he'd only known her a week and they'd only kissed once. She hadn't even mentioned it again. But as he drove back to the vineyard, he glanced across at her and saw her looking out the window, lost in a daydream, trailing the rose across her cheek to inhale its scent absently, a smile curving her lips. It warmed him through and made him anxious at the same time, but he tried to put his anxiety to one side. It was just a flower, a nice gesture, and she was so lovely, she deserved it.

That evening was one of the nicest he'd spent in a long time. Relaxed after his conversation with Kev, Gene gave in and agreed to a wine tasting, and the two of them listened to the talk given by the vineyard owner as they sipped at samples of Pinot gris, Sauvignon, Chardonnay, Shiraz, and Merlot, arguing good-naturedly about which was the best.

Then they returned to the restaurant and spent a long while over a couple of platters of cheese, meat, and seafood, and he allowed himself one glass of Sauvignon as they watched the sun sink gradually toward the horizon. The air was warm and a little sultry, and Callie's skin glowed, a combination of the wine and the heat bringing a flush to her cheeks.

She still hadn't mentioned the rose, and she wasn't overly familiar toward him or anything, but her manner was relaxed. Whenever she met his gaze, the look in her eyes sent a tingle running through him from the roots of his hair to the tips of his toes.

Tonight, she wore a long summer dress in a bright blue the color of her eyes, covered with shining darker blue and green swirls like a peacock's feather. It was hardly revealing, but it clung to her curves as she leaned forward to lift her drink, drawing his gaze repeatedly to her breasts, the dip of her waist, and the swell of her bottom when she sashayed away to the ladies' room.

The fever that had begun days ago grew to a raging heat for her that refused to be quenched. It couldn't be alcohol, he thought, because he'd only had the tasters and one other glass. But he felt dizzy with lust, desperate to pull her into his arms, to feel his lips on hers. What was wrong with him? He was a grown man, more than able to control his desires. Why did he feel like a teenage boy with his first crush?

He tried to make the evening last as long as he could, but all good things come to an end, and eventually, as stars began to pop out against the fading darkness, they finished their drinks and walked slowly back to their rooms, lit by the solar lights strung along the path.

"What a gorgeous evening." Callie looked up at the stars. Somewhere in the distance, a morepork hooted from a tree, mournful in the night. *More pork. More pork.*

"It is. Made more beautiful by the delicious company." He couldn't stop the compliment falling from his lips.

She paused outside her room and turned an impish gaze up to him. "Delicious? Interesting choice of adjectives. You sound as if you could eat me up."

He couldn't ignore the suggestiveness behind that comment. He gave a short laugh, and her lips curved up, her eyes glittering in the semi-darkness. "I could," he said, his heart thudding. He moved closer to her, hands behind his back so he wasn't tempted to touch her. "And I bet you taste sweet, like strawberries."

"Shame you won't get to find out," she said.

His heart pounded, and his breaths came quickly. The notion of stripping Callie naked, kissing down her body, and sinking his tongue into her folds had him hard as a rock in seconds.

But he shouldn't. He couldn't. He wouldn't. He was here to protect her, and he couldn't do that if he was sleeping with her.

Callie didn't move toward him, but neither did she move to open her door. She was going to leave it up to him.

He had to stay strong. For heaven's sake, he'd coped for months as a single man, in the desert, miles from the nearest desirable and available woman, without a second thought. He could gather the strength to resist one girl for one evening. Even if she did smell divine. Even if her lips did look soft and red as the petals of the rose he'd bought her. Even if she was looking at him with yearning in her eyes. He might not have been old enough to be her father, but he was older than her, and he was a man—he should be the one to exhibit restraint and be wise enough for the both of them.

Callie moistened her lips with the tip of her tongue, and something popped inside Gene's head.

Fuck it.

Bringing up a hand to cup her cheek, he moved forward until they were only an inch apart. Callie didn't move, but her breasts rose and fell quickly, and her eyes widened, the pupils huge in the semi-darkness.

"Tell me to stop," he said huskily, pausing when his lips were a fraction of an inch from hers.

She didn't move to kiss him this time, but waited, her breath whispering across his lips, and gave an almost undetectable shake of her head.

"Please," he demanded. He wasn't strong enough. He was weak—possibly the weakest man of all time, a slave to his senses, a self-indulgent fool who would undoubtedly regret this in the morning, but who, right now, could no more walk away from this woman than he could turn his back on someone who was drowning.

Callie still didn't move. When she spoke, her voice was soft as the summer breeze that was stroking the back of his neck. "Why would I do that, when it's what I want more than anything in the world?"

Gene groaned, slid his hand into her hair, and lowered his lips to hers.

Their previous kiss had been feather-light, tender and gentle. But this time, he was too hungry to rein in his passion.

He claimed her mouth, hot and hard, conscious he could almost be bruising her with his ardor, but she didn't complain or move back. Quite the opposite—she lifted her arms around his neck and pressed herself against him, tipping her head to the right to change the angle of the kiss. He brushed his tongue across her bottom lip, and she moaned and opened her mouth to him, welcoming the slide of his tongue inside with little thrusts of her own.

Gene's thoughts and emotions spiraled together, becoming a jumble of sensations. He couldn't think about anything but the sensual slip of her tongue against his, the feel of her silky hair sliding through his fingers, the softness of her flesh beneath his hand when he laid it on her waist. As he'd guessed, she tasted of strawberries, the prominent flavor of the rosé she'd been drinking, touched with the earthy richness of the chocolate pudding they'd eaten at the end of their meal.

He moved his hand to the small of her back, pulling her against him, feeling the press of her breasts against his chest. *Slowly*, his mind scolded him—this was just a kiss, and he didn't want to insult her by assuming it would lead to anything more. Which of course it shouldn't.

Pull away now, his brain yelled. *Say thank you and wish her goodnight, and retire gracefully before you make a fool of yourself.*

But it was hard to stop when she'd tugged his shirt from his trousers and had slipped her fingers beneath it. Her hand was warm on his back, her nails grazing as she explored his muscles, and when she scored them lightly around his ribs and stroked over his nipples, Gene nearly exclaimed out loud.

Callie moved then, stepping back, and with surprise he realized she'd opened her door and was backing into her room. He paused, about to say something, but she took his hand and pulled him with her, leading him inside.

He went, because he was too confused and excited and hot to refuse, but as she let the door close behind her and continued to back up to the dresser against the wall, warning bells rang in his head, and he opened his mouth to say something.

Callie pulled him hard toward her, though, hard enough to make him stumble, and he fell against her, jolting the dresser and making the leaflet on the vineyard that stood there fall over.

"Sorry," he began, "I should—"

But she turned, and with one arm swept the leaflets, cards, pens, and other knickknacks onto the floor. Backing up, she rested her bottom on the edge and lifted herself onto the top. Then she pulled up her dress to her knees, parted her legs, and yanked him toward her.

"Callie," he said, resting his hands on her knees, but any warning he might have given vanished at the feel of her soft skin beneath his fingers and the temptation of her silky thighs lying just within reach.

"Kiss me," she whispered, reaching up a hand to slide into his hair, and she clenched her fingers in the short strands. Her nails scraped across his scalp, and Gene was lost.

"Fuck," he said, and crushed his mouth to hers.

Callie gave a long, low moan deep in her throat that reverberated right through him. He delved his tongue into her mouth, hungry now, wanting to consume her, possess her, more than anything he'd ever wanted in his life, he was sure.

Slowly, he slid the skirt of her dress up her thighs, his fingers finding soft, warm, silky skin. It was warm in the room as she hadn't turned on the air conditioning, and her skin felt a little moist to the touch, the same way he knew sweat would be dampening his hair at his temples and the nape of his neck. He wanted to run his tongue up her body, to taste the salt, but she was widening her thighs to give him better access, and of their own accord his fingers hooked in the elastic of her panties and slipped around between her legs.

He lifted his head and watched her as he moved his thumb down over the soft skin, where it slid easily through her slippery folds to the already-swollen bud of her clit. Her mouth opened and she inhaled, but she didn't push him away. He moved his thumb down to collect some of her moisture, then returned it to circle over her clit, pressing lightly on the small swelling.

"Oh…" Her teeth tugged at her bottom lip. "Gene…"

"Is that nice?" Fuck, it was heavenly, feeling her, knowing she was aroused, seeing her eyelids drop to half-mast with pleasure at his touch.

"Yes…" she hissed.

Keeping his gaze locked on hers, he lifted his thumb to his mouth and sucked it. There might have been a very small chance of him stopping a few minutes ago. It had rapidly shrunk to miniscule when he'd touched her. And now he'd tasted her, there was no question it was zero.

"I want you," she said. All signs of humor and teasing had vanished from her eyes, which glittered with a dark passion that made his erection strain at the seam of his trousers.

"Good," he replied, and kissed her again.

Chapter Seventeen

Callie pushed herself off the dresser, then lifted her arms as Gene held the bottom of her dress and drew it up her body. He did it slowly, almost reverently, as if excited to reveal her inch by inch, feasting his eyes on what lay beneath as the material peeled slowly up her skin.

Her heart thumped against her ribs as the dress reached her hips, her waist, skimmed over her breasts, and then she felt her hair lift as he drew it over her head. He draped it over a nearby chair and turned back to rest his hands on her hips.

She fought the urge to cover herself up and instead leaned back against the dresser, her body burning under his heated gaze.

"Pretty," he said, running a finger across the top of her bra. His finger hooked over the lace, brushing her skin. "But not as pretty as what's underneath."

She wore one of Rowan's creations—a comfortable but stylish orange-colored set with blush-red lace and golden embroidery. It always made Callie think of a sunset on a warm February night.

"Why does everything about you remind me of summer?" he whispered as if reading her mind, sliding his hands around her back to her bra strap. One neat twist and the clasp opened, her breasts dropping a little as the elastic released them. Drawing the straps down her arms, his gaze rested on her breasts as they were gradually revealed.

"Jesus." He tossed the bra behind him without looking to see where it landed. She liked that—it was as if he couldn't bear to spare the few seconds it would take to look away. Cupping her breasts, he felt the weight of them on his palms, then stroked his thumbs across her nipples. "You're so beautiful." He circled the pads of each thumb around the edges of her nipples a few times, watching as they tightened, then took the resulting beads between his thumbs and forefingers and tugged gently.

"Oh…" Already fired up, Callie gave in to her need to kiss him and pressed her lips to his, sliding her hands to his waistcoat. He stepped back, however, undid the buttons of his waistcoat himself, and let it slip down his arms before tossing it onto the chair. Then his lips were on hers again, and this time when she removed his tie and started to unbutton his shirt, he let her.

Suddenly everything became urgent. The previously gentle presses of his lips turned into a heated and demanding capture of hers, and Callie welcomed his hot kisses, hungry for him, wanted to consume and be consumed by him. Her fingers fumbled in their rush to see him naked, and it took her a few goes to get all the buttons of his shirt undone. Reaching the bottom, she pushed both sides of the shirt apart and groaned at the feel of his warm skin beneath her fingertips.

"You're driving me mad," he said, his voice husky with desire.

"I want to." She slid her hands up under his shirt, skating across the smooth skin of his back. She felt giddy with lust, desperate to have his naked skin next to hers. Pushing his shirt off his shoulders and letting it drop to the floor, she wrapped her arms around his waist and pressed herself against him. "I want you, Gene. I'm aching for you. I want you inside me. I haven't been able to think about anything else all day. I don't care if I'm moving too fast or being reckless. Life's about the here and now and, here and now, I want you."

"I want you too. I have since the moment I walked into your office." He kissed down her neck, his tongue hot and wet on her skin, tracing down to her breasts, where he covered a nipple with his mouth. Callie clenched inside as he sucked, tightening her fingers in his hair and groaning. He swapped from one nipple to the other, teasing them with his lips and tongue until they looked like pebbles on the beach, wet from the sea, hard and shiny.

"Stop," she said with a gasp as she felt the first flickers of an orgasm approaching, way off in the distance. "I need you inside me. Please."

He straightened, admiring the effect he'd had on her nipples for a moment before hooking his thumbs in the elastic of her panties and drawing them down her legs. She stepped out of them and lifted herself back onto the dresser, parted her knees, then pulled him toward her by the waistband of his jeans.

"Have you got a condom?" she asked. She had one in her handbag if he didn't, but was relieved when he nodded. Her fingers fumbled at the button of his jeans while he retrieved it from his wallet, and once he'd found it, he helped her out, undoing the button and sliding down the zip.

Callie inhaled at the sight of his erection jutting out from his jeans, encased in thin black cotton briefs. She'd dreamed about this moment since he'd walked into her office, all smart and sophisticated, with those sultry, knowing eyes that said, *One day you'll beg me to take you, and I'm going to enjoy every minute of it.*

Suddenly, the full realization of what they were about to do hit her. This wasn't teasing, or flirting, or making out on the sofa. This was naked, raw, adult sex. Gene wasn't a teenager—he wasn't even like Jamie, a young man with more hormones than sense. He was a grown man, a hundred percent XY chromosome—possibly more so than any man she'd ever met. Once they'd done what they were about to do, there would be no going back. They'd never be able to undo the memory of his body sliding into hers, of their baser instincts taking over. Of being locked in ecstasy together.

She swallowed hard as he ripped the packet off the condom. Was she being foolish? It might be the twenty-first century, and women had a lot more sexual freedom than they used to have, but that didn't mean they should sacrifice their self-worth to achieve it. If it had been up to him, he would have walked away and returned to his own room. He had principles, but he was still a man, and she'd pushed him past his limits until nature had taken over from the civilized soul inside him. Would he regret this in the morning?

That might indeed be the case, but she couldn't stop now. Just as his body had shifted into autopilot, so Callie's had become pure sensation. It was like being drunk, even though she'd only had a couple of glasses of wine, but the thrumming in her blood, the desperate urge to have him inside her, made everything else fade into the background until the world consisted only of the man before her, with his hard muscles, his hungry mouth, and the stiff shaft he was now releasing from his briefs that strained eagerly toward her.

He hadn't removed his trousers, and as he pushed down his briefs, she caught a glimpse of puckered skin on his hip—the wound he'd received in Afghanistan. She wondered briefly whether he was worried about her seeing the scar, but then all thoughts fled as he lifted the elastic of his briefs over his erection.

Callie fought not to pant out loud as he grasped it and stroked himself a couple of times before rolling on the condom. Fuck, this guy knew what he was doing, and that was so sexy she nearly melted into a puddle. She widened her thighs as he moved closer to her and parted her folds with the tip of his erection.

Then he paused, cupped her chin, and lifted it so he looked into her eyes.

"Are you sure?" he murmured.

"I'm sure."

He kissed her, and then he pushed his hips forward and sank slowly into her.

Callie closed her eyes and tipped back her head as he filled her. He didn't stop until his hips met her thighs. She tightened her internal muscles, and she could feel him all the way up, so thick and hard she nearly came on the spot.

He groaned and began to move with cautious thrusts at first to make sure he was lubricated. He slipped his hand into her hair to cup the back of her head, his lips finding hers again with deep, searching kisses that took her breath away. His fingers were gentle on her hair and where he held her hip, but firm, and as his thrusts grew bolder, his kisses harder, she had the blissful feeling of him taking over and guiding them both toward the ecstasy of fulfilment.

He slid inside her so easily now that she knew she must be wet and swollen, all her senses turning her on. The feel of him as she rested a hand on his arm, admiring the movement of his biceps beneath her fingers, like rock beneath the satin of his skin. The sexy sound of him inside her, slick and sensual, and the deep murmur of his voice in her ear as he told her how beautiful she was while he made love to her. The taste of him, sweet as wine, and the smell of his aftershave mingled with the smell of sex. And the sheer sight of this gorgeous man taking her, his body painted silver with starlight.

"Callie," he whispered, pulling her close, shifting his stance. He thrust even deeper into her, but clearly it wasn't enough, because after a few moments he slid his hands beneath her and lifted her. She squealed, flinging her arms around his neck, but he held her tightly with one around her waist, and within seconds she found herself on her back on the bed with Gene leaning over her, supporting himself on his hands and casting her in shadow.

She wrapped her legs around his waist, lifting her hips, and he groaned and thrust forward, burying himself deep inside her. "Fuck," he said, and did it again, setting up a fast pace, grinding against her clit every time he moved.

He bent and captured her mouth with his, his tongue hot and wet against hers, and Callie felt the world falling away around her. She moaned against his mouth, and he lifted his head, his gray eyes glittering in the moonlight.

"Come for me," he whispered, still moving, and kissed down her neck to her breast. He swirled his tongue over her nipple and plucked at it with his lips, and it was enough to tip her over the edge.

"Oh," she said, half conscious that he'd lifted his head to watch her as she came. But there was nothing she could do about it, because the orgasm had her in its grasp, and she could only cry out and give in to the fierce clenches. They seemed to go on forever, and while her body pulsed, without thinking she dug her fingernails into his back and scored down it.

"*Aaahhh...*" Gene shuddered and lifted up to thrust harder, giving in to his climax just as hers released her. She forced her eyes open to watch him stiffen, his muscles hardening even more, if that were possible, as if his body had been turned to stone, a frozen monument of the perfect moment. His hips jerked and he cried out, pushing forward so hard she imagined that he would pierce her right through to the mattress.

"Fuck." He almost yelled the word as his body finally relented and released him. His breaths came in great gasps, and when he opened his eyes, Callie was shocked to see them filled with anger.

Moving back, he held the condom as he withdrew, sat back on his haunches and disposed of it, then flung himself onto his back and covered his eyes with an arm.

Callie looked up at the ceiling, her own breathing gradually slowing, and tears pricked her eyelids. He was angry with her, because now the paroxysm of lovemaking had subsided, his better nature had returned. He hadn't wanted to give in to their obvious desire for each other, but she'd made him, or at least he felt that she'd provoked him until he'd been unable to say no.

She clenched her jaw until her teeth ached. Well that was bullshit, because he was a grown man, and at any point he could have stopped. She might have encouraged him, but she'd hardly stripped naked on the front step. And even if she had, that didn't mean he had to take advantage of the moment. She hadn't forced him to make this choice. He'd lost control, and that wasn't her fault. Like all men, he'd been led astray by his own desires.

She rolled her head to look at him. His arm lay over his face, and his chest was still heaving. His other hand rested on his stomach, clenched into a fist. His body looked like a black-and-white photograph in the moonlight, all silver muscles and shadowed hollows, and part of her wished she had the courage to reach for her phone and take a photo of him to remind herself of this night. He'd tucked himself back into his briefs, but his trousers still lay open, the top of the scar on his hip just visible. Would she ever get to see the rest of it? Somehow, she thought not.

Listening to his breathing gradually leveling out beside her, his arm still over his face, she fought not to let the tears fall. She might not have forced him into this, but that didn't mean she wasn't foolish. She should have guessed he'd feel this way afterward. Whatever happened now, she had to bear some of the blame. Men were weak, and she'd been an idiot not to take that into account.

Chapter Eighteen

Gene's heart was pounding on his ribs as if it were trying to break through and escape across the room, but after a few minutes it began to slow and his breathing gradually returned to normal.

Still, he didn't move. His arm blocked out the shine of the moon through the window, and also the view of Callie lying next to him.

He knew he was being rude. He'd just made passionate love to possibly the most beautiful girl—both inside and out—that he'd ever met, and since he'd come, he'd done the equivalent of rolling over and going to sleep. She didn't deserve that.

The mattress lifted beside him, and he felt Callie roll off and heard her pad over to the bathroom. The door closed.

He lowered his arm and stared up at the ceiling, then got to his feet and walked over to the window. The vineyard rolled away from him in stripes of silver and black. Far above, the Milky Way looked like spilled milk across the glittering sky.

Leaning on the window, he rested his head on his forearm. *You fucking idiot.* Getting involved with a client was number one on the personal protection officer's What Not To Do list. Being a bodyguard was about solid concentration, about not getting distracted, and the worst thing he could have done was give in to his lust. He despised himself for being so weak. Not only was he risking Callie's safety, but she deserved so much more than a one-night stand, especially considering what she'd been through with her ex. It didn't matter that he hoped to date her once Kirk was caught. He'd deceived her by not telling her the truth about his true reason for being there. Once she learned that, she might not want to see him, and by seducing her, he'd only served to confuse things more.

No doubt she thought it was her fault for flirting with him. She wouldn't understand that even though he'd expressed his desire to wait, he'd seduced her nevertheless, by having dinner with her, drinking wine with her, and buying the fucking rose. Why the hell had he done that? How was that maintaining a business relationship?

It was entirely his fault, and now he could only blame himself if everything went tits up.

The bathroom door opened behind him. He pushed off the window and turned to see Callie exiting the room. She looked at the bed first, stopped as she saw it empty, sighed as she presumably thought he'd left, then inhaled sharply when she saw him standing by the window.

"I thought you'd gone," she said.

"I wouldn't do that," he replied softly.

She walked forward to stand by the window. The moonlight slanted across her. Her golden hair became a sheet of silver, her body like a marble statue of a Greek goddess. She crossed her arms over her breasts, telling him she felt uncomfortable with him because of what he'd done.

"I'm sorry," he said. He stepped close, wrapped his arms around her, and turned his back to the window, not liking her being exposed to anyone lurking in the shadows. *Bit fucking late for that,* he thought, but all he could do now was thank his lucky stars that she was safe, and make sure he protected her better in the future.

She stayed stiff in his arms, although she rested her forehead on his shoulder. "Don't be angry with me," she whispered.

"With you? Honey, I'm angry with myself, not with you. I could never be angry with you." He kissed her hair, stroking her back.

"I thought you resented me coming on to you."

"No." He closed his eyes, enjoying the feel of her silky skin beneath his fingertips. "Of course not. I'm flattered. I'm cross with myself because it's unprofessional to become involved with you. I told myself that many times, but I suppose it says something about how attracted I am to you that I couldn't keep away."

She placed her hands on his chest and pushed back to look up at him. Her face was dry, and her eyes held a touch of rebellion. "Don't regret this," she said. "It's the best thing that's happened to me for months."

"I won't," he said, although he did, because he couldn't shake the feeling that he'd jeopardized his chance of a future with her. "But it can't happen again, Callie."

"I know." Her eyes looked like the night sky, the pupils encompassing almost all of the irises. He couldn't tell what she was thinking. Was she just saying what she wanted him to hear? Or did she truly believe that? Something twisted inside him. What a hopeless situation.

He touched her cheek, and when she didn't pull away, he kissed her, long and lingering. Her lips were dry and soft beneath his. She remained passive, letting him kiss her, but not returning it, with no sign of the passion that had been evident while they'd been making love, which had been better than he'd fantasized, and he had a pretty good imagination. The memory of plunging into her warm, wet body was making him hard again, and he didn't want her to be aware of that, so he moved back reluctantly. "I'd better go to my own room."

"Okay."

He released her and slipped his shirt and then his waistcoat on, and shoved his feet back in his shoes. Finally, he collected his phone and wallet.

When he turned back to her, he saw that she'd pulled on the sweatshirt he'd loaned to her in Christchurch. "It's cozy," she protested when he raised an eyebrow. "I'll give it back to you when we get to Wellington."

"Keep it. It looks better on you than it does on me." There was something sexy about a woman in a man's clothes.

She accompanied him to the door and held it open for him. He hesitated in the doorway. "Thank you," he said. He was grateful not just because she'd given herself to him, but because she hadn't argued when he'd tried to explain why he was angry. That boded well for the future, he thought.

She rested her head on the doorjamb. "See you for breakfast?"

"Of course." He scratched the back of his neck. "I know I have no right to ask a favor of you, but can you not tell Neve about what happened tonight?"

She blinked, her eyes inscrutable. "I won't be telling anyone, Gene." She pushed off the doorjamb. "Sleep well."

"'Night."

The door closed.

*

The next morning, as he sipped his coffee at the breakfast table, Gene glanced at Callie's face and thought that she looked as if she'd had even less sleep than he'd had. Her usually flawless complexion bore a dark smudge beneath each eye.

He was relieved that she'd smiled at him as they'd walked into the restaurant, but he noticed that she only ordered a bowl of muesli, and now she was stirring the oats and fruit with her spoon while she read from her iPad, unusually quiet compared to the bright chatter she usually exhibited.

"So, off to Nelson today," he said.

"Yes. The final city on our whistle-stop tour." She ate a strawberry, and Gene found himself watching her lips move as she chewed, his body tightening when her tongue peeked out to catch a drop of milk from her lip.

He lowered his gaze and concentrated on his bagel. "Three appointments there, isn't it?"

"Yes, that's right. All in the afternoon."

They were as polite as strangers. Nobody listening would have guessed that the night before they'd done the most intimate thing two people could do together, naked in the heat and the dark.

Well, what had he expected? Had he thought she wouldn't be affected by his attitude and the way he'd acted?

I won't be telling anyone, Gene. Was she ashamed of what they'd done? Did she wish it hadn't happened? And yet she'd also said, *Don't regret this... It's the best thing that's happened to me for months.* Maybe she just wanted to keep it private. He hoped she wouldn't tell Neve anyway. He knew girlfriends often confided in each other, but he didn't want the feisty Neve telling Phoebe he'd let them both down.

He pushed away his plate, the bagel half-eaten, and Callie did the same, fruit and oats still swimming in the milk.

"Shall we go?" she said.

He nodded, and they left to retrieve their cases.

As he took the road west out of Blenheim, he wondered what he could say to make things better, but he couldn't think of anything. He'd been so stupid. He didn't know which part of his actions was worse—sleeping with someone he'd promised to protect, or rejecting her once he'd done so.

There was no point in apologizing again—he was sure that would only irritate or annoy her. He couldn't say that his declaration that it couldn't happen again was wrong, because he had to distance himself from her now and remain professional. Telling her how wonderful it had been to take her to bed would be rubbing salt into what was obviously a sore wound. So what was there to say?

Still, his heart ached as the fields and vineyards disappeared in his rearview mirror and the countryside became wild and mountainous. The road wound up thickly forested hillsides and down into valleys that glistened with deep green rivers.

Gene would have liked to have discussed the views, but something in Callie's reserved manner made him keep his mouth shut. They stopped at a place called the Crab Pot Café for lunch, but in spite of the glorious food, neither of them ate much, and it wasn't long before they were on the road again.

Callie remained quiet, and in the end Gene put on some classical music and just drove, leaving her to her own thoughts and cursing his idiocy all the way. Although it was a winding road, it wasn't long before the road dipped and turned toward the coast, and suddenly there was Tasman Bay before them, sparkling a gorgeous blue in the summer sun.

"Oh," Callie said, the first word she'd uttered for about thirty minutes.

"Beautiful, isn't it?" He couldn't help but comment, desperate to get her talking to him again.

"It is. I love Nelson. I could easily live here." She sat up straighter in her seat, peering past him to look at the sea. It couldn't have been a more beautiful day. "The sun always seems to shine here."

"You're right. It has its own little micro-climate, and it's the sunniest place in New Zealand. We're staying in a villa near Tahunanui Beach, if you'd like to have a walk along the sands later." He tried to keep a pleading note out of his voice, but he wasn't sure he'd succeeded.

She nibbled her bottom lip. "I don't feel we did lunch justice, either. Maybe we should go to a seafood restaurant tonight."

He glanced across at her. Her eyes were guarded, but hopeful. Maybe she was eager for the atmosphere between them to improve as much as he was. They'd come to enjoy a relaxed camaraderie that he hoped she was missing too.

"I'd love that," he said. "A huge bowl of green-lipped mussels swimming in white wine and cream with garlic bread."

"Oh... now you're talking." Her eyelids fluttered dreamily, not unlike the way they had when she'd come.

Gene stifled a sigh. Best not to let his mind wander down memory lane again. He could think about that moment forever and never get bored.

He navigated the busy roads to the middle of the city and parked, and they spent the next few hours finishing off the South Island appointments. Callie was in good spirits by the time she finished. Again, two of the stores agreed outright to stock the Four Seasons brand, and the manager of the third hinted the answer might be yes once she'd checked with her head office.

Gene drove them to the villa, which turned out to be a cream-colored colonial-style building with a white portico and a picket fence surrounding neat gardens, only a short walk from the beach.

"Walk first or dinner?" Gene asked. "It's nearly six o'clock."

"Ooh, dinner. I'm starving."

So they walked a short distance to a seafood restaurant that jutted out into the ocean, and sat at a table by the window, looking down at where the sea lapped at the legs of the pier and the dark shapes of fish slithered beneath the surface.

Callie's reserved mood seemed to have passed, and they spent a long while dipping into a huge bowl of mussels, soaking up the liquid with bread, and then finishing off with strong coffee while they talked.

She appeared to have forgiven him for the way he'd acted, and she seemed keen to move on, keeping him talking by asking lots of questions about his interests, steering clear of the Army and anything else he supposed she thought might upset him. She was a talented conversationalist, putting him at ease, and he began to see why she was obviously doing so well with her business, winning her customers over with her sheer charm.

Gene knew he should have been delighted. They were getting on again, and it looked as if the faux pas he'd been responsible for hadn't prompted her to end their business relationship, which meant he didn't have to tell Phoebe or Neve or anyone else that he'd screwed up. He'd spoken to Kev that morning, and Kev had said everything was still quiet, and the STG had reassured him they were hours from finding Kirk. Everything was going well.

So why did he feel so terribly forlorn? He wanted to slap himself around the face. He was like a moon-sick calf, staring at Callie longingly the way a person on a diet might gaze in the window of a chocolate shop. He wanted her, and although he'd thought having her might sate his hunger, all it had done was give him a taste of her, and he wanted to taste her again.

After finishing the last drop of her coffee, Callie replaced the cup in the saucer. "Well, shall we take that walk along the beach?"

"Yes, sure. It's a lovely evening."

It was the understatement of the year, he thought as they left the restaurant and took the steps down to the sand. The sun was sinking toward the horizon, but it was warm enough to combat the sea breeze. The golden sand stretched away as far as the eye could see, and the ocean sparkled blue. The sky looked like a Turner watercolor, all blues and oranges and purples. But it was the woman by his side who held all his attention.

For once, Gene had forgone his suit, relaxing a little now he knew the STG were onto Kirk, and he wore jeans and a short-sleeved blue shirt, open at the neck, smart and yet relaxed, too. Callie had also changed from her business clothes into a long sundress that brushed her feet, the tie-dyed purple and orange color a mirror image of the sunset. She looked beautiful enough to make his heart ache, and her curves made his hands itch to touch them.

For God's sake, he scolded himself as they bent to remove their shoes and let the cool sand sink between their toes. He couldn't make the mistake of giving in to his lust again. He had to remain strong and fight his hormones.

He watched the breeze lift her blonde hair off her neck and imagined placing his lips there, and felt a sweeping sense of despair. He was pathetic. Hopeless. So, so weak. Because he wanted her, and his desire for her was so strong he knew he couldn't fight it.

Chapter Nineteen

Callie bent to pick up a piece of shell, straightened, and turned it over in her hands. It was paua, the outside a dull stone color, the inside a beautiful blend of shining blue and turquoise. For some inexplicable reason, it made her feel happy.

She welcomed the emotion, because she'd woken up feeling very flat and not at all her usual self. She'd scolded herself for it all morning, both during breakfast and on the trip to Nelson. What had she expected, for crying out loud? That Gene would declare his love for her and get down on bended knee? They'd had sex. It was purely a physical thing and hadn't involved their feelings at all. And it had been great. They'd been carried away by lust, as if they'd placed a pan of water on the stove to boil, and now they'd removed it from the heat, things would simmer down and then return to normal.

The problem was that things weren't simmering down. She couldn't shake images of last night from her mind. They paraded repeatedly through her brain as if they were suitcases on an airport conveyor belt that someone had forgotten, going around and around. And not just images, but sensations... the memory of his lips on hers, his tongue sliding into her mouth, the smell of his aftershave, the way he'd picked her up and carried her to the bed so he could thrust deeper and carry her away to ecstasy.

Sex with Jamie had been good, and she couldn't complain about any of the partners she'd had before him, but there had been something about the intensity of sex with Gene that had been different. Her previous relationships had led gradually to the bedroom, sometimes after months of dating. She'd never felt such dark desire, such an intense need to possess a person, and to be possessed in return. It had shocked her, and she didn't know what to make of that shock.

She'd tried to reason with herself that it didn't mean anything. Traveling with him had led to a false intimacy between them, like when actors worked with makeup staff on a movie set. They didn't really have anything in common, and no doubt when Becky returned and he left to continue with whatever he ended up doing, they'd never see each other again.

She felt as if every relationship she'd experienced in the past had been childlike compared to last night's, even the one with Jamie. Although she knew she was being ridiculous, she felt like a little girl who'd been playing at having boyfriends, as if she'd understood nothing about men and sex until this moment. She'd grown up thinking that sex should only be an expression of love between two people, and although she would never have said so, she hadn't understood when some of her friends had indulged in one-night stands, not understanding why someone would desire sex without the comfort of a steady relationship.

She hadn't understood the pull of desire, and the sheer craving for someone that could overwhelm everything.

But even though she told herself it meant nothing, and she had to be grown up about this, and she couldn't press Gene for more because he'd made his feelings clear, her heart wanted more, and that was what made her sad.

So she welcomed the small flutter of happiness as she turned over the shell, and she looked up at Gene with a smile.

The look on his face made her catch her breath and inhale sharply. "What?"

He shook his head, apparently speechless, and then before she could say or do anything else, his arms were around her, his lips were on hers, and he was kissing the living daylights out of her.

Callie gave a muffled exclamation, but he didn't release her, and in the end she went limp in his arms. Closing her eyes, she gave in to the embrace and just accepted the kiss, opening up her senses and making the most of him while she had him.

The warm water washed over her feet, and as she curled her toes, they sank into the cool sand. The smell of the salty sea mingled with the aroma from a barbecue someone was having further along the beach, the smells of summer, bringing with them a lightening of her heart and a curve to her lips.

Gene's hands were warm on her back, and when he realized she wasn't trying to pull away, his kiss grew gentle, his lips moving tenderly, while his tongue played with hers.

It took him a long time to finally move back, and when he did, Callie held on to his arms, afraid that if she let go her legs would give way.

"Um…" Her brain felt like a ball of knotted wool. "Kind of getting conflicting messages here."

"I know." He cupped her face and tucked the strand of hair that fluttered in the sea breeze behind her ear. "I apologize."

"It's okay."

"It's not, and I am sorry. But I can't keep away from you. I thought that after last night all our passion would have vanished, but I can't stop thinking about you." His thumb brushed her cheek, his voice turning husky. "It wasn't enough. I want you again. I want more of you. Last time was hard and fast because I was afraid my brain wouldn't let me finish before the guilt took over. I want you again, but slowly this time. I want you naked on the bed so I can kiss every inch of your skin. I want to taste you and make you come on my tongue, then take you and make you come while you look into my eyes. Will you let me, Callie?" She shivered, and he groaned. "Do that again and I'll take you here on the sand."

"Gene…" Her heart pounded and her cheeks had grown hot. "I don't understand. What's changed?"

"What's changed is that I've accepted I'm weak. I'm fooling myself if I think I can stay away from you."

She tried to slow her breathing so she didn't hyperventilate. The look in his gray eyes was so intense it turned her to mush inside. "I… I don't know. Last night was so hard when you left, and I've only just talked myself around."

"I know, and I'm sorry. I won't do that to you again. I thought I was doing the decent, honest thing, but I was wrong. We'll talk about where we go from here, I promise. I won't make decisions for both of us. Just… come to bed with me again."

Callie felt dizzy. "Oh…"

He moved closer to her again, and slid his hands onto her bottom so he could pull her hips to his. His erection pressed against her mound, leaving her in no doubt as to his desire for her.

"Let me make love to you," he murmured. "Let me see if you taste like strawberries and cream, like I suspect."

"Gene!" Her cheeks flamed.

He gave a sexy chuckle and nuzzled her ear. "Let's go back to the villa, and we'll open the balcony doors. I'll slowly remove your clothes, and then you can just lie there and be pleasured in the evening sun. How does that sound?"

"Fucking marvelous," she said, worried she was dribbling.

He laughed. "Nicely put."

"On one condition, though. We both remove our clothes."

He opened his mouth to protest, but the look on her face obviously convinced him she was serious. "Callie…"

"Once was impulse," she said. "If we have sex again, it means there's more between us, and whatever happens, I want to start off the right way. No secrets, Gene."

He glanced away, looking out to sea, his smile fading.

"I know you have a scar," she whispered, resting her hand on his hip. "Don't be ashamed of it. It's part of you, part of your past. Don't shut me out." She didn't say what she was thinking—that he'd obviously shut Angela out, and that had brought about the end of their relationship. There was no way of telling how things would pan out between them, but she didn't want to begin with them hiding more than they had to.

She cupped his cheek and rubbed a thumb across his lips. "Deal?"

She felt them curve up. "Deal," he said.

"Come on, then." She took his hand and they walked back across the sand, then up the grassy bank and along the road to the villa. They didn't say much as they walked, but excitement rode bareback on her blood through her veins, and she could feel his tension and knew he was experiencing the same sensations.

Still, she couldn't eradicate a small amount of doubt that lingered like sea spray in the air. Was she doing the right thing? The more times she slept with him, the more she was going to fall for him. She wasn't the sort of person who could indulge in casual sex and remain untouched emotionally. How would she feel if, once again, he brought her to the dizzy heights of pleasure and then rolled over and cursed?

Nibbling her bottom lip, she unlocked the door to her room and went in, and he closed the door behind him. As he'd promised, he crossed to the far windows and opened them wide, letting in the evening sun, smells, and sounds. The cry of seagulls and the sound of music filtered through—someone was playing Barry White on the beach.

Gene laughed as he came back to her. "It sounds as if I've set that up, but I promise I haven't."

Callie smiled, leaning back against a chest of drawers, then moving forward hastily as she remembered what had happened the previous night.

He tipped his head and studied her, then turned away and walked over to the minibar. "How about a glass of wine?"

"Just a small one." She felt suddenly nervous, and not at all sure she wanted to go ahead with this. The heat of passion was one thing, but the things he'd told her he wanted to do to her made her hands shake as she accepted the glass half-filled with Sauvignon.

"Try to relax." His doubt appeared to have vanished, she wasn't sure why, and he seemed full of confidence as he took her hand and led her over to the window. "Look at that lovely view."

It was gorgeous, the ocean reflecting the copper-colored sky, the sun still holding enough heat to warm her as she sipped the wine, then tilted her face up to let the cool liquid slide down her throat.

"You're so beautiful."

She looked up at him, her heart racing. He was so much taller than she was, and although she loved his suits, in his casual shirt and jeans he looked rakish and relaxed, like a cowboy who'd won a lasso competition and was now claiming his prize.

"You don't have to do anything you don't want to." He lifted a hand and rested a finger on her bare shoulder, then slid it down her arm. "But I promise you'll want to."

Callie shivered, aware she was being seduced. Last time, without meaning to, she'd done the seducing, by enticing him with suggestive looks and encouraging him to give up his principles to take her to bed. This time, though, he was the one doing the seducing. She knew that if she said no loudly, he would accept it and wouldn't push her— he was a gentleman, after all. But he wouldn't take her indecision or her silence as proof that she wanted him to stop. If she didn't want to end up in bed with him, she was going to have to make it quite clear.

His finger reached her free hand, and he lifted and turned it, then drew a spiral on her palm. She lowered her gaze to watch his strong, tanned hand move up to brush the sensitive skin of her inner wrist, then further up the ticklish skin to tease the crook of her elbow. She shuddered, then bit her lip, conscious of what he'd said the last time she'd shivered. *Do that again and I'll take you here on the sand.* What a thought. Making love outdoors in broad daylight, the risk of being discovered only adding to the excitement coursing through her veins.

He swallowed another mouthful of wine, then traced up to her shoulder, over the neckline of her dress, then across to the other arm, continuing his gentle exploration of her body. She looked up and met his eyes, feeling a sweeping sense of helplessness at the determination within them. She could read the thoughts passing through his mind, because he'd already told her them on the beach.

I want you naked on the bed so I can kiss every inch of your skin. I want to taste you and make you come on my tongue...

How could she fight against such a beautiful seduction? Callie was lost, and there was nothing she could do about it.

Chapter Twenty

Gene could tell the moment Callie surrendered and made up her mind to stay with him. In spite of her encouraging reply on the beach, as they'd entered the room she'd turned stiff and reluctant, not pushing him away but not completely welcoming his touch, either. He guessed she was wary because of what had happened last time, and he cursed himself for being so selfish and cold toward her.

It wouldn't happen again. He was determined. He'd fought with his principles, but they weren't strong enough to overpower his attraction to Callie, and now he'd finally accepted that he wasn't going to hold back.

He'd consoled himself by thinking that being this close to Callie was even better for her safety, because he wouldn't be leaving her alone at night. He'd know if she wanted to go out for a walk, or if someone knocked on her door, or if there was someone prowling outside, and he'd be able to take steps to combat that.

Being emotionally involved with a client might not have been the smartest thing, but he was over berating himself for it. From now on, he would stop wrangling with himself, and put all his energy into showing her how he felt about her.

And he could see when she came to a similar decision, because her shoulders loosened, her arms slid around his waist, and she leaned against him as she reached up to kiss him properly.

Her mouth was sweet with wine, and he gave a long sigh, enjoying not only the sensation of her pressed to him, but also the anticipation of what would happen over the next few hours. What could be better than spending a summer evening with a gorgeous, naked blonde and having his wicked way with her as often as he could manage it?

Except she wasn't naked yet, and it was about time he rectified that situation.

Gently, he took her nearly finished glass of wine and placed it with his on a nearby table, then gathered the hem of her sundress in his hands and lifted it up. Callie's eyes widened, but she just raised her arms as he pulled the dress up her body and over her head, and then let it flutter down onto the table.

Today she wore a gorgeous bra and panties set, the satin material the color of the paua shell she'd picked up on the beach, a blend of turquoise, blue, and purple swirls, outlined in purple ribbon and with a turquoise bow between her breasts. "Another of Rowan's designs?" he asked, running the tip of his finger beneath the ribbon along the top of her right breast.

She nodded, her gaze fixed on his face, a small smile on her lips.

"Pretty." He traced across to her left breast. "So pretty I'd love to leave it on, but I'm afraid that's not going to happen."

She laughed, not complaining when he moved his hands behind her back to unfasten the clasp of her bra. He loved what happened when the elastic of a bra revealed a woman's breasts—how the boned and shaped garment collapsed in his hands and released her body, her muscles relaxing and settling to her natural shape. In Callie's case, her breasts were on the large side but still youthfully high, and he cupped them with his palms and squeezed gently, incredibly turned on just by the feel of her, so soft and yielding in his hands.

Tossing back her hair, she pulled back her shoulders and arched into his touch, and he sighed. Her nipples were the color of the sky to the west, a rose pink, and they felt softer than the rest of her, swollen in the heat, large and round and just begging to be teased. So he did, running a finger around the outside, which slowly contracted like a flower closing its petals for the night.

It was no good—he needed to get his mouth on them. Wanting her to be comfortable, he took her hand and led her across to the bed, then gestured for her to climb onto the mattress while he unbuttoned his shirt. She did so, but remained kneeling as he stripped, and just sank onto her haunches while he undid his jeans and, with a deep breath, slid them down his legs and stepped out of them.

He hated undressing in front of someone, whether it was a woman or a doctor or a friend at the pool, but Callie's words about starting off the right way had rung home. *No secrets, Gene.* His hands hesitated for a brief second, the secret he still kept hanging between them like an opaque curtain, but he swept it aside and removed his briefs, returning to stand before her naked.

Her gaze rested on his hip, soft and light as a butterfly. Slowly, as if reaching out to a wounded animal—which he supposed he was, in a way—she lifted a hand and pressed her fingertips to the scar. He looked down, embarrassed by the puckered skin, the jagged scar that was still a dark pink and stood out starkly against his tan. A bullet had smashed through his pelvis, and it had been a miracle he'd had no lasting damage to his crown jewels. It had taken several long and extensive surgeries to rebuild the bone, and he bore enough metal pins to set off the detector in an airport, but he was immensely grateful that he'd regained ninety percent of his movement. He'd worked hard to get to that stage, practically learning to walk again, but it had been worth it.

Callie trailed her forefinger across the scar, her face showing no sign of the revulsion he'd worried would appear there. Her finger continued moving, and he caught his breath as she closed her hand around his erection.

"Impressive," she said. Gently, she stroked him, her hot gaze studying the way she revealed and then closed the skin over the bulbous tip.

"Jesus." He swelled in her hand, closing his eyes for a moment at the blissful sensation. She continued to stroke, gentle and yet firm, and he bore her touch for as long as he could before he opened his eyes and carefully removed her hand by the wrist. "Lie back," he instructed. "My turn."

Callie shifted up the bed, her arms above her head, stretching elegantly, wearing nothing but her tiny panties. Her skin glistened in the warmth of the room. "Mmm," she said, obviously enjoying the feeling of the sun across her like a golden blanket.

Climbing onto the mattress, Gene stretched out beside her, propped up on an elbow, and looked down at her dips and curves as she wriggled like a cat beneath him.

"I'm so turned on," she said breathlessly. "You have a fantastic body."

"Thank you." He was genuinely flattered by her comment.

"Mmm." She ran a hand up his arm, admiring his muscles, and down his chest, exploring his pecs and abs. "I'm so lucky."

"You're lucky? I feel as if I've won the lottery." Placing a hand on her thigh, he stroked up her body, following the way it curved out over her hips, then into her waist, then out again to her breasts. She closed her eyes, moving beneath his hand, her lips parting with a moan. It took every ounce of self-control he possessed not to just mount her and thrust them both to oblivion, but he forced himself to hold back. He wanted this to be an exploration of each other, and he wanted to draw out her pleasure until she was begging him to let her come. He wanted her crazy for him, again and again, until she couldn't bear to be apart from him.

So he spent a while just stroking her, learning the landscape of her body, like a sexual Marco Polo, discovering every freckle and hair, where she was ticklish, and which erogenous zones made her sigh and squirm beneath him. Eventually, when he couldn't wait any longer, he kissed her lips, delving his tongue inside, then kissed around to her ear and sucked the lobe into his mouth. He brushed his lips down her neck, finding the spot with his tongue where her pulse raced just beneath the surface, and sucked there, giving a satisfied smirk when he lifted his head and saw that the skin in that spot had flushed pink.

His blood rising, he kissed down to her breast, cupping it with a hand to lift the nipple to his mouth. They'd relaxed again from the warmth of the room, and when he covered each one with his mouth, it was like sucking on a soft truffle, the velvety texture making his mouth water. He squeezed them gently with his tongue to make them contract, and then he flicked and nibbled and teased with his lips until they hardened and lengthened to shining beads.

Callie was moaning and writhing beneath him by now, and he thought it was about time that he turned his attention to the lower half of her body. So he brushed his lips slowly down her ribs, tasting her skin with his tongue, kissing over her stomach, then from hip to hip across the line of her panties. At the same time, he stroked up the inside of her thigh to cup her mound, and he pressed gently with his fingers, massaging her folds through the satin material.

As he'd suspected, she was swollen and wet, her panties quickly becoming soaked with her moisture, but he continued to stroke, turned on by the way the material became slippery.

Eventually, though, he shifted on the bed and moved between her legs, kneeling up to pull her panties down. They left her wet flesh reluctantly, and she gave a little moan as they peeled away, fidgeting on the bed beneath him while he made himself comfortable.

"Stop wriggling," he scolded, pushing her knees wide to expose all of her to his gaze.

She groaned and covered her face with her arms, and he gave a short laugh. Let her be embarrassed at his lustful stare. He couldn't have stopped for the world.

For a moment, he just studied her, admiring the glisten of her folds, the shimmer of her skin. Then he lifted a hand and stroked down either side, enjoying the feel of her silky soft body. Finally, he used both hands to part her folds, exposing her clit to his gaze.

Lowering his head, he covered the swollen bud with his mouth. Callie gave a long, sexy moan. Slowly, he began to explore her most secret area with his lips and tongue, finding out what pressure she liked, and whether she responded to light and fast, or slow and firm licks.

At first, her thighs remained tense on either side of him, the muscles tight, but the more he licked and sucked, the more she relaxed, her thighs loosening and her movements becoming more uninhibited.

Only then did he add his fingers to the mix, and he slid two down and into her, slow and careful so he didn't hurt or alarm her. There wasn't much chance of that, though, because she was incredibly wet, and she gave small but obvious thrusts of her hips to match the movement of his fingers, encouraging him to stroke more firmly.

"Oh…" she said, dropping her knees to the sides and surrendering to his mouth. "Gene…"

It was the best thing in the world as she began to tense around him, her autopilot kicking in and her body taking over, but he wasn't ready yet. He withdrew his fingers and lifted his head, and just blew softly on her hot flesh.

"*Aaahhh…*" She writhed beneath him, trying to push her hips up to meet his mouth.

He waited for about fifteen seconds, kissing across her hips and thighs, before he lowered his head, letting her body loosen before he began with his fingers and tongue, teasing her once more to the edge.

Yet again, though, after about half a minute as she began to tighten, he withdrew his fingers and lifted his head.

"Argh!" She lifted up on her elbows and glared at him. "Gene!" Her cheeks were flushed, her eyes blazing with unspent desire.

He fixed his gaze on hers. "Lie down."

Her chest heaved and she continued to glare at him for a moment, then flopped back and stared up at the ceiling.

Hiding a smile, he kissed the insides of her thighs, waiting for her to relax, and only then returned his mouth and fingers to begin stimulating her again.

By now, her slippery moisture coated his hand and her clit was firm and hard as a button, and as he sucked it, she gave a long moan almost like a cry and writhed beneath him. Taking pity on her, this time he didn't stop but went with her all the way, and was rewarded when she tightened around his fingers and wailed as her orgasm claimed her with thick, hard pulses, her head lifting up and her features creasing with pleasure.

He kept his mouth there until she groaned and collapsed back onto the mattress, and then he carefully withdrew his fingers and took a few moments to place soft kisses and light licks, tasting the aftershocks that rippled through her until her breathing slowed and her body relaxed.

Chapter Twenty-One

Callie lay high on a haze of sexual endorphins, limp and spent. It seemed that Gene hadn't finished with her yet, though. He was kissing her thighs, and across her hip, slowly moving up her body, teasing and tantalizing with his lips and tongue as he went.

"Mmm." She felt as if she were swimming in a huge bowl of melted chocolate, rich and sated. "That was nice."

"It was." He moved to lie beside her. Eyes closed, she felt his fingers slip down between her legs, gathering her arousal. Then, to her shock, he smoothed it across a nipple before lowering his mouth to suck it off.

"Gene! Jeez."

"What?" He did it again, to the other nipple.

"I... oh..." She'd thought she was completely spent, but to her surprise her body began to stir again.

He kissed up her neck to her mouth, wrapped his arms around her, and rolled onto his back, taking her with him. Callie pushed herself up to sit astride him, feeling his erection like a wooden pole between the cheeks of her bottom.

"Mmm." She rubbed against it, liking the way his eyelids fell to half-mast with desire. "It feels as if you're ready for action."

"Always, when you're around." He pulled her down to kiss her, and she gave in and opened her mouth to his searching tongue, wanting to turn him on as much as he'd done to her. It didn't seem to be a difficult task. In less than a minute, he was reaching for his wallet, and she helped him out, removing the condom, tearing off the wrapper, and rolling it on for him.

She did it slowly, taking time to stroke him as she went, and by the time she maneuvered herself so the tip of his erection parted her folds, he was breathing deep and fast, and his eyes were hot with passion.

Pushing down, she welcomed him inside her, closing her eyes as he slid in easily. His hands landed on her hips, pushing up the final inch, and she tipped her head back with a groan, enjoying being filled like this, being impaled.

Holding her hips firmly, he began to thrust hard beneath her, but Callie didn't want that. He'd drawn out her pleasure, taking time to arouse her, and she didn't want this to be all about the destination. The journey was where the fun lay.

So she took his hands, linked their fingers, and moved them up to pin them above his head. He could have wrestled himself free with little effort, but he chose to play along, and let her hold him down while she began to ride him with long, slow thrusts, rocking her hips to slide him almost out before she lowered herself again. He said nothing, but his gray eyes fixed on hers, filled with an emotion she couldn't quite decipher—admiration? Affection?

"I could get to like this," she whispered, bending to kiss him. "Having you at my mercy."

He closed his eyes while she pressed her lips to his, and she felt them curve up. "Hmm," he said when she eventually moved back.

"Yes." She could feel the tension building inside him, and she slowed her movements, enjoying the sensual slide of his rock-hard erection through her swollen and sensitive flesh. "Maybe I'll buy some handcuffs and chain you to my bed at home, and keep you there for when I feel like using you for my pleasure."

His eyebrows rose. "Handcuffs?"

"Mmm. I'm sure Neve has a few sets in her displays. I'd cuff each hand apart, and your legs, and bring you food so you never had to leave."

"I can think of worse ways to live." His voice had grown husky— the game was turning them both on.

She leaned over him, grazing her nipples over his lips. He opened his mouth obligingly and sucked first one and then the other. She kissed around to his ear, feeling his deep groan rumble through his chest as her breasts brushed along it. The wet, hard beads of her nipples scraped through the hair on his ribs, sending tingles right through her body, down to her clit. "Oh…" Her orgasm wasn't far away, but she wanted him to come first—he deserved it.

Lifting up again, she kissed him, making sure her thrusts were slow and regular, knowing he was close when his breathing grew ragged and his hips thrust involuntarily. He made as if to loosen their hands, and she knew he wanted to toss her onto her back and thrust hard to relieve the ache inside him, but she shook her head and tightened her fingers on his.

"Just wait," she instructed. "Let it take you slowly. I want to watch."

He blinked a few times, then gave a small nod, so she straightened her arms and continued to move, teasing him further to the edge with each push of her hips. At one point, she let him slide almost out of her and just teased the tip of his erection, in and out, watching his chest heave and his face contort with pleasure, and then she sank down, taking him all the way, and carried on with her slow thrusts.

It didn't take long after that. With delight, she watched his climax take him with the wash of a long, gentle wave that gradually grew in strength rather than a tsunami. She saw his fierce frown, his lips part with a groan, his body tense beneath her, and felt him swell inside her as his body pulsed.

Only when he'd finished and relaxed back into the pillows, gasping, did she thrust a little harder, grinding her clit against him until her own orgasm hit, and she clenched around him, trying not to laugh as he swore and complained while she squeezed his hyper-sensitized shaft.

"Ow," he said when she finally released his hands and fell forward onto his chest.

She gave in to the laughter and giggled away, enjoying the warmth of his arms when he hugged her. "Sorry."

"I think you've milked every last drop out of me."

"Mmm. I hope so."

He sighed and kissed the top of her head, and they lay there like that for as long as they could before they had to move. He withdrew and disposed of the condom, and she shifted to the side, her heart racing at the memory of how he'd been the last time they'd done this.

But this time he turned her so her back was to his chest and wrapped his arms around her, and she nuzzled into his embrace, enjoying the slide of their warm skin from the heat of the room. His arm rested tightly under her breasts.

"Thank you," she said.

She felt him chuckle. "You're welcome."

"I mean for not leaving immediately. I appreciate it."

He kissed her hair. "I'm sorry about last time. I have to tell you, though—I'd rather go back to my own room in a while, if that's okay."

The sun had set now, and the sky was turning a darker blue and purple, with the first stars appearing—Orion to the north, and Sirius the Dog Star shining brightly to his side.

Callie swallowed hard. "Of course."

"It's just... I sleep very little, and I'm quite restless. I wouldn't want to wake you."

"It's okay," she whispered. "I don't mind."

"Thank you."

So they lay for a while, not saying much, and then he kissed her goodnight, gathered his clothes, and left the room.

Callie curled up in the big bed, but it was a long time before she finally fell asleep.

*

Gene was still awake, sitting at the table in his room and working through the latest reports from his office, when his mobile rang on the bedside table.

Holding it up to his ear, he answered, "Hello?" as he walked over to the window. For a moment, he didn't register who was calling, taken aback by the beauty of the view. The sky was filled with stars that had turned the ocean a stunning mixture of black and silver. It took his breath away—or was he just seeing things differently through the eyes of a man smitten by the gorgeous blonde lying in the other room?

"Gene?"

He snapped back to the present. "Kev?" He frowned. It must have been close to midnight. "What's up?"

"Bad news, I'm afraid."

"What's happened?"

"Philip's just rung." That was their contact at the Special Tactics Group. "Within the space of about an hour, two members of the jury that convicted Kirk have been shot and killed. Philip admitted Kirk's slipped the net."

Cold slithered through Gene's veins, making him inhale sharply. "Fuck."

"Yeah. I can't believe it. I was convinced he was on the verge of being found."

"You and me both."

"I'll inform Ms. Hawke in the morning. I assume she'll contact Ms. Summer and update her."

"Yes, I'm sure she will." Would it have any effect on Callie? She'd not raised the subject of the threat on her or her mother's life at all. Neve had suggested Callie didn't take the threat seriously. Would this make a difference? "All right. Stay frosty. Send me through any details. We'll talk more in the morning." Gene hung up.

He leaned on the window and rested his head on his arm. All of a sudden, he wanted nothing more than to confess to Callie and discuss the situation with her. If she was aware of who he really was, maybe he could convince her that his presence there was essential, and there wouldn't have to be any more secrets between them.

But what if he told her and she still refused to take it seriously? If she broke off their... relationship, or whatever it should be called, sacked him as her PA, and told him to get lost? His heart sank. He couldn't risk it. He wouldn't be able to protect her properly from a distance.

Then he gave a wry laugh. *That's not exactly the truth, is it?* The reason he didn't want to tell her wasn't just because he was worried about protecting her, although that was important. He didn't want to tell her because he didn't want to risk losing her. Not now. Not when they'd begun something that had made him feel the best he'd felt in years.

Chapter Twenty-Two

"What's he doing here?" Rowan glanced over her shoulder to where Gene stood by the drinks table, topping up glasses from a bottle of bubbly for a group of Willow's friends.

Callie had just finished filling her, Neve, and Bridget in on the successful appointments she'd had over the past week. They were all thrilled that so many stores were willing to stock the Four Seasons designs, and she thought that for the first time since they'd begun their venture, the rest of them were finally beginning to believe in her vision of how far they could go if they gave it their all.

She followed Rowan's gaze, admired Gene briefly in his black tux and bow tie, and then looked back. "Neve suggested he come and be a waiter for us. I thought it would be funny to see how he reacted in this kind of situation."

"He seems to be doing all right." Bridget sipped her wine and grinned as the women around him burst into giggles at something he'd said.

"Yes, he does," Callie said wryly. She was slightly surprised by that. There was something straight-laced about him at times, and she'd half expected him to get flustered and embarrassed in a group of women, but the opposite appeared to be happening. If anything, he seemed to have relaxed more, losing the ex-soldier ramrod stance and becoming quite the flirt.

"He's rather gorgeous." Rowan nibbled nervously at some peanuts. "I have no idea what to say to him."

"Dear Rowan," Callie said with affection. "He's perfectly normal. Just talk to him like you talk to us."

"Oh, I couldn't. What would I say?"

Neve gave an unladylike snort. "I don't know why you always go to pieces when a good-looking guy turns up. Looks don't mean anything. It's what's inside that matters."

"What's Gene like inside, Callie?" Bridget asked. "Spill the beans." Her expression was a little too innocent. Rowan giggled.

Callie met Neve's steady gaze and knew she suspected what was going on between them. *Can you not tell Neve about what happened tonight?* Gene had asked that the first time they'd slept together.

"He's very nice," she said.

Bridget rolled her eyes. "Aw, come on…"

Callie laughed. "Nothing's happened between us."

"You're kidding me." Rowan's eyes nearly fell out of her head. "He hasn't made a move on you? More importantly, you haven't made a move on him?"

"Not at all. We have a professional, working relationship."

All the other three women snorted.

"I'm telling the truth," Callie said softly, not liking that she was lying to her friends. Was she putting Gene's feelings above theirs? What did that mean? "I like him, of course I do, and I think he likes me, but he made it clear on the first day that he's here to work and that nothing's going to happen between us before Becky comes back."

"And when she does?" Rowan asked.

Callie shrugged. "We'll have to see. I'm in no hurry anyway. I'm still in post-Jamie gloom." That was only partly true. Gene was rapidly dispelling it. "What about the rest of you?" she asked in an attempt to draw attention away from herself. "Any news on the romance front? It is Valentine's Day tomorrow, after all. Are you expecting cards and flowers from anyone?"

"No," all three of them said at the same time. They all laughed.

"We're hopeless." Rowan sighed and sipped her wine.

"Speak for yourself." Neve finished off her glass of vodka. "I don't want any of that stupid romance stuff. I'm going clubbing tomorrow night, and I'm going to find myself a man for the night for some tawdry sex."

"Neve!" Bridget scolded. "You love to shock us all, don't you?"

"I might join you," Rowan said enviously. "I haven't had sex for a millennium."

That made them all laugh. "Somehow I can't imagine you in a nightclub on the prowl," Callie teased.

"I know." Rowan swirled the last inch of wine around in her glass, watching the bubbles rising and popping on the surface. "Nightclubs terrify me."

"Everything terrifies you."

"True. But I know I'm never going to meet anyone sitting behind my desk. I have to put myself out there a bit, I am aware of that. The other day, Hitch said 'nothing ventured, nothing gained,' and although it's a cliché, it really made me think. He's right. If I don't take risks, I'll never meet the right man."

"My brother knows precisely nothing about romance," Bridget advised her. "For God's sake, don't let him give you advice."

"Oh, I don't know." Callie wasn't sure she agreed. Bridget's brother was a nature photographer who spent almost every waking hour of his day covered in tree ferns and hiding in the middle of the bush somewhere, photographing possums and kiwi and other nocturnal creatures. About eight feet tall, gorgeous, and funny, he was obsessed with his work, and Bridget was right in that his track record with women was abysmal, extending to brief bouts of concentrated sexual activity before he disappeared once more into the wild, invariably leaving a bawling woman in his wake. In spite of that, though, he was very down-to-earth, and Callie could think of worse people to give the romantic, idealistic Rowan advice.

"Can I get you ladies anything?"

Callie glanced up to see Gene standing there, a bottle of bubbly in one hand and a dish of miniature chocolate eclairs in the other.

"Ooh." Neve took three eclairs. "Thanks."

Callie held up her glass. Gene's eyes met hers for a brief moment, and then he rested the lip of the bottle on the rim of the glass and tipped it up.

When they'd met up in the morning, he'd been quiet but hadn't pulled away when she'd hugged him. He'd continued to be a little reserved while they'd driven back to Picton, where they'd left the car to be returned down south and had taken the ferry to Wellington. Catching a taxi back in the city, Gene had instructed it to take Callie back first, and he'd left her with a promise to attend the party the next day.

They hadn't discussed how what had happened would affect them once they left for their journey north. Callie supposed she would have to wait and see once they arrived at their next destination.

He hadn't asked her to keep quiet about their relationship again, but when she'd arrived at Willow's place, he hadn't greeted her with anything more than a formal nod of the head, either, so she'd assumed he wanted to keep it beneath his hat for the moment.

He wandered to the next group with the bottle, and Callie sipped from her glass.

"How's your mum, by the way?" Rowan asked. "Any news on the death threats?"

"I'd rather not talk about it," Callie said. "If that's okay."

Rowan's expression softened. "Sure. But you're all right?"

"I'm fine," she lied. Phoebe had rung earlier to tell her that Kirk hadn't been captured, and that a couple of people had been killed. She'd tried to convince Callie to postpone her tour, but Callie had been adamant that she wasn't going to let some idle threats stop her doing her job. They'd argued, and in the end Callie had hung up and thrown her phone across the room. It was the last subject she wanted to discuss tonight.

"Pressie time," Willow announced loudly, providing a welcome distraction.

Gene finished filling up the others' glasses and promised to get Neve another glass of vodka, and the girls moved their seats to form a close circle around Willow with the other ten or so young women whom Willow had invited to her baby shower.

The mother-to-be looked her usual bohemian self, Callie thought, smiling with affection at Willow's pretty, rainbow-colored tunic that hung in soft folds over her maternity jeans. Her long brown hair hung around her shoulders in gentle waves, and she was the very picture of motherly beauty.

Although she and Rowan were identical twins, they were so very different. But then, most of that was nurture, Callie mused. Rowan had told her once—late at night, after a party at university, and when they were both drunk—what lay at the root of her problems. They hadn't referred to it since, but it haunted Callie sometimes. Things had happened in Rowan's past that had molded her into a very different girl from her laidback sister. It was amazing that Rowan was sane at all considering what she'd had to deal with over the years.

"Are you nervous?" Callie asked as a couple of her friends moved the table of presents closer to Willow.

"Not really. I'm excited. It's all planned." Willow perched on the edge of the sofa, her cheeks flushed with pleasure. "I'm having a natural water birth, with no drugs, if at all possible."

"Sheesh." Neve pulled a face. "I can't think of anything worse. I'll be, like, give me a fucking epidural and get that thing out of me!"

They all laughed, including Gene.

"Do you want kids, Gene?" Bridget asked him.

He raised an eyebrow as they all turned to look at him. "Of course. When I meet the right girl."

"You haven't met her yet?" Bridget enquired.

He smiled at her. "When I do, you'll be the first to know."

Callie reached across to the sausage rolls on the nearby table and took one. He hadn't looked at her when he answered, and now he was helping Willow get comfortable on the sofa, fetching her a cushion and then a glass of lemonade. He'd sidestepped the question admirably, so Callie had no idea of knowing what was going through his head. Was he thinking, *Jeez, that's the last thing on my mind, hope Callie doesn't get any ideas...*? Or did the thought of a future with her give him a tingle, the way the notion of seeing more of him in the future did with her?

She put it all to the back of her mind. This evening they had to concentrate on Willow, and there would be plenty of time in the future to work things out.

Willow started with a present from her sister, squealing at the sight of Rowan's handmade baby jumpsuit in neutral yellows and oranges because Willow and Liam had chosen not to know the sex of their baby.

"And it'll also remind him or her of me," Rowan said, "as autumn."

"I love it." Tears shone in Willow's eyes and she stood to give Rowan a hug. "Thank you."

"I've made lots more clothes, but these are the prettiest," Rowan said huskily. "I'm so glad you like it."

Neve nudged Gene, who was standing next to her. "You realize after this you're going to have to go out and do incredibly manly things just to negate all the estrogen you've been exposed to."

"I plan to chop logs and hunt wild boar while listening to loud rock music straight after I leave here," he advised.

Everyone giggled, and Callie grinned. The idea of watching the sexy Mr. Bond chopping logs naked from the waist up wasn't the worst proposition in the world. He glanced over at her, his lips curving up, and raised an eyebrow as if to say, *What do you think?* She shrugged, *meh*, but thought that her eyes probably held a little of the lust that coursed through her at the thought.

It took Willow quite a while to open all the presents. Gene moved around the room while she did so, refilling glasses and taking around plates of food to keep everyone occupied.

"Fancy a nibble, ma'am?" he murmured to her at one point when he bent to offer her a selection of tiny pastries.

"Mmm, yes please," she replied, determined not to blush, and well aware that Neve still had her eye on them. "Thank you, Mr. Bond."

He moved on, but not before they'd exchanged the briefest of glances, and she saw the warmth in his gray eyes.

After the present opening, Willow made a short speech thanking her friends and family for their support, then announced that they were going to have a bit of fun with the Four Seasons lingerie party. The women all clapped, thoroughly enjoying themselves by this point.

It was Neve's turn to take over. Callie had been to many of Neve's parties, so she was well aware how skilled her friend was at being the host, but as always she found herself admiring Neve's confident manner, the way she managed to include everyone in the evening, and how she made it fun and a little risqué without picking on anyone who might have been embarrassed or nervous at some of the things she brought out of her suitcase.

First she handed everyone a catalogue of the Four Seasons brand and brought out displays of lots of their lingerie and swimwear, which the girls all cooed over. Many of them took pieces to try on in Willow's bedrooms, and Callie had to suppress her usual pleasure and excitement at seeing the order list get longer and longer as the girls emerged with pleased squeals. Even Willow chose a few pieces, because Neve had purposely included some maternity bras that Rowan had made—beautiful as ever, but with practical clips that meant a nursing mum could remove the cups.

"What do you think, Gene?" Neve directed the question at him and held the bra with her fingertips, giving it a slight shake in his direction. She'd had a few vodkas now and was growing increasingly naughty, and Callie knew she'd do her best to tease him. Rowan coughed into her wine, always the most easily embarrassed of the lot of them.

But he appeared impossible to shock and just nodded. "Easy access," he said. "I approve."

Everyone laughed, and Neve gave a wry smile.

Bridget nudged her as he turned away to fetch a new bottle of wine. "Leave the poor man alone."

"Why? I want to see what it takes to make him blush."

Callie knew she should stop her, but she had a sneaky feeling that it was her friend who was going to come out the loser in this battle. Gene was proving to have a better sense of humor and a higher degree of unflappability than she'd realized.

The test came when everyone had finished looking at the lingerie. Neve produced another case and grinned as she placed it on the table. By now, all of them except Willow had been drinking for a few hours, and the mood was high and a tad raucous.

"Ready for a little fun?" She popped the lid.

The women all squealed at the array of vibrators and other sex toys on display. Callie, who was used to this, glanced up at Gene. He was looking with interest at the range of objects, but as if he'd known she would be looking at him, his eyes rose to meet hers, and a small smile crept onto his lips.

"Right," Neve said, and rubbed her hands together. "Time for some demonstrations."

Chapter Twenty-Three

Spending an evening with a crowd of rowdy young women would normally have been Gene's idea of hell, and he'd been on the verge of turning down Neve's suggestion of acting as a waiter for the night. That afternoon, however, after he'd gotten the taxi to drop Callie home, he'd walked into the Safe & Secure offices to learn that Phoebe had received a new death threat.

"It's just as nasty as the previous one," Kev had said. "But that's not the only bad news." He'd shown a copy of the note to Gene, who'd read it with growing distaste. As well as threatening Phoebe, it ended by describing exactly what he was going to do to her and her daughter when he got hold of them, in great and disgusting detail.

"What do you want to do?" Kev had asked with concern.

Gene knew he had to sort himself out. No more wearing casual clothes—it had to be the bulletproof vest at all times, and from now on he had to make sure he was completely focused on her safety. He couldn't afford to get distracted with romantic thoughts when he should be concentrating on analyzing the threat at all times.

He couldn't tell Kev that, though. Instead, he'd said, "I think it's time to upgrade the threat on Callie from low to medium." They'd labeled Phoebe's case as 'very high' from the start, but because the threat to Callie had been indirect, they'd kept hers rated as 'low' until now. "And it's time to send someone ahead of us to do risk assessments of the places we'll be staying, and to do covert protection from a distance to catch anything I might not be aware of."

"You really think he'll come after her?"

"No," Gene had said, although he'd not been sure if that had just been wishful thinking. "I think it's a scare tactic rather than a real threat. But we can't risk that, of course."

After leaving the office, he'd gone to the gym for a while and had tried to lose himself in the heat and sweat of physical exercise, but all it had done was made him think of Callie's hot skin next to his, her soft moans in the darkness, and to imagine how terrible he'd feel if something happened to her.

How stupid he'd been to give in to his desire. Her life was in danger, and all he could think about was taking her to bed and tasting her again, and losing himself in her sweet warmth.

To punish himself, he'd agreed to go to the party, certain he'd hate every minute. Oddly, though, he discovered he was quite enjoying himself. Willow's friends were fun without being over the top, a little embarrassed to have him there but half enjoying it, too, and it was interesting to be on the inside of women's lives for once and watch how they interacted with each other once they semi-forgot he was a guy.

It was nice to get to know Callie's close friends as well. Bridget was bright and bubbly, Neve outwardly mischievous and wicked, but inwardly—he suspected—soft as mush with a heart of gold. Rowan was a bit harder to fathom, as she barely said two words to him, and she seemed the shyest of the four of them.

He also enjoyed watching Callie with her friends. She didn't seem any different, sunny and warm, open and fun. Presumably, her mother had kept her informed of recent events regarding Darren Kirk. Was Callie concerned about the increasing threat on her life? She didn't look it, appearing very relaxed, and she didn't seem nervous or distracted.

He'd wondered whether she'd be able to avoid the temptation of telling her best friends what had happened between them while they'd been away, but although she met his gaze once or twice during the evening, and something passed between them like a radio wave from her eyes to his, she didn't make any reference to their brief relationship. He was relieved, and a tiny bit disappointed. Of course he didn't want it coming out into the open, he scolded himself. But it didn't stop him wondering where it was going. Was this just a bit of fun for her? A holiday fling to amuse herself while they traveled? Or was it something more? He surprised himself by hoping it was the latter.

The only time she reacted to his presence with more than a flick of her eyes was when Neve opened the case containing the sex toys. Callie obviously knew what the case contained, but as he perused the contents and then raised his gaze to hers, he caught her watching him, and saw a deep blush spread from the apples of her cheeks across her face, like two drops of scarlet paint dropped onto a plate of cream.

His lips curved up. That, at least, boded well.

"Now, this is my favorite," the indefatigable Neve said, holding up the rabbit vibrator. "Shaped for your pleasure, ladies." She proceeded to explain to them the various delights of the toy.

Gene retreated to the drinks table to pour another round of wine glasses and walked discreetly around the room to hand them out, trying not to laugh out loud at the squeals and shrieks of the women as they handled the toys. From what he could see, they consisted mostly of vibrators of various shapes and sizes with a few anal devices, no nipple clamps or whips or anything too scary or painful that might have been too much for anyone who hadn't been brave enough to purchase any toys before. He felt a sudden surge of affection for Neve, who was managing to make everything seem both erotically naughty and yet perfectly normal, too. Even Rowan was having fun investigating the options, although she completely refused to look him in the eye.

He tried not to stare too long at the contents, knowing he'd get himself hot and bothered at the thought of trying them out on the strawberry blonde currently examining the types of lubricants available. She didn't really need any of those, he thought, remembering how wet and swollen she'd been, then closed his eyes briefly and forced himself to think about arctic conditions and having his wisdom teeth out and anything else that would dampen his ardor.

Luckily, nobody seemed to notice his discomfort, their attention distracted by Willow, who was complaining that she was too fat even to see below her navel, and that once the baby came she was sure it would be at least six months before she and Liam would have the energy to try out any of the toys.

Neve had apparently finished going through all the items in the case. The women were busy flicking through catalogues, purchasing items that were available from Neve's small stock and writing down their orders for those items she didn't have, most of the girls apparently brave enough to treat themselves to at least one item.

Neve turned her wicked smile on him. "Gene? Can I put you down for anything?"

Everyone giggled. He took her over a plate of chocolate truffles and bent to offer them to her. "Actually, I'll take one of those. Looks like fun." He tapped the list in her hand.

Neve's eyebrows shot up, and all the women went "Oooooh!"

"For anyone we know?" Bridget asked.

"Yes," Neve said, "anyone we know?" Her eyes were hard.

"For my special someone," he said. "A lady who's been in my heart for a very long time."

He saw the disappointment flicker across Bridget and Rowan's faces, and surprise on Neve's at the acceptance that it was someone he'd known for a while.

"Well, she's a very lucky woman," Bridget said brightly, glancing at Callie. He didn't follow her gaze, but out of the corner of his eye he saw Callie turn to talk to Willow, showing her apparent disinterest in his love life.

The party went on for maybe another thirty minutes, but by then Willow was noticeably flagging, almost dozing off in her chair, and everyone began to gather their purchases and their handbags.

"I'll ring for taxis," someone called. "How many do we need?"

"Hitch is taking us home," Bridget said, indicating the four of them. "I just need to phone him to come and pick us up."

"Will we all fit in his car?" Neve asked doubtfully. "It's a very old Mini," she explained at Gene's quizzical look.

"I'll take Callie and Rowan home," he said. "As I'm still officially on PA duty."

"Don't worry about me," Rowan said. "Hitch is going to drop me at the supermarket. I want to pick up a few bits and I can walk from there."

None of them seemed interested in the fact that he was taking Callie home. He glanced at her. She was busy saying goodbye to Willow, but didn't reject his offer, so he guessed she didn't mind.

While he waited, he emptied any food remains into the rubbish bin, rinsed the plates and stacked them with the glasses in the dishwasher, and tidied up so Willow wouldn't have much to do when everyone had gone.

Closing the door to the dishwasher and pressing the start button, he looked up to see Callie leaning against the doorjamb, watching him. "Ready?" she asked.

"Yep." He picked up his car keys, wallet, and slipped the purchase he'd made into his pocket, and followed her out to where the others were saying goodbye. "Bye," he said to Willow, bending to kiss her on the cheek.

She threw her arms around him. "You cleaned up! You can come again. Thank you so much."

He gave her a quick hug back. "You're very welcome. I hope things go well for you."

Callie waved goodbye too, and then they all went out onto the street.

A tall, dark-haired guy was leaning against an old racing-green Mini, but he pushed off the car as they approached.

"Gene, this is Bridget's brother, Hitch," Callie said. "Hitch, meet Gene. My... PA." She left the slightest pause between the final two words.

"Hey." The two guys shook hands. Hitch turned to the girls. "Who's coming with me? Might be a squash." He winked at Rowan. "You can sit on my lap if you like."

"That would be rather dangerous, don't you think?" she pointed out as she walked around to the passenger seat, completely missing the flirty nature of his comment. Hitch met Gene's eyes and gave a wry smile.

The other girls got in, yelling at Callie to keep in touch about the rest of their trip, and then Hitch drove away, pretending to bang into a nearby lamppost and making them all squeal before he righted the car and disappeared around the corner.

Callie blew out a long breath.

"Ready to go home?" Gene asked.

"Yeah."

As they walked the short distance to his car, he crossed behind her to walk on the road side of the pavement.

"What are you doing that for?" she asked.

"So I can protect you with my weapon."

"I'd like to see that."

He smiled, and her lips curved up a little, but she seemed subdued.

"Are you okay?" he asked as they reached his car.

"Fine, thank you." Polite as strangers again.

They got into the car, and he started the engine and pulled away.

"Callie," he said as he headed out of the city center toward her house, "you realize that when I mentioned I'd bought that stuff for my special someone, I was talking about you, right?"

He glanced over at her. She'd turned startled eyes to him, eyes that glistened like the sun in the evening sky.

"Oh," she said.

"Seriously?" He returned his gaze to the road. "After what we've been up to the last few days?"

"You said it was for 'a lady who's been in my heart for a very long time.'"

He pulled up at some traffic lights and looked at her again. "I think maybe you have. Or the idea of you, anyway."

"Why, Gene, that's a very romantic thing to say on the eve of St. Valentine's Day." Her expression had softened, and her eyes had warmed. She'd really thought he'd been referring to someone else.

It would be stupid to make any declaration of love. Not when he was supposed to be protecting her. And not after only a week. Common sense told him to keep his distance emotionally, even if he couldn't physically.

But as he looked into her eyes and she smiled, all he could think was that he was crazy about this woman, and it wasn't getting any better.

He pulled up outside her house and left the engine running.

She studied him for a moment. "Do you want to come in?"

He wanted that more than anything in the world, but he knew that one of his team was currently sitting outside her house, waiting to take over when he left, and he didn't want anyone guessing that something was developing between them. And Rowan would be home soon too.

So he shook his head. "I can't tonight. I've got a few things to do before we leave tomorrow."

Disappointment flickered on her features briefly before she smothered it. "Oh, of course. I still feel bad about going away on your birthday. Are you sure you wouldn't be doing anything? Your family wouldn't have planned you a surprise party or anything?"

"I very much doubt that," he said wryly. He'd be lucky if they even remembered it was his birthday, let alone how old he was. "They know I'd hate that. I'd much rather spend it with you, having dinner."

She smiled. "Okay."

She hesitated, and he wondered whether she was expecting him to kiss her goodnight. Fuck. This was awkward. And if the threat on her life increased, it was only going to get worse, because he couldn't be seen being intimate with her at all. If he had to increase the number of officers shadowing her, it was going to make things very difficult between them if he couldn't even hold her hand.

But she turned, opened the door, and got out of the car. "I'll see you tomorrow, around two o'clock, then?"

"Sure."

She shut the door and walked toward the house.

He waited until she'd gone in and closed the door. Giving a brief nod to Ian, who was parked across the road in his car, Gene drove away.

Chapter Twenty-Four

The next day promised rain, the sky heavy with gray thunderclouds, lending a humidity to the air that Callie knew would only get worse as they traveled further north.

"I think the skies are going to open soon," Gene observed as they passed the sign for Napier. It had just gone five, and they'd been traveling for a few hours.

"Hopefully we'll get to the hotel before it comes down."

Their first appointment wasn't until eight the following morning. It was an early start, but the manager of the largest clothing store in Napier was leaving at nine for a flight to Australia. It was the only time she'd been available to meet on the day, which was the main reason they'd driven up the afternoon before.

"So," Callie said as he checked the GPS for directions to the hotel, "are you excited to discover what your birthday present is?" She'd wished him happy birthday when she'd first gotten in the car, and had promised he'd get his present later.

He glanced at her, his lips curving up. "I think so."

"You'll like it, I promise. A birthday and Valentine's Day present rolled into one."

He returned his gaze to the road, continuing to smile, but she sensed wariness behind it. Not for the first time, doubt flickered inside her. Was he regretting becoming involved with her? His words the night before had been encouraging, but he was so reticent, so withdrawn and private, that it was difficult to know what was on his mind.

She cleared her throat. "I feel I should make something clear. We had a great time last week, but I'd like to say that if you've changed your mind and would rather we held back from a... physical relationship while we are away, I understand." The fact that he'd not stayed in her room that night still played on her mind, and she didn't want to assume.

He glanced at her again, and this time his smile was warmer. "Are you saying you don't want to sleep with me anymore?"

"Um, no." Her face filled with heat.

He surveyed her reddening cheeks, grinned, then looked back at the road. "Good. Because I have a little Valentine's Day gift for you, too."

Pleasure filled her. "Oh?"

"Something I bought at Willow's party." He looked impish then, and suddenly younger, throwing off all the cares and worries that appeared to weigh heavily on him at times.

"Oh…" Callie hadn't asked Neve what he'd bought, not wanting her to be suspicious about them, but now she was intrigued. "What is it?"

"If I told you, it wouldn't be a surprise, would it?"

"I hate surprises," she grumbled.

He just laughed. "Too bad."

He refused to tell her more, even though she spent the next five minutes badgering him, so in the end she gave up and decided she'd have to wait until later. Together with her own present, it promised to be an exciting evening.

Gene found the hotel without too much hassle, and he parked outside and they checked in. Rebuilt after an earthquake in 1931, the city boasted some distinctive art deco architecture, and the hotel on the waterfront was a terrific example of this. The front bore the distinctive clear, simple lines associated with Manhattan during this period, and its decor was filled with sunbursts and fountains symbolizing the dawn of a modern age. The foyer boasted a skyscraper mural on one large wall, and when they went up to their rooms, Callie discovered they were decorated in black and gold with the geometric shapes that characterized the period.

"I'll call for you at six?" Gene asked her after they'd admired the decor.

"Okay. See you in a bit."

Gene went into his room and closed the door.

Callie walked into her own room and sat on the bed, feeling a bit flat. Part of her had wondered whether he would suggest they only book one room while they were away. But then, they weren't a couple, she reminded herself, not yet. Maybe he was the sort of man who liked his own space. Or maybe he didn't want her to assume anything, not this early on in their relationship. She would just have to wait and see how things developed.

So she took the opportunity of being alone to shower, slather herself in cream, and sort out his birthday present to be ready for when he hopefully came back to her room at the end of the evening. If he chose not to, well, she'd worry about that then.

At six o'clock, a knock came at the door, and she answered to see him standing there. As usual, he wore his three-piece suit, apparently intent on remaining professional even on his birthday.

"Wow." His gaze slid down her and made her tingle all over. "You look fantastic."

"Thank you." She'd made an effort that evening. Not that she didn't normally take care of her appearance, but usually she wore comfortable, classic cuts and kept her makeup to muted skin tones. Tonight, though, she wore a sleek little black number that reached to just above the knee, with thigh-highs and black high heels, and she'd used smoky gray on her eyelids and emphasized her lashes with black mascara. Her dark red lipstick matched the clutch she carried.

He offered her his arm like Cary Grant. "Shall we?"

She slid her hand into the crook of his arm. "Yes, let's. I'm starving."

Luckily, Gene had possessed the foresight to book, because as the waitress showed them to their table, she informed them that they were completely booked right up until nine because it was Valentine's Day.

Callie flicked through the menu, her eyes going straight to the barbecued ribs, which she adored. She sucked her bottom lip as she debated. There were unspoken rules about what to choose to eat for a romantic meal. Spaghetti, or anything else with sauce that could be flicked or dripped down one's clothes, was a big no-no. Ribs could never be eaten daintily either, but then it wasn't as if they were two ordinary lovers, was it?

"I feel such a fraud," she said.

Gene gave her a quizzical look. "Why?"

She shrugged. "Well, we're not exactly sweethearts, are we? More like..." She'd been about to say fuck-buddies, but the look on his face made the words trail off.

"I'm sorry I can't be all hearts and flowers," he said quietly. "I would like to be, and it's only what you deserve. It's really important to me that I stay professional while we're working together. Just for a while. I hope you can understand that."

"Including not sleeping in the same room?"

He looked pained. "I know that makes me sound like I'm taking advantage of you. I honestly don't want it to be like that."

"Gene, it's okay. I'm not criticizing. This situation won't last forever. I know you didn't want to give in and go to bed with me, and it's kind of flattering that it happened anyway. But I understand that you want to keep your distance for a while. We can be grown up about this, can't we? I like you. And you like me. We're having fun while we're traveling. For now, isn't that enough?"

His lips curved up. "No. But I think it has to be, for now."

"That's fine. It's more than enough for me to deal with, I can assure you." She rolled her eyes and studied the menu. "Now, then, what sounds good?"

"They've won lots of awards here," he said. But when she looked up, he was still watching her, his eyes filled with the affection he couldn't—for his own reasons—portray.

As the evening drew on, the restaurant grew busier, but Callie didn't mind, because the lively, romantic atmosphere made it easier to pretend she and Gene were involved, even if they weren't.

The trouble was, it felt as if they were. He might not have held her hand or told her he loved her, but throughout the evening, his gray eyes hardly left her face and they were filled with warm amusement and genuine affection.

After a whole week where they'd hardly been apart, Callie felt that they were beginning to feel comfortable with each other, and to delve beneath the initial conversations of who liked what music and their favorite foods to deeper issues. They discussed politics for a while, discovering their views were close enough to ensure they were unlikely to argue about many substantial issues. The same was true when it came to religion and family values, both of them having a modern approach, but with an underlying sense of tradition that kept them from wanting to be too revolutionary.

"I think tradition's underrated," she said as she made her way through the barbecued ribs stacked high on her plate, interspersing them with crispy fries and the wonderful chipotle slaw. "As long as you accept that change is a necessary thing, and it's important not to think that the past is always better than the present, there's something about traditions—family ones and national ones—that give you a sense of belonging, of roots, don't you think?"

"I do. I would love to have had some." He looked up from cutting his medium-rare Angus fillet steak with blue cheese sauce and laughed.

"What?"

"You have barbecue sauce on your cheek."

"Of course I do. The better the ribs, the more sauce you have to have on your face." She wiped delicately at her cheek. "What did you mean, you would love to have had some traditions?"

He chewed the steak thoughtfully and shrugged. "I can't think of any family traditions. My folks weren't keen on that sort of thing."

"Oh, come on. You must have. What about dressing the Christmas tree, for example? Everyone has a tradition around that."

"Not me." He speared a carrot with rather more force than was necessary, she thought. "We didn't have one."

"Oh." She frowned. "Why not? Because your mum died?"

"No, even before then. Dad hated the commercialization of that time of year and said the tree was a British creation he had no intention of following." Gene had explained that his father disliked being reminded of New Zealand's European roots and wanted the country to break free from the Commonwealth.

"Actually, it was a German creation," Callie pointed out, "but whatever he thought, it seems cruel to take away the pleasure of dressing the tree from your children."

"Well, his children's pleasure was always low on his list." Gene ate another piece of steak, his expression guarded.

"And your mum? Did she never contradict your father?"

"I remember one year, when Freddie and I were small, she baked some tree-shaped cookies for us to decorate with icing. Dad refused to eat any of them."

"Good Lord."

"Yeah."

"Did you have presents?"

"Yes. But they weren't left at the bottom of the bed or anything. There was never any attempt to pretend that Santa had delivered them."

Callie finished her last rib and dipped her fingers in the bowl of water, rubbing them with lemon. "That makes me sad."

"You had a better experience, I presume?"

She dried her hands and then speared a few fries with her fork. "Yes and no. Dad was in the Army, so we moved around a lot. But we had a Christmas tree, and they kept up the pretense of Santa as long as they could. I didn't have a bad childhood. I was brokenhearted when my parents broke up."

"When was that?"

"About... ten, eleven years ago now. They'd lived apart for a long time, since I was about seven or eight, I suppose. Mum made the decision to stay in New Zealand with me when Dad was away. She didn't want me to have to keep switching schools. Plus, of course, she had her own career by then as a lawyer, and she was getting very good at it. She used to go out to visit him, and they seemed quite content with their arrangement—they had their own space, but the security of being married, I suppose. I think she wanted him to leave the Army, but he refused—the Army was his life."

"He's a major, isn't he?"

"Yes, although he's retired now. Anyway, that year he was stationed in Afghanistan. She'd been away visiting him, but I remember her coming home a week early, and she announced she'd left him. I never did find out exactly what happened. There was some sort of accident—she fell down a flight of stairs or something. She looked awful, bruises everywhere. She wouldn't talk about it. My guess is that it was the straw that broke the lawyer's back—she needed his support and begged him to leave, and he wouldn't. So she walked out."

Gene ate the last mouthful of steak and pushed his plate away. For a long moment, he was silent.

Callie raised an eyebrow. "What?"

He took a long swig of his Diet Coke. She had the strange feeling he was trying to decide whether to tell her something.

He put down his glass and wiped his mouth on a serviette. "So," he said. "Dessert?"

Chapter Twenty-Five

Gene knew he'd paused for too long. Callie was too astute not to notice his hesitation. But she didn't quiz him, maybe understanding that if he hadn't caved, it meant he'd decided to keep it to himself.

Would he ever tell her the truth about what had happened in Afghanistan? He leaned back in his chair as the waitress came to clear their plates, sadness settling over him like a wet mist. He couldn't shake the feeling that once the truth about everything came out, Callie wouldn't want to see him.

He accepted the dessert menu, half wishing he'd told Phoebe that he didn't take protection jobs himself anymore. As director of the firm, he'd been within his rights to farm out the work to one of his agents, and there were plenty who would have done a great job—a better job than he was doing, he thought gloomily. But he had a soft spot for Phoebe, and he'd been unable to say no to her.

"Why so sad?" Callie leaned forward on the table. She'd rested her breasts on her forearms, pushing them up in the process. The dress wasn't low cut, but it gave him a perfect view down her cleavage, and he had to fight not to look at it.

"Just thinking about the past."

"Army life is a strange dichotomy, isn't it? I would imagine it's the same in the other defense forces. When you're away, you can't wait to get home, and when you're home, you're constantly thinking of going back."

"Maybe. I don't miss it, though."

"You think you made the right choice leaving?"

"Oh yes. It's a good life for a young single man, but as you've mentioned, not so great when you get older or have a family."

"Would you like to have a family?"

He smiled. "One day. You?"

"Oh yes. I think I'd be a terrible mum, though. I'd never remember their lunches, and I'd forget to pick them up from school."

"You'd make a great mum," he said, meaning it. The thought of Callie curled up beside him, pregnant with his child, gave him goosebumps.

She looked into her glass of wine for a moment, and he watched as a light blush filled her cheeks. She was so gorgeous. He wished he could lean forward and press his lips to hers.

She glanced to one side as a movement a few tables across caught her eye, and she smiled. He followed her gaze to see a guy lowering down to one knee as he proposed to his girlfriend. The young woman pressed her fingers to her lips and burst into tears, nodding furiously. Everyone around the restaurant cheered, and the guy stood, his face bright red and beaming.

"Aw," Callie said. "How romantic."

"You think?" Gene drew his brows together. "I can't imagine proposing in a restaurant. Imagine how embarrassing it would be if the girl turned you down."

He'd not given much thought to marriage before, but he decided that when he eventually proposed, it would be just the two of them, him and his chosen girl, somewhere quiet.

His brain transplanted Callie into the picture, giving him a vision of kneeling before her. Her words rang in his head: *we're not exactly sweethearts, are we?* It made him sad, and he looked away.

The waitress returned for their order, and Callie requested the ice cream trio, while Gene just wanted coffee.

When she'd left, Callie leaned on the table again. "Tell me about Lisa," she said.

That startled him. He was surprised she even remembered Lisa's name. "What about her?"

"What was she like?"

He played with the salt shaker, turning it around in his fingers. "Shortish. Long, dark hair she wore in a bun most of the time. Pretty. Feisty. Brave. She loved animals—dogs, cats, horses, anything we met went straight to her." He knew why—she'd had a magnetic personality that had pulled everyone and everything toward her.

"How long had you been dating?" Callie asked.

He stared at her. Then he put down the salt. "What makes you say that?"

"It's obvious, Gene. It doesn't take a mind reader to see your pain."

"I'd have been upset at the loss of any colleague."

"Sure. How long?"

He sighed. "Only a few months. It wasn't serious—it had only just gotten going, really. Maybe that was worse, never having the chance to discover whether it would have worked. I don't know."

Callie covered his hand with her own. "I'm sorry."

He left it there for a moment, but he was too worried that Ian—the agent who'd preceded them to Napier to carry out a threat assessment, and who'd be keeping an eye on the surroundings—would see them, so he carefully slid his hand away and picked up his drink. "Thanks."

He hated doing this, pushing her away, and cursed himself for being so weak. She finished off her drink, though, and smiled at him, suggesting she wasn't upset.

"Let's change the subject," she said. "Where are we off to after Napier?"

She kept the conversation light after that, talking about the towns they were due to visit and places she'd been to while she dipped her spoon into her ice cream and ate it slowly. Gene was content to listen to her and watch the spoon filled with creamy mixture slide between her lips, her tongue occasionally protruding to remove any drips.

He wished they were a couple, and she would ask if he wanted a taste of her ice cream, and feed him spoons of it, looking into his eyes with adoration. But she didn't ask, and although she smiled a lot and her eyes were friendly, she was careful to keep her hands to herself, and to steer the conversation away from anything too intimate.

But it was as if the more he tried to remain professional, the more he hungered for her. By the end of the evening, he ached with longing.

After they'd eaten, they went for a short walk through the streets of Napier to let their dinner go down, and it was all he could do not to take her in his arms, strip her of the dress right there in the street, and feel her hot skin against his.

"It's going to rain any minute," Callie said, looking up at the heavy gray sky. "Jeez, it's humid."

He couldn't even take her hand, because he knew Ian would be following them at a distance, keeping a watch out for any suspicious characters. This really was like torture, and even though he hadn't drunk a drop of alcohol, he felt slightly dizzy, consumed by lust and need for her.

Something landed on his cheek—a large drop of rain. "You're right," he said. "We should get back."

They began to walk more quickly, but Callie was wearing high heels and couldn't stride out as fast as him.

"We're not going to make it," he said as the raindrops increased and began to turn the pavement a dark gray.

"Hold on." She stopped walking and bent to ease her heels off, then squealed as the heavens opened. "Quick!"

She ran beside him in her stockinged feet, but they were still soaked by the time they reached the steps to the hotel. "So much for the elegant makeup," she said, dripping onto the tiles as they walked across the foyer. "I bet I look like a panda."

"You look wonderful." It wasn't false flattery. Her cheeks were flushed and strands of wet hair clung to them, but she looked young, fresh, and full of life. It was only at that point he realized that, in spite of his relationship with Angela and a few other girls, Lisa had haunted his memories for a long time, and it was nice to be with someone who banished his dark thoughts, at least for a while.

She didn't reply, and they made their way to the elevator, just catching a half-filled cubicle about to go up. They stood to one side of it as the doors closed, and she looked up, meeting his eyes. She was quite a bit shorter than him without her heels, and he discovered he could see down her cleavage from this angle.

Heat flooded him, and it must have shown in his eyes because her lips parted. Their gazes locked, and suddenly Gene knew that in seconds she'd be in his arms, naked, and it wouldn't be much longer afterward that he'd be sliding inside her, losing himself in her warmth.

The elevator dinged at their floor and they broke their gaze and walked out. There was another couple in the corridor, talking, and so they walked straight to their rooms, not saying anything. Callie swiped her card and opened her door, went in, and waited.

He glanced over his shoulder. The couple had disappeared. The corridor was empty. Ian would have taken a room on the same floor, but he would continue to keep an eye out in the foyer for a while before retiring for the night.

Turning back, Gene followed Callie into the room, and the door closed behind him.

She walked to the bed, flicked on the bedside lamp, then turned to face him. He closed the distance between them, until they were standing only an inch apart. Outside, the rain hammered on the streets and pounded on the window, but inside the room it was warm and quiet, the only sound their fast breathing and the tick of the clock on the wall.

Callie looked up at him. "Can I touch you now?" she said softly.

He undid the buttons of his jacket, slid it off, and hung it over the chair. Then he did the same with his waistcoat, because he didn't like her touching it in case she discovered how thick it was and started asking questions.

Then he came back to her, cupped her face, and lowered his lips to hers.

Oh… it was heavenly to kiss her after an evening of having to keep his distance. She gave a little moan, and he slid his arms around her and pulled her against him, reveling in the feel of her soft body against his. Brushing his tongue across her bottom lip, he was rewarded when she opened her mouth, and they exchanged a long, slow kiss, his hand sliding down to her bottom, hers beginning to unbutton his shirt.

Reaching the hem, she thrust the sides of the shirt aside and slipped her hands underneath, onto his skin. "*Aaahhh*," she sighed, scraping her nails lightly across his ribs. "I've wanted to do this all evening."

He shuddered, and suddenly everything was taking too long. He needed her naked, wanted to feel her against him, to have her beneath him. Turning her, he caught hold of the zipper at the top of her dress and slid it down, then eased the dress off her shoulders and let it fall to the floor in a whisper of material.

Eyebrows rising, he turned her back to face him. An impish smile crossed her face. "Happy birthday. And happy Valentine's Day."

She wore a set of Four Seasons underwear he'd seen in the catalogue, made from black lace with a shiny red ribbon threaded through the tops of the demi-cups. The same red ribbon wove through the fabric of the panties, culminating in a neat bow at the front. It was grown-up and sexy at the same time—not the cheap sort of underwear a girl bought and wore once before relegating it to the back of the drawer because it was too uncomfortable, but the type a woman bought and wore all the time because she wanted to feel good and look sexy for herself as well as for her man.

"Wow." The erection that had been half there all evening now sprang to attention. Turning her away from him, he moved closer and slid his hands from her hips up to cup her breasts. "You look fantastic," he murmured, kissing down her neck to where the pulse beat, and covering the spot with his mouth. He sucked, and she groaned and leaned her head on his shoulder, arching her back to push her breasts into his hands. Taking the hint, he took each nipple between his thumbs and forefingers through the fabric and tugged a little, and she moaned again and covered his hands with her own.

"I need you," she whispered, turning to throw her arms around his neck. "I want you, Gene. I've wanted you all evening. I can't bear it any longer. Make love to me."

He didn't need to be told twice. He pushed her onto the bed and gestured for her to climb onto the mattress, which she did, lying on the pillows, her breasts rising and falling fast with her rapid breaths. He let his shirt drop to the floor and quickly removed his trousers and his underwear, then went to his jacket and took out a small velvet pouch before returning to the bed.

Her lips curved up. "Is this my present?"

"Well, it's a present for both of us." He climbed on and stretched out beside her. "I wouldn't have bought a toy without consulting you, but I thought these might be acceptable." He handed her the pouch.

She unclipped the popper, opened it up, and took out the two small bottles of lube. "Oh!" Her face lit up with pleasure. "His and hers!"

"Yeah. This one is a warming gel. This one makes things... tingle. And together they combine to provide some interesting sensations, apparently."

She met his gaze and smiled. "Thank you."

"Not that I think you need it," he teased, laughing when she blushed prettily. He moved close to her, pulling her thigh across his so she was practically wrapped around him. "God, I want you," he said huskily. "It's all I've been able to think about."

"Have me, then." She pulled him on top of her and hooked her ankles behind his back. "Take me, Gene. I'm all yours."

Chapter Twenty-Six

Callie was so fired up that she would have been happy if Gene had slid straight inside her and thrust her all the way to a blissful conclusion. But even though he was obviously as turned on as she was, he appeared to have other ideas.

He started off by kissing her, long, slow, deep kisses that started a fire in her belly and fanned it until it became a roaring inferno. His hot, hard body only increased her desire, and she rocked her hips against his, aching for fulfilment.

He lifted his head and kissed her nose. "Slowly," he said, amused. "I haven't waited all day to have this over in seconds."

"But I ache," she said with a groan.

His gray eyes surveyed her for a moment, and then he lifted off her and moved to the side. Puzzled, she went to rise, but he pulled her against him, and, before she could say anything, covered her mouth with his and moved his free hand down her body. Lifting the elastic of her panties, he slid his hand underneath and pressed his fingers into her folds.

"Oh…" She inhaled sharply, her mouth opening under his, but he just plunged his tongue inside, his fingers mimicking its thrusts as they gathered up her moisture and then circled over her clit.

Already turned on, it took only moments before all her internal muscles tightened, and she gave in to the orgasm, exclaiming against his mouth while his fingers teased her until she lay gasping and spent.

He lifted his head, withdrew his fingers, and kissed her lips. "There," he said. "Now we can start properly."

"Fuck," she said, heart pounding, her chest heaving.

"Give me a chance," he scolded, rolling her toward him so he could undo the clasp of her bra. "Talk about demanding."

She laughed and kissed him again, letting him draw the bra down her arms and toss it onto the floor. Then he removed her panties, leaving her lying there naked, before he reached for the velvet pouch.

SERENITY WOODS

"This is fun." He pulled out the bottle of warming lube and popped the top. "Like a scientific experiment."

"So I'm a guinea pig, am I?" Her body felt like a guitar string, still thrumming with her orgasm, and when he smeared a small amount of the lube on each nipple, it was as if he'd plucked at the string again, sending a vibration that rippled all the way through her.

"Yep." He closed the lid of the bottle, folded his arms, and leaned forward until his mouth was an inch from her breast. Taking a deep breath, he blew out over her nipple.

"Ooh!" She squirmed beneath him at the strange sensation of warmth.

"Nice?" He leaned across her to try the other one, doing the same, blowing out across the sensitive skin.

"Mmm. Oh yes." She closed her eyes in bliss.

He chuckled and covered the nipple with his mouth, and her eyes flew open again. "*Aaahhh.*" The lube intensified the heat of his mouth, making the skin ultra-sensitive and sending tingles through her all the way down to her clit.

He concentrated on her breasts for a while, licking and teasing them and fanning the flames inside her until the ache began to build once more. Then he shifted down and reopened the bottle of lube. Pouring a little onto his fingers, he stroked it through her folds.

"You really don't need this," he said, his fingers sliding easily through her already wet, swollen skin.

"Gene..."

"Not a complaint. Just stating a fact." He moved two fingers deep inside her, and her hips lifted automatically, pushing toward him.

Leaning over her, he blew a soft breath from her clit down between her legs, then ran back up with his tongue.

Callie groaned and covered her face, feeling as if she'd stepped into a warm bath. "I can't take much more of this."

He tutted, continuing to blow on her skin and following up with light strokes of his tongue. "This is too easy. You're not much of a challenge."

"Sorry to disappoint." It was just too lovely, and she was going to come again if he didn't move away. She pushed at his head and rolled over. "Stop it!"

Laughing, he moved back. "Lightweight."

"Yeah, well, the shoe's going to be on the other foot now." She took out the other bottle of lube from the pouch and flipped open the top. "About time I had some fun."

Gene sighed, lay on his back, and tucked his arms under his head. "If you must." His eyes met hers, hot and amused. "Help yourself."

"Mmm." What an offer. His erection stood proud of his body, the top glistening, begging to be licked. "I intend to." She poured a decent amount on her hand, made sure her fingers were well lubricated, and then closed them around him.

He closed his eyes, his eyebrows rising as he gave a helpless groan. Callie's lips curved up, then she turned her full attention to her hand. His erection was thick, her fingers barely meeting as she circled the shaft. And he was hard, so hard, like rock, covered in a sheath of fine, soft skin.

Gently, she slid her hand down, revealing the swollen tip, and rubbed her thumb across it, smearing the lube all over him before beginning to give him long, slow strokes. He held his breath for a moment, then blew it out in a rush.

"How does that feel?" She twisted her fingers as she stroked, massaging him carefully, covering him in lube until her hand was sliding with little effort, slick and smooth.

"*Aaahhh*... It tingles. Feels hot and... sensitive..." Not so relaxed now, he moved his hands from under his head, linked his fingers, and rested them on his forehead. "Jesus. That feels good."

Glad she was giving him pleasure, she stroked him for a while longer, then—making sure his eyes were closed—she lowered her head and covered the tip with her mouth.

"Fuck!" He jumped beneath her, and she had to stifle a laugh as she slid her lips down the shaft. "What the... Jesus... Oh fuck." He lowered a hand to rest on her head, and threaded his fingers into her hair. "Callie... That's amazing..."

The lube tasted of strawberries, and Gene tasted of hot, musky male, and Callie would have groaned herself if her mouth hadn't been full. She washed her tongue around the head, teasing the slit at the top, then took him deep inside her mouth again, her thighs growing wet with her own moisture the longer she spent arousing him.

He bore her touch for as long as he could, but eventually he tugged on her hair, and she lifted her head and looked up at him, catching her breath at his expression. All humor had gone now, and the heat and desire in his eyes sent a shiver down her spine.

Lifting up, he reached for his wallet. She put a hand on his wrist, though, stopping him as he went to retrieve a condom.

"Wait a minute," she said. "Isn't it supposed to be extra nice when the two lubes combine?"

He tipped his head at her. "Yeah…"

"You want to try it? Just briefly? It's up to you." She knew she was clean, and she trusted him and knew he wouldn't attempt it if he wasn't.

"You're sure?"

She was on the pill, so there was little-to-no chance of getting pregnant. "Go for it."

Eyes blazing, he rolled her onto her front and then pulled her up to her knees. Callie rested on her elbows, steadying herself as he moved behind her and positioned the tip of his erection between her folds. She closed her eyes, biting her lips as he pushed his hips forward.

Both of them were so slippery that there was no friction at all, and he slid right inside her in one easy thrust.

They both let out a long, heartfelt sigh. The heat from her lube combined with the sensation from his, making everything feel sensitive, hot, and tingly.

"Wow," he said, confirming he felt the same. He pulled back and thrust again, the position taking him deeper than before.

"That's amazing," she whispered, widening her knees to encourage him to push forward. He did, beginning a series of long, deep thrusts that had them both groaning within minutes.

While he moved, he stroked down her back, over her ribs, and cupped her breasts, playing with her nipples until she felt the first stirrings of an orgasm. She moistened her lips, anticipating the build, but at that point, Gene stopped moving and withdrew. She sighed, but it was only a temporary pause, and a few seconds later, he'd applied a condom and was back inside her.

"Mmm, Gene…" It was a shame not to be skin on skin, but it still felt great, and she grabbed a pillow and rested her forehead on it, pushing back against him.

"Oh, Callie…" He began to thrust harder, his body obviously taking over from his wish to make it slow. She'd never felt or heard anything so sexy, the air filled with the slick sounds of their flesh sliding together, the sound of his hips meeting her bottom as he really began to move. "Oh fuck," he said, "tell me you're close."

"I... oh..." She couldn't even get the words out before her climax hit her, and she clamped around him and cried out into the pillow as the intense pulses claimed her.

"Thank God." He thrust hard, riding out her orgasm, and then groaned as he came. "*Aaahhh...*"

Callie could only wait, aftershocks still rippling through her as he continued to thrust deep inside her. His already hard muscles seemed to have turned to rock, and they locked together for what seemed like forever before their bodies finally released them, and they collapsed in a tangle of limbs, limp and spent.

"Oh my God, oh my God, oh my God." Callie knew she would never be able to move again. She felt as if she'd run a marathon, swum ten miles, and then cycled halfway up a mountain. "I'm exhausted."

Gene lay heavy on her, pressing her into the mattress. "Mmm," was all he said, still breathing heavily.

Callie didn't complain. She rested her lips on his hands and pressed light kisses there as their bodies relaxed, the sensitivity of her skin fading to a beautiful glow.

She tried to take a mental snapshot of the moment to take out when she needed a pick-me-up, concentrating on the taste of strawberry in her mouth, the aroma of the lubes mingled with the smell of sex, the hum of her body, the feel of him beneath her fingertips. And the look in his eyes when she eventually turned her head, filled with warmth and, for want of a better word, love, or at least a deep affection that gave her goosebumps and made her want to cry.

He kissed her, then withdrew and disposed of the condom before taking her in his arms. They lay there in the glow of the bedside lamp for a while, just relaxing and letting their breathing return to normal, basking in the afterglow of shared bliss.

Eventually, though, she had to pee, and extricated herself reluctantly from his arms to visit the bathroom.

When she came out, he'd retrieved a bottle of water from the minibar and had drunk half of it. He held it out to her, and she sat on the bed next to him and finished it off, enjoying the slide of the cool liquid down her throat.

She put the lid on and tossed the bottle into the bin, and rested her hands on the edge of the mattress, mirroring his pose.

He bumped shoulders with her. She wrinkled her nose and bumped him back.

"I'd better go," he said.

She nodded, having expected that. He met her gaze, then leaned forward, and they exchanged a long, slow kiss.

Gene moved back, his expression showing his reluctance, and maybe frustration, too, at having to go. It took every piece of willpower she had not to beg him to stay.

He got up and started getting dressed, pulling on his underwear and trousers. "I'll see you for breakfast?"

"Sure. Seven o'clock?"

"Yes, of course. Early start. See you then." He pulled on his waistcoat over his open shirt and put his jacket over his arm. Then he paused. "Happy Valentine's Day."

"Happy birthday."

He winked at her. Then he opened the door. She watched him look outside and scan the corridor before he slipped out, closing the door behind him.

She sat there for a bit. Then she took his sweatshirt out of her case and pulled it on. It fell to her hips, the sleeves falling over her hands. She smiled as she tugged them up to her elbows, walked over to the window, and leaned against the post.

The sea glistened in the moonlight. If a boat were to sail in a straight line east from Napier, it would cross six thousand miles of the South Pacific until it hit the coast of Chile. So much ocean, vast and dark and deep.

She rested her head on the window, and sighed.

Chapter Twenty-Seven

For Gene, the next few days were a blur of towns and cities and hotels as he escorted Callie to her appointments, while his evenings followed the pattern of dinner and late walks followed by hours of sensual delight as they explored each other's bodies. Every day, Gene tried to convince himself to stay professional, and every evening his resolution crumbled at the temptation in Callie's eyes.

But he never told her he loved her, and he never stayed the night.

He spent the late hours in his room, going over the reports from his office and gradually growing more concerned as events began to escalate. Two more members of the jury that had convicted Darren Kirk were injured in attacks on their life, and a third was killed, bumping the case up the STG priority list until it was flagged as a nationwide alert. Reports came in thick and fast from his crew of repeated sightings of the same men around Phoebe's office and home, and she now had two personal protection officers with her at all time, and another four covert officers working out threat assessments of places she went and generally trying to keep her safe.

Gene knew that Phoebe had spoken to Callie about what was happening, but she never mentioned it to him, and so he didn't feel that he could ask her what she felt about it all, because he wasn't supposed to know. In bed, their intimacy deepened, but outside the hotel room they only seemed to grow further apart, as what was happening became an elephant that had not only entered the room but that sat between them on the table and refused to budge.

He now had Ian, another protection officer, working covertly, advising him on routes in and out of the hotels, checking out the stores before Callie went into them, and shadowing them both at a distance while they drove up to Gisborne, Whakatane, Tauranga, and Hamilton, occasionally stopping at other smaller towns on the way when Callie discovered a lingerie store existed there.

Gene worked for hours each night making sure that Callie could continue her tour and remain as safe as possible while still being

SERENITY WOODS

unaware of her protection. It would have been difficult even if they
hadn't shared a bed, trying to answer phone calls out of her hearing
and scanning shops and streets as unobtrusively as he could while
they walked. But becoming romantically involved made things a
hundred times worse, not in the least because Gene knew he was
lying to her.

As they entered the city of Auckland, even though they were
nearing the end of their tour, Gene was beginning to consider telling
her. The night before, in Hamilton, they'd spent hours in bed making
love, lying there talking, then making love again until they were both
wrung out and exhausted. But as usual, he'd had to get up and go to
his own room so he could work, and once again he'd had to cope
with the fleeting look of disappointment on Callie's face before she
smothered it with a smile.

She never asked him why he left, or begged him to stay, but he
knew that every time he walked out, he hurt her, and that was
beginning to be more of a problem than anything else.

Because he was falling for her. He knew that now. It was too soon
to say he loved her. Love was like the plant he'd once read about that
grew in the Bolivian mountains, a bromeliad that took a long time to
grow and bloom. It wasn't like bamboo—it couldn't grow overnight.
But being in love—that was something different. And Gene was
rapidly coming to the conclusion that he was falling in love with
Callie.

If that was the case, and he wanted to stand any hope of
continuing their relationship once Kirk was caught, how was he
going to explain why he hadn't told her the truth before now? Telling
her he'd been worried for her safety might sound a great reason in his
head, but for a woman who'd been cheated on and for whom truth
and honesty were two of the most important things in a relationship,
keeping the news to himself could possibly be the worst decision he
would ever make.

If he told her, he might risk her life if she refused to have another
personal protection officer, and he told himself that was the main
reason he continued with the ruse. But deep down, he knew he was
scared of losing her, and every day that passed he became more and
more terrified.

For better or for worse, things came to a head when they reached
Auckland. The biggest city in New Zealand, although not the capital,

Auckland was large and sprawling, its oldest park based around an extinct volcano, its distinctive waterfront and skyline giving it the nickname 'City of Sails'.

By now it was mid-February, equivalent to mid-August in the northern hemisphere. The mornings bore a touch of autumn, but by midday the sun was high and hot, and it was growing increasingly humid this far north. Gene sweltered in his shirt and waistcoat every day, but there was no way he could drop the waistcoat, so he just had to put up with it.

After Napier, partly because Callie seemed to enjoy him being there and partly because of his growing concern, he'd begun to accompany her into her meetings. She introduced him as her PA, which often induced jokes and humorous comments from the store managers, but Callie just let that ride over her, and then she would launch into her spiel.

It was only then that Gene began to realize why she was so successful at her job. She had a way of putting a person at ease immediately, and the combination of her professionalism, her friendliness, and her beauty, he was sure, meant that the majority of times she came away with a promise to stock the Four Seasons brand and a new friend in the bargain. She filled out an entry on her phone for every client, noting some personal details about him or her—for example 'supports the Blues,' 'has a son at Massey University studying photography,' or 'has baby twins, one boy, one girl.' Gene knew she'd check these entries before she rang the client when she returned to Wellington, making the connection with them again when she spoke to them. It was a simple trick, but a clever one, and it only added to his admiration for her.

Their first day in Auckland was busy, four appointments all within three hours across the city, and by the time he reached the last one at four thirty, Gene was tired, stressed, and slightly irritable. Thus, when his phone rang halfway through their last appointment, he was tempted to cancel it, but as he apologized to Callie and the store manager and pulled out the phone, he saw the name Phoebe Hawke on the screen and knew he had to take it.

"Excuse me." He walked out of the office and along the corridor, letting the door close behind him so he couldn't be overheard before answering it. "Hello?"

"Gene?"

"Yes. Hi, Phoebe. Are you okay?"

"Yes. Well, no. I mean, I'm not hurt or anything." She sounded flustered, not like the Phoebe he knew at all."

"Spit it out," he said wryly. "What's up?"

"I've had another email."

He frowned, puzzled as to why she'd phoned him and Kev hadn't. "When?"

"Ten minutes ago. I've forwarded it on to you."

"Okay, hold on." He lowered the phone and brought up his emails. She forwarded all the threats she received on to his office, and they'd been trying to track down the origin of the emails, although the sender had gone to great lengths to hide his tracks.

He brought it up. It was the usual bullshit, meant to intimidate and induce fear. They never failed to make Gene angry, but it was the last paragraph that made cold slither through him as if he'd swallowed an ice cube whole.

Did your daughter enjoy her kingfish last night? I hope so. Because it might be her last.

The final two sentences went on to describe what Kirk was going to do to Callie when he finally got his hands on her.

Gene wanted to throw up. The night before, Callie had indeed eaten kingfish in the hotel restaurant. Kirk—or one of his men—had been there, unspotted by either Gene or the other PPOs.

"Fuck," he said.

Normally, Phoebe would have mocked him for that, but today she just said, "I know," in a husky voice. "He's watching you, Gene. He's watching my baby. Until now, I haven't really been scared—I don't care what this man says to me, I refuse to be scared for my life, but I am scared for Callie. I don't know what I'd do if someone hurt her because of me."

"They won't." His voice was hard as flint. "That's what I'm here for."

"I want to double her cover, Gene. I don't care how much it costs. I want at least two people with her at all times, and a proper team following her."

Although he knew she was right, his heart sank. There would be no more creeping into her room at night. "Of course."

She took a deep breath. "And I want you to tell her, Gene. I want her to know who you really are."

He closed his eyes. "But what if she tells me to go?"

"We'll deal with that if it happens. I don't think she will—up until now she hasn't taken the threat seriously, but now we know she's definitely being followed, I think it will make her think differently."

Gene wasn't so sure, but at least the decision was made now. He had to tell her. "Okay. I'll let her know."

"I'll call later, once you've had a chance to speak to her and to make the arrangements with your office."

"Okay. I'll get some people to fly up overnight for our last couple of days away. It'll be easier once we're back in Wellington."

"Thank you, Gene."

He blew out a long breath. "And how are you? Are you okay?"

"I'm fine. You know what I'm like. Nobody's going to get the better of me."

His lips twisted wryly. "Yeah. Glad to hear it."

"Thank you for taking care of my baby."

He examined his shoes. "You're welcome. She's a lovely girl."

"She's a sweetie. Make sure she stays safe."

"I will."

"I'll speak to you later."

He hung up.

For a long moment, he just stood there. Outside, the sky was heavy and gray, promising rain. There was no air conditioning in the corridor, and he was already beginning to soak his shirt with sweat.

He'd been living in a fantasy, caught up in Callie's spell, but it was time to return to the real world. *Some things are more important than sex, Gene!* he scolded himself.

But that filled him with shame. This wasn't just about sex. What he had with Callie was more than a series of one-night stands, and to refer to it like that, even in jest, was doing her a great disservice.

"Gene?"

He turned to see she'd finished her meeting and was walking toward him with a smile.

"You okay?" she said, observing him with her wide blue eyes.

"Fine." He managed a tight smile. "Sorry about that. How did you get on?"

"All good. Yet another success for the Summer School of Charm!" Her cheeks flushed with pleasure, and he felt an ache begin deep inside him at the thought of the conversation they had to have.

"Shall we go, then?" he asked.

"Please. I'm knackered. I'm desperate for a shower and something to eat."

He drove them back to the hotel, with Callie talking constantly, making it difficult for him to get a word in edgeways. She continued to talk all the way up to their floor in the elevator, and was still talking as they reached their room, swiping her card before he had a chance to say anything. She just managed to promise to meet him for dinner before the door swung shut.

Gene cursed himself for drawing this out, but it was too late now. He consoled himself by ringing Kev, discussing the threatening email, and going through the new plan, organizing to have four more agents fly up that night. Then he showered and changed into a fresh shirt, put his waistcoat back on, and was ready to knock on her door at six o'clock. He'd planned to blurt it out immediately, but she came out looking beautiful, young, and fresh in cropped jeans and a pretty orange shirt, and somehow the words wouldn't come.

And then it was time for dinner, and he didn't want to spoil that either, so he bit his tongue, cursing all the while, and promising himself that he'd tell her as soon as the meal was over.

"Shall we go for a walk?" Callie said once they'd finished their coffee.

He hesitated. He didn't want her going outdoors now unless she had to, but equally it would be easier to tell her when they were alone rather than in the restaurant, just in case she went ballistic and made a scene. He couldn't imagine the calm, good-natured Callie making a scene, but there was a distinct possibility it wouldn't end well.

So he said, "Okay," and they left the restaurant and walked along the waterfront. At any other time, it would have been a beautiful evening—it had rained briefly for a while, but the clouds had cleared, and the evening sun had painted all the boats in shades of orange and red. But he could take no pleasure from it, his stomach in a knot, sweat breaking out between his shoulder blades at the thought of what her reaction would be.

"Gene?" she spoke softly. She never held his hand in public, never made the effort to act as if they were a couple, but she touched him now, on the arm, gentle and concerned. "What's the matter? You've been quiet all evening. Is something wrong?"

He opened his mouth to reply, and at the same time he saw the man approach out of the corner of his eye. The guy was walking fast, straight toward them, and Gene's professional training kicked in without a second thought.

He turned and stepped in front of Callie, briefly registering the man's startled look before he grabbed his arm and twisted it behind his back. Quickly, Gene propelled him forward to the nearest wall and slammed him up against it. He pushed the guy's arm hard up his back and forced his knee between his legs, using his superior height and weight to pin the man there.

"One twitch of your eyebrow," Gene said fiercely, "and you're fucking dead, you understand me?"

"All right, all right!" The words tumbled from the guy's mouth where his face was squashed against the brick.

"Oh my God!" Callie appeared suddenly beside him.

"Summer," Gene yelled. "Back off."

"It's Jamie," she snapped, tugging at his arm. "It's my ex!"

Chapter Twenty-Eight

For a moment, Callie's words didn't register in Gene's head, and all he could think was that the person he'd pinned to the wall was an enemy, the bastard who'd lain out in detail the cruel, disgusting things he wanted to do when he got his hands on the beautiful woman by his side. Behind him, Ian appeared out of nowhere, ready to help him take him down.

She tugged his arm again, though, and yelled, "Gene! It's okay. It's Jamie. Let him go."

Her ex. Shock filtered through him, and he stepped back and let go of the guy's arm. Both he and Ian hovered, though, the instinct to protect too strong to make them immediately back up.

Callie pushed between them, looking up at her ex in concern. "Jamie, jeez, I'm so sorry."

"What the fuck!" The young guy massaged his shoulder and glared at him. "You'd better explain yourself quick or I'm calling the police."

"It's not his fault," Callie insisted. She didn't look at Gene. "Mum's been getting death threats, and they've threatened me, too— he thought you were going to attack me."

Jamie's eyes widened. "Death threats?" he said. "Seriously?"

"Yeah. It's a guy she put away ages ago, some kind of psychotic mobster, and he's threatened her and her family." She put a hand on his chest. "Don't worry about it, I'm fine. What are you doing here?"

While Jamie told her something about a history course he'd been sent on at the Auckland War Memorial Museum, Gene glowered, his stomach boiling with shame, rage, and jealousy at their intimate touch. This was the guy who'd slept with someone else while he'd been dating Callie. He'd cheated on her. What a fucking imbecile.

The two of them spoke quietly as if he and Ian weren't there, Jamie even turning his back on them, cutting them out of the conversation.

When Jamie laughed at something Callie said, though, and placed his hand on her arm, Gene saw red and knocked the guy's arm away.

Jamie spun around, furious. "Jesus, man! What the fuck do you think you're doing? I'm her friend."

"Some fucking friend." Gene put both hands on the guy's chest and shoved him hard enough to make him stumble. "You cheated on her. You come near her again, I'll shove your teeth down your throat, regardless of whether you've anything to do with the death threats."

Ian's hand tightened on his arm. "Gene," he said urgently.

Callie's cheeks had gone scarlet, and for a brief moment Gene thought she was going to tell him to leave her alone with her ex. Nausea rose in his throat, and he ran his free hand through his hair, trying to get his emotions under control.

Callie's eyes were cool. But to his surprise, she didn't tell him to fuck off, as he'd thought she might. Instead, tearing her gaze from his, she turned to Jamie. "You'd better go," she said. "Sorry about this. It was nice to see you."

Jamie backed away, not taking his eyes from Gene's. Four inches taller, thirty pounds heavier, and a whole lot madder, Gene glared back, and eventually Jamie just rolled his eyes and walked off. Once he was ten feet away, he turned and said, "I'll call you," to Callie, glancing at Gene with a final twist to his lips before he disappeared around the corner.

Gene twitched, but Ian's hand was still on his arm. He didn't follow Jamie, but he jerked his arm away, his chest heaving with anger.

Callie cleared her throat. Ignoring Gene for a moment, she turned to Ian and held out her hand. "I'm very sorry about that. We haven't met. I'm Callie."

"Ian," he said wryly, and shook her hand. "Nice to meet you, ma'am."

She gave a short laugh. "Yeah, I'm sure."

"I'll leave you to it." Ian's eyes met Gene's briefly before he walked away. Gene knew from that look that he'd guessed there was something between them. Well, that was the least of his worries right now.

His breaths still coming fast, adrenaline continuing to course through his veins, he looked at Callie, who watched Ian walk away before bringing her gaze back to him.

"Do you still have feelings for him?" he snapped.

"For Ian?"

"Don't be so bloody dense. You know who I mean. Are you still in love with Jamie?"

She lifted her chin, and her eyes blazed. "Of all people, you have an incredible nerve asking me that after what we've shared."

His chest heaved. He was so fucking screwed up. He had to tell her the truth or he was going to explode. "Callie…"

She looked at him, her blue eyes as clear as the water in the harbor behind her. And slowly, like the sun coming out, he realized what she'd said.

Mum's been getting death threats, and they've threatened me, too—he thought you were going to attack me.

She understood that he knew about the threats, and that he'd been trying to protect her.

His jaw dropped.

"You know," he whispered.

She blinked a few times and sucked her bottom lip.

"You know who I really am," he said.

She looked at him for a moment longer. Then she shrugged, her eyes holding a hint of amusement. "Of course I know."

He couldn't have been more baffled if she'd hit him with a frying pan. "What… how…?" He walked backward until luckily his legs met a bench, and he sat heavily. "Did Phoebe tell you?"

She shook her head.

"Neve?"

Another shake.

"Who, then?"

"You did." She came to sit beside him, looking extraordinarily calm, while his heart raced at a million miles an hour.

He'd told her? "What do you mean?" he demanded. "When?"

"The first day we met. You had a notepad on your desk. It had some kind of threat assessment of the office."

He stared at her. His brain had turned to sludge. "But… I wrote that in shorthand."

She gave a sexy little shrug of her shoulders.

"You can read Teeline?" he said, aghast.

"And Pitman." Now she was trying not to laugh. "Sorry."

It *was* funny, but Gene was too upset to laugh with her. He stood and walked up to the railing, gripping hold of it until his knuckles were white.

Behind him, he heard her soft sigh, her footsteps crossing to him. "Gene?"

"I can't believe it." He kept shaking his head. "You knew. All this time, you knew who I really was. I can't get my head around it." He turned to face her, chest heaving. "Why didn't you tell me? I've been tying myself up in knots for being unprofessional, for getting involved with you when I should be protecting you. For not telling you the truth. And all this time you knew!" It made him want to howl like a dog left in the car.

Her smile faded as she saw how distraught he was. "At first," she admitted, "I wasn't sure what to think. I didn't want protection, and I was mad that my mother had organized it without asking me. I presume it was her, anyway." He gave a sharp nod. She rolled her eyes. "I knew it. I was going to come in the next day and finish it. But..." Her lips curved in an impish smile. "I liked you. I didn't want you to go."

"But..." His head was starting to hurt. "You could have said at any time. You must have known how hard it was for me to leave every night."

"Why do you think I didn't ask you to stay? Or demand to know why you had to leave? I knew you had to go."

"I don't understand why you carried on with it when you didn't want protection."

"I was angry with Mum, but for the first time, I began to understand how serious this was. For her to go to that trouble, for you to keep up the pretense of being my PA... To go to the lengths you have done to keep me safe... I knew it must be serious."

He slid his hands into his hair, tugging at the roots. "I still don't get why you didn't just tell me. Callie, I've been going mad. I've been so angry with myself."

"I know." A hint of shame crossed her features. "At first it was fun. I'm embarrassed to say I enjoyed it. I was interested to see what you did, and how you handled it. But the longer I was with you, the less like a game it became. I realized what you were risking, and how you were so torn between being with me and doing your job. I was sure that if I told you I knew you were some kind of bodyguard, you'd tell me you couldn't do the job anymore. You'd have to get someone else in, because you wouldn't have been able to carry on doing something you shouldn't when I was aware of it."

He stared at her. She was right. That was exactly what he would have done. He couldn't have acted as her bodyguard and continued to sleep with her if she'd been aware of what he was doing. Wrangling with his own angst was one thing, being openly dishonorable was another.

And then he realized she'd been going through exactly the same as him, tying herself into a million knots because she'd wanted to keep him at her side, knowing she should tell him the truth but not wanting to lose him.

In a second, all his anger and anguish drained away.

"Well, well," he said softly. "Aren't we a pair?"

She met his gaze. Her lips curved slowly up. "Aren't we?" Her eyes filled with humor. "You were very impressive the way you handled Jamie."

He scratched the back of his neck, embarrassed. "Shit. I'm sorry about that."

"Gene, it's okay. You've been protecting me for two weeks. Putting your life on the line for me. Do you not think I appreciate that?" Her eyes were filled with wonder.

"I…" He felt as bashful as a schoolboy and couldn't think what to say.

She took his hand and led him back to the bench. The warm evening sun had dried up the rain, and he could smell the jasmine growing in a pot around a nearby restaurant. Music filtered over to them, some folksy jazz, and his muscles started to let go of some of the tension. She knew now. He didn't have to make a decision anymore. That, at least, was something, whatever happened now.

They sat quietly for a while. He didn't interrupt her thoughts, wanting to let her think.

"So Ian's a part of your team?" she asked eventually.

He nodded. "He works for me."

"He works for you? Are you, like, a team leader?"

"I run the company, Callie. Safe & Secure. It's my company. I set it up after I left the Army."

Her mouth formed an O of surprise. "I didn't realize that. But… why are you acting as my bodyguard? Why didn't you send one of your guys to do it?"

"I saw the file," he lied. "Your picture. Couldn't resist."

Her eyes appraised him. She wasn't fooled. But he wasn't about to give away Phoebe's secret, not yet.

"You should know that I'm flying four more operatives up tonight," he told her. "You'll have another PPO—that's personal protection officer—from tomorrow, and Ian and three others will be around to carry out threat assessments and watch from afar."

"Why the increased protection?"

He told her about the new death threat, and the fact that someone was obviously following them. "I was going to tell you who I really was anyway, because from now on we need to take more care of you. Up until now, it was a low to medium threat—I didn't really believe Kirk was interested in you. But knowing that someone's following you has changed everything."

She glanced around her, scanning the people walking along the waterfront, glancing up at the buildings. "He could be anywhere," she whispered.

"I know. That's why I'm here. I can type at eighty words a minute. But I'm also an ex-soldier, and a personal protection officer. I'm trained in surveillance, in threat recognition and assessment, in first aid, in overt and covert protection, and in offensive and evasive driving. I'm trained to operate under extremes, to prevent, detect, avoid, counter, and combat all threats to the principal. I'm trained in unarmed combat, and in handling ballistics, edged weapons, and explosive devices, and I had to pass high-level physical tests."

"Are you trying to turn me on?"

He gave a short laugh. He was crazy about this woman. She was smart, sexy, funny, and she still seemed into him. Maybe there was hope for them yet. "I told you not to boast, but so that you know I'm not some two-bit cowboy. I'm here to protect you, and whoever's following you will have to go through me to get to you."

They studied each other for a long moment. It was as if a storm had stirred the silt up from a riverbed, but now the storm had subsided, and the silt was gradually settling again, leaving the water bright and clear.

"What do you want to do now?" she said.

"Personally or professionally?"

She smiled. "Both. I think at the moment they're too closely linked to be separated."

"Maybe. I suppose the main question is whether you would like to continue our relationship considering I've lied to you for the past two weeks."

She rested her elbow on the back of the seat and leaned her head on a hand. "I would."

The last dregs of tension left him in a rush, and he let out a long, shaky breath. "Okay. Right. Good."

She wrinkled her nose. "So, where from here?"

"We've only got a couple of days left on your tour, and as I said, I'm flying up a team to increase your protection. So for the next few days, I'd like to concentrate on your safety. I want to get you back to Wellington in one piece."

She nodded. "Okay," she whispered.

He felt a sweep of relief that she was happy to comply. He'd miss her at nights, and would long for the touch of her body against his, but for now it would make things easier for him professionally to concentrate on her protection. "I'm still hopeful the STG will catch Kirk soon, and then it will all be over. You'll be able to hire a new PA, and then… well… we can concentrate on our personal lives."

"I can't wait." Her eyes glowed. "I'm crazy about you, Gene. I hope you know that. I think about you all the time." Her expression turned sultry. "I want you. I miss your hands on me, your mouth on mine. But I'll wait for you. And I can't think of anyone else I'd rather have protecting me."

"Okay. I think we should get you back to the hotel now."

"Come on, then."

They stood and began walking back. Callie chatted on about the journey to Whangarei and then the Bay of Islands the next day, and Gene half listened, relieved and happy that he hadn't lost her, and excited to think of the future they might have once all this was over.

But first he had to eliminate the threat on her life. A seed of unease lodged in his stomach. Kirk and his henchmen were still out there. Someone was still watching Callie. Someone who wanted to do very unpleasant things to her, and who wanted to end her life. This was the most important job he'd ever done. And he just wanted it to be over so he could get on with his life.

Chapter Twenty-Nine

The next two days were both exciting and borderline scary for Callie.

When she'd read Gene's notepad on the first day he'd come to her office and had realized he was actually an undercover bodyguard, she'd been angry at first, then curious to see how he would carry out the role when he thought she didn't know. So she'd observed him discreetly over the past few weeks almost as much as he'd been watching her, she was sure.

She was well aware how he always scanned a room before he walked into it. How, even after they started sleeping together, his gaze wouldn't be on her for more than ten seconds before it left her to glance around the room, observing anyone who might have walked in, checking exits, constantly assessing the risks. She was aware how whenever they were out walking, he would cross to the roadside to protect her from anyone in a car. How he always placed his body between her and anyone who came up to speak to her. She'd watched him react to incidents on the road and knew he had lightning-fast reactions. And she'd known that when he left her room at night, it was to work, even though he desperately wanted to stay by her side.

The fact that they'd become intimate hadn't stopped his professionalism, whatever he thought. Part of her was still a little resentful at having him there, because it implied she couldn't take care of herself, and she refused to be intimidated and scared by the bully who was stalking her mother. But equally, she wasn't stupid. Gene did this for a living, and if he thought the threat was real enough that she needed protection, she wasn't going to argue with him.

The morning they left Auckland, Gene introduced her to the four other agents who, with Ian, would be with her at all times from now on in shifts. Julia, the female PPO, was to work with Gene and stay close to Callie at all times, while the other four would work at a distance, two of them travelling ahead to carry out threat assessment prior to their arrival, the other two following behind to provide at-a-distance protection.

When they stopped at the small city of Whangarei and she visited two stores there, Julia stood outside the manager's office while she had her appointment, while Gene came in with her each time.

Now Gene didn't have to carry out the pretense of being her PA, and Callie could only watch and admire him as he directed his team. He was still warm and a little flirty with her when they were alone, but as soon as Julia was with them he turned strictly professional. No longer did he let Callie get away with anything. He refused to let her go out without either him or Julia glued to her side. His firm gaze brooked no argument when he demanded someone go with her to a shop or even to the bathroom in a restaurant. She'd thought him impressive when he'd acted secretly, but as an overt protection officer he was amazing, and she couldn't fault him.

"Is he looking after you?" Phoebe asked the question at lunchtime, not long after they'd arrived at Kerikeri in the Bay of Islands. They'd dropped their stuff off at a motel on the outskirts of town, and they were now in the town center catching some lunch before her final appointment at the large lingerie shop just along the street from the café. The town was busy, and felt very subtropical with the palms lining the streets, the bright sunshine, and the extremely humid weather.

Callie had answered her phone and walked a short distance to the nearby fence surrounding the café's garden, intending to keep the call private. Julia sat at a nearby table, but Gene had followed her, and now leaned on the fence next to her. She flicked her fingers at him, telling him to give her some space. He just raised an eyebrow above his sunglasses. She stuck her tongue out at him. His lips curved up at the corners in a sexy little smile. Her cheeks grew warm as she remembered the pouch with the two lubes and what they'd gotten up to, and his smile turned into a grin.

"Callie?"

She snapped back to the phone call and looked away. "Oh. Sorry. Actually, he's being a pain in the arse right now. He won't leave me alone."

Phoebe laughed. "Good. That's what I'm paying him for."

Callie had told her that Gene had confessed who he was. "I have one question," she asked curiously. "Why did you ask him to be my bodyguard? I mean, why him in particular? He's the director of the company—surely one of his men would have sufficed?"

To her surprise, her mother fell silent for a long moment. It was rare that Phoebe couldn't think what to say, and Callie's brow furrowed. She glanced up at Gene, who was looking away across the street.

"Mum?" she prompted.

"I... I can't tell you. But... you... you should know."

"What do you mean? What's this about?"

"Put me on to Gene."

Callie hesitated, then passed the phone to the man at her side. He took it and pressed it to his ear.

"Hello?" He watched the shoppers strolling along the pavements as he listened. Callie slid her gaze down him, admiring the way his shirt sleeves clung to his impressive biceps, and the fit of his superbly cut suit. He'd revealed to her that the reason he wore a three-piece was because the waistcoat was a bulletproof one. For some reason that turned her on. She had no idea why.

"Are you sure?" He was frowning now, and he glanced at Callie. Then he said, "Of course. I will. Yes. Speak to you later." He handed the phone back to her.

"Okay, darling, I've got to go," Phoebe said breezily.

"What's going on?"

"Gene's going to tell you, because I can't. Darling, I'm so very sorry."

"Mum..."

But Phoebe had hung up.

Callie slid the phone into her pocket and frowned at Gene. "What the hell's going on?"

"Hold on." He collected their two mugs of coffee from the table and brought them back to the fence. "Here." He gave hers to her, and they both leaned on the fence.

"Why won't Mum tell me what this is about?" she demanded.

"She's embarrassed and ashamed," he said. "And it's hard for her, because she knows you adore your dad."

"My dad? What's this got to do with him?"

"It's about something that happened in the Army, a long time ago. You told me about the time your mum came home early, and she'd had an accident?"

"Yes. That was when she said they were getting a divorce."

To her surprise, he took off his sunglasses and tucked them in his trouser pocket. His eyes were gentle, concerned. Her heart began to race.

He sipped his coffee. "I was a lieutenant then. I was stationed in the same place as your father. Normally, he would have rented a private place, but he'd only arrived the week before with your mother and they'd been given temporary married quarters on the base. That night, I happened to be walking past the officer's block when I heard a woman scream. I ran into the block, and found Phoebe… She was lying at the bottom of the stairs. She was conscious, but badly injured. The worst thing, though, was that she told me she'd been arguing with your father. He was drunk, and she'd told him she was leaving him. He'd hit her, and that was what had caused her to fall."

Callie stared at him. "What?" Her head spun. "Dad hit her?"

"I helped her up and took her to the first-aid tent, and they patched her up, but she refused to go back to your dad, and she left the next day."

"Oh my God."

"You should know that I don't think he meant to push her down the stairs. They were arguing—I think maybe she'd said she was going to leave him and had been making her way from their quarters, and he struck out in a fit of temper, and she lost her footing and fell. She didn't press charges against him, but she did use it in her divorce application. The thing is, I gave evidence in court to back up her application. We kept in touch, and she knew when I started up my own security company. She trusts me, and that was why she wanted me to protect you."

Callie felt nauseated. "Jesus. Why didn't she tell me?" She couldn't believe her mother had kept it quiet all these years.

"Because she knows you love your father, and she didn't want to spoil that relationship."

"For fuck's sake." She banged her hand on the fence. "When will she stop making decisions for me?"

Gene looked pained. "I'm sorry. I would have told you, but I didn't feel it was my secret to tell."

She wasn't angry with him—in fact, the thought of him being there for her mother was strangely comforting. It was the whole situation, and the thought of her father doing something so awful.

"I…" The sentence she'd been about to say trailed off. Walking toward her, through the garden of the café, were two men. Normally, she wouldn't have thought twice about it, but there was something about them that made her catch her breath. Maybe it was the look of determination in their eyes, or the hard, mean look on their faces. Or maybe it was the fact that Ian was running at full pelt along the road toward them.

The next few seconds passed in a blur. Ian yelled, causing Gene's head to snap around. Julia leapt to her feet. The two men separated, moving fast to either side of her, the one on the left slightly in front.

Gene acted immediately, intercepting him before Callie could blink. She wasn't sure how he did it—an elbow to the stomach, the heel of his hand to the man's chin, maybe—but in seconds the guy was on the ground with Julia on top of him, yelling in his ear as she pinned him to the floor.

The other man dodged around some startled customers, and then he came for her. Ian leapt over a table, scattering cups and plates everywhere, but he wasn't fast enough. Leaving the man on the ground to Julia, Gene spun and turned to step in front of Callie just as she saw the approaching man's arm come up, something glinting in his hand.

She knew Gene was wearing a bulletproof vest. And she knew he was there to protect her. But all Callie could think was that the man had a gun, and Gene was standing in the way of the bullet.

She shoved him, hard. Taken by surprise, he stumbled, just one step, but it was enough.

There was a flash of light. An incredibly loud noise. Something thumped into her shoulder with enough force to spin her around and send her tumbling to the floor.

Someone screamed. She saw the guy who'd shot her fighting with another man. Hands were on her, pressing something against her shoulder, moving her, talking to her. She heard Gene's voice, calm, urgent, directing, instructing, and then his face loomed into view.

"Hold on, Callie," he said. His gray eyes bored into hers, hot and fierce. "You crazy girl. Hold on."

She wanted to tell him she loved him, but she couldn't get her mouth to form the words.

Then everything went black.

Chapter Thirty

Callie's eyes fluttered slowly open.

At first, nobody noticed. A couple of nurses were talking quietly opposite her, discussing something on a chart. She was in a large room with several beds, although those on either side of her were empty.

She felt tired, and her shoulder throbbed with a deep ache so intense it made her feel nauseated. Her throat was dry, and she swallowed with difficulty.

At that moment, one of the nurses looked around and smiled, and they both walked over to her.

"Hello, Callie?" The first nurse bent over her. "How are you feeling?"

"It hurts," she whispered.

"We'll give you something for that." The other nurse was already doing something to the side, and within seconds, Callie felt a rush of something through her veins and everything went hazy. Morphine, she thought.

She licked her lips. "Can I have a drink?"

"Of course. Just a few sips." The nurse held a straw to her lips and she took a few sucks of icy cool water. It was the most beautiful drink she'd ever had.

She laid her head back on the pillow, conscious that she was moving slowly, as if she were drunk. "What happened?"

"You've had an operation," the nurse said. "To repair your shoulder. You were shot."

"Shot?"

"Yes. Luckily, the bullet missed anything major. The operation went well and you're going to be fine."

She'd been shot. In New Zealand! For some reason, she found that extraordinarily funny, but when she tried to giggle, it came out as a groan.

"Nice and quiet, now." The nurse checked her drip and adjusted something. "We'll take you up to the ward in a little while."

She wanted to ask what had happened at the café, but was aware that the nurses probably wouldn't know.

"Just rest," the nurse said, so she closed her eyes and went back to sleep.

*

When she woke again, she was somewhere else, in a room on her own. It was dark outside the window, and in the corridor the lights had been dimmed to reflect the late time of day.

"Callie?"

She rolled her head on the pillow to see her mother sitting beside her. Phoebe stood as she saw her daughter was awake and leaned over her.

"Sweetheart." Phoebe cupped her face, her eyes filled with concern. "How are you?"

"Sore," Callie whispered. Her shoulder throbbed again, a terrible, dragging pain that made her want to moan.

"Here." Phoebe pressed something into her hand, a little tube with a button. "Press this and it will give you a shot of morphine."

Callie did so, and within seconds she felt the now-familiar rush, the lightening of her head, the release of the pain. "Oh. That's better."

"Do you want me to fetch a nurse?"

"No, I'm okay." She gestured to the water on the table, and Phoebe brought her a cup to sip.

"There." Phoebe replaced the cup and perched on the edge of the bed. "I'm so glad you're awake. I was terribly worried."

Callie looked up at the ceiling, trying to get her thoughts in order. She remembered the man striding toward her, Ian yelling, the flash of the gun, the thud in her shoulder. But the rest was a jumble of sights and sounds, the smell of spilled coffee, the taste of something bitter in her mouth. Adrenaline, she thought. "What happened?"

"One of Kirk's men shot you. You pushed Gene out of the way and took the bullet yourself. He's furious with you."

"I bet he is." Had she really done that? No wonder he was mad. It had been instinct—she'd just wanted to keep him safe. "Did the men get away?"

"No, darling. Gene's agents took them down. They're in custody now, telling the STG all about Darren Kirk."

"Will they catch him?"

"Hopefully very soon, and then we can put this horrid business behind us."

"Where is he?"

"Kirk?"

"No." Callie's brain was muddled. "Mr. Bond."

"Gene?"

"Is he at the office?"

"No, darling, he's standing outside, ready to rugby tackle anyone not in a white coat. He hasn't left your side since you were shot. He feels terribly guilty, I think. Do you want to see him?"

"I don't know. How do I look?"

Phoebe eyed her shrewdly. "Why should that matter?"

Callie gave a sulky shrug.

Phoebe's lips curved up. "I see."

"No you don't."

"It's all right. He's a great guy, and I think he's in love with you."

Callie stared at her, the words sinking into her morphine-addled brain like a stone sinking into treacle. "What?"

"It's written all over him, darling. He's out of his mind with worry about you."

"Oh my God." How could she face him when she was in this condition?

Phoebe squeezed her hand. "I'll go and get him."

"No, wait." She swallowed painfully. "He told me about you and Dad."

"Oh." Regret crossed her mother's features. "I'm sorry you had to hear that."

"You should have told me." For years, Callie had blamed her mother for her parents' breakup. She felt terrible knowing the real reason for it.

"I didn't want to come between you and Dad."

Callie knew there was an awful conversation coming with her father, but she wasn't going to worry about that now. "I just wanted to say sorry for what you had to go through."

"Don't talk about that now. You need to concentrate on getting better. I'll go and get Gene. I know he'd like to see you."

"No, I…" But it was too late. Phoebe had opened the door and slipped outside.

Callie attempted to feel if her hair was in order, and gave in when she found it spread all over the pillow. It wouldn't be so bad if she could get her mouth working in conjunction with her brain.

The door opened again, and Gene came in. He paused, then walked up to the bed, his hands in the pockets of his trousers. He obviously hadn't shaved for a day or two, and stubble darkened his usually clean-shaven jaw, while dark patches lay under his eyes.

"My God," she said sleepily, "you look awful."

He gave her an exasperated look. His eyes blazed with anger. "You can talk. Look at you! Getting shot in the shoulder. Seriously. What a stupid thing to do."

"I saved your life," she said, a little sulkily.

"Do you expect me to feel pleased that you acted so foolishly?"

"No, Mr. Bond, I expect you to laugh." She stifled a giggle.

He glared at her. "Is that supposed to be funny?"

"Kind of. I'm high as a kite."

He glared at her. "It's my job to keep you safe. What on earth made you push me out of the way?"

"I thought the man was going to shoot you."

"He was!" His voice rose. "I was wearing a bulletproof vest!"

"It might have missed it." Against her will, her eyes filled with tears. "Don't yell at me. I just wanted to keep you safe."

He blew out a breath as she became upset, and he took his hands out of his pockets and came up to the bed to hold her hand. "Callie… I didn't mean to yell. I am angry that you didn't let me do my job, but what you did was wonderful and brave, and I'm touched beyond belief that you would risk your life for me. You crazy, crazy girl."

She sniffed. Her shoulder pounded, and she clicked the morphine button again. Her eyelids drooped. "I'd do anything for you."

"And I'd do anything for you. You mean more to me than anything else in the whole world." He leaned over her and pressed his lips to hers.

"I love you," she said, and fell asleep.

*

"Morning."

Gene looked up from his iPad to see Callie awake, her head turned on the pillow toward him.

"If it is morning," she said, looking at the window. "I've lost all track of time."

"It's morning." He put down the tablet, rose, and went over to the bed. "How are you feeling?"

"Better."

"Does your shoulder hurt? Do you want the button?" He lifted the device and held it out to her.

She pushed it away. "God, no. Never again. I was all over the place. I can hardly remember last night at all." She brushed a strand of hair from her face and gave him a wary look. "Did I say anything stupid?"

His lips curved up. "Not at all."

"Oh." She sighed. "Good." She tried to push herself up the bed, and failed. "Can you help me sit up?"

"Of course." He slipped an arm around her and lifted her carefully, raising the end of the bed to support her. "Is that better?"

"Thank you, yes." She rearranged the covers and then patted the side to encourage him to sit. "You look better today."

He sat beside her. "I went back to the hotel room, had a shower and a shave." Phoebe had also convinced him to catch a few hours' sleep, and he'd agreed once he'd been able to see for himself that Callie was okay.

"I seem to recall you telling me off last night." Her face was pale, but her blue eyes weren't glassy the way they had been the night before, and now they danced with laughter.

"Sorry," he said. "I'm sure that was the last thing you needed." He hadn't been able to stop himself. He'd been out of his mind with worry for hours, from the moment he'd realized she'd been shot until they'd told him she'd come around.

"It's okay. I understand. I didn't mean to do it. What I mean is, it was instinct. I didn't think of myself. I just wanted to make sure you weren't hurt."

"You'd make a good protection officer," he said.

She smiled.

He picked up her hand and held it between both of his. "I'm so glad you're going to be all right."

"Me too."

"I mean it. I don't know what I would have done if something had happened to you." He lifted her hand to his lips and held it there for a moment, fighting with his emotion.

"Aw." She squeezed her fingers. "I'm going to be okay."

"I know. But I should have protected you better. I should have forced you to stay inside, or to—"

"Hey," she said sharply, "nobody forces me to do anything. You knew I didn't want to live as if I was in a cell, and you did the best you could while taking account of your client's wishes. You mustn't be too harsh on yourself."

"But if we hadn't gotten involved…" He looked out of the window, across the tops of the trees and buildings of Whangarei. "If I'd had more self-control, maybe I would have noticed that guy before he got so close to us."

"If ifs and ands were pots and pans…" she said. "It's done, Gene. Besides, we both know I'm irresistible. You didn't stand a chance."

He had to laugh at that. She gave him an impish smile.

"I'm not proud of myself," he whispered. "But equally, I don't regret what happened between us."

"I'm glad. Because meeting you is the best thing that's ever happened to me."

He met her gaze. Her last words to him from the night before rang in his head, *I love you.* She hadn't meant it, of course. Maybe one day, in the future, they'd be able to say it properly to each other, but last night she'd been high on morphine, and he couldn't take anything she'd said as the truth.

But even so, clearly she had feelings for him, and that warmed him more than the rays of the early morning sun pouring through the window.

"As soon as you're able, we'll fly you back to Wellington," he said. "Now we have one of Kirk's henchmen, I'm sure it won't be long before he's caught, and then we'll be free to date properly. If you want to."

"I want to," she said, eyes shining.

"Good." He checked over his shoulder, then leaned forward and pressed his lips to hers.

She lifted her good arm and slipped her hand into his hair, holding him there, and the peck turned into a long, slow smooch that had his heart hammering by the time she eventually released him.

"Mmm," she said dreamily, pressing her lips together.

"You're supposed to be an invalid," he scolded. "Excitement like that might put you into cardiac arrest."

"I don't care." She slid down the pillows with a happy sigh. "I've never felt so happy."

And she looked it, her cheeks now bearing a healthy flush, her eyes filled with affection. She was going to be okay. Gene wished he could burst into tears like a five-year-old girl, but he satisfied himself with gritting his teeth and squeezing her hand tightly.

"Get well," he said. "Get well soon."

Chapter Thirty-One

It was five days before the hospital decided that Callie was well enough to fly home. She was still sore, but the pain had lessened to a manageable level with painkillers, and luckily it was only a couple of hours to Wellington with a change at Auckland.

Still, she'd underestimated how tired she would feel after even that small journey, and by the time they touched down in Wellington, she was dozing off on Gene's shoulder and desperate to get home.

Ian collected their cases while she sank onto a seat, the ever-present Gene by her side, keeping a sharp lookout across the airport. Her eyes closed again, and she sagged against him. His arm came up around her shoulders, gentle against her bandaged wound but holding her tightly to him.

"Ian might see," she mumbled, trying to stay upright.

"Don't give a fuck," Gene replied. "I'm past caring what everyone thinks."

Callie looked up at him. Phoebe had had to leave after a couple of nights, but Gene had barely left her side in the hospital. She'd guessed what he felt for her was more than the concern he might have felt for a client, but it was nice to hear him confirm it.

"Really?" she murmured.

He lowered his head and gave her a quick kiss before straightening to scan the lounge again. "I still want to wait until it's over. But I don't care if everyone discovers my feelings for you."

She nestled against him, smiling as she closed her eyes.

"Did you speak to your dad?" Gene asked.

She opened her eyes again, her smile fading. She'd called Peter Summer the day before, and it had been a long and difficult conversation that had ended with her in tears and her father choked up with shame. "Yes. Possibly the worst telephone call I've ever had to make."

"How did you end it?"

"We're still talking, but I can't say I've forgiven him. I feel bad for blaming Mum for the breakup of their marriage all this time. I know she isn't easy to live with, and I'm not saying everything is his fault, but of course hitting someone is never acceptable."

"Did you tell him about me?"

"Yes," she said softly. "He didn't say much, but to be honest, I think you've impressed him by the way you've stood by Mum all this time. And he wanted me to pass on that he was grateful for the way you've looked after me."

"Apart from the fact that you got shot."

"Yes, apart from that."

He kissed the top of her head. "I'm going to spend the rest of my life making sure nothing horrible ever happens to you, Callie Summer."

She swallowed hard. It was the first time either of them had suggested that what they had might be more than a fling.

Something was niggling her, though, and she had to say it. "Gene... You're not just saying that because you feel guilty that I got shot, are you?"

"No."

She looked up at him.

He raised an eyebrow.

She put her head back on his shoulder. "Okay." It seemed there was no more to be said on that topic.

*

The next few days she spent resting, sleeping for a few hours before getting up and mooching around her house, watching TV, and sitting out on the deck, reading. Rowan kept a close eye on her, making sure she didn't want for anything.

It felt as if she was in limbo, physically and emotionally, and she began to feel a rising restlessness, which wasn't helped when firstly Phoebe received yet another death threat, and then another member of the jury that had convicted Kirk was shot dead not far from them in Wellington.

Everything seemed to turn ultra-serious after that. For the first time, Gene left her side and returned to his office to coordinate his teams and to work with the STG, although he visited her often. Julia and Ian took turns to stay in the house at all times. Two other agents patrolled outside. Both Callie and Phoebe were advised to stay at home until Kirk was caught.

By day three, Callie was pulling her hair out. She'd spoken to Neve and Bridget frequently, keeping them updated on what was going on, but she hadn't seen them yet and she was bored witless. "Please come around!" she wailed that afternoon, and so within an hour the four of them were sitting on the deck under the large umbrella, sunning their legs and drinking iced lemonade in the sultry heat.

Julia took a seat at the bottom of the garden and walked around the perimeter every now and again, making sure nobody was hanging around. Apart from that, Callie could almost believe she was living a normal life.

"How's Willow?" she asked Rowan. Liam had rung the night before to announce that her sister had gone into labor early.

"No news yet." Rowan bounced in her seat. "I'm going to be an auntie. I'm so excited."

Callie smiled, although she felt a twist in her gut at Rowan's genuine enthusiasm. Her friend had a hundred reasons to be envious and resentful of her twin sister's good fortune, and yet the lovely Rowan—beautiful in body and mind—never showed anything but joy at Willow's happiness.

"Childbirth, though," Neve said, wincing. "Ouch."

"Yeah, but think what she'll get at the end of it," Rowan said, misty-eyed.

"You mean stitches, a saggy tummy, and no sleep for the next three years?" Neve said.

Rowan rolled her eyes. "You're so bloody..."

"Practical? Realistic?"

"Unromantic."

"Oh, stop it, you two," Callie said good-naturedly. "Don't argue. Not today."

"How are you feeling?" Bridget gestured at her bandaged shoulder. "Does it hurt?"

"Only when I do my physio. I'm down to painkillers twice a day, and it's manageable now. Just a bit stiff."

"I can't believe you were shot," Neve said. "That's so cool."

"I know." Callie prodded her bandage. "I'll have something interesting to tell my grandchildren, anyway."

"Speaking of which... I've been talking to Phoebe." Neve's look turned mischievous.

"Oh?" Callie's heart began to race as the others' faces turned curious.

"Yeah. She told me he's got the hots for you."

"I don't know what you're talking about."

"You're blushing," Bridget said. "Come on, spill the beans."

Neve grinned. "What were the 'his and hers' lubes like?"

Callie's face burned, and they all laughed. "Stop it," she scolded, fanning herself.

"How did it start?" Rowan wanted to know.

Callie decided there was no point in denying it, especially when they were going to see each other after the whole business wrapped up. "I don't know. It just happened. He told me that you warned him not to get involved, Neve. And before he realized that I knew who he was, it tore him up—I could see that. He knew he shouldn't. But neither of us could keep away from the other."

"Aw." They all looked a mixture of envious and pleased for her.

"So is he staying here?" Bridget asked.

"No. His discovery that I knew came at the same time as that horrible death threat where the guy mentioned he was watching me. We made the decision to keep apart after that so Gene could concentrate on protecting me."

"It's so romantic," Rowan said dreamily. "I'm so happy for you."

"Maybe you need to start designing her wedding dress," Neve teased.

"Good grief, let's not jump the gun," Callie said hastily. "We've not even discussed dating again properly yet."

"But you think there's a possibility he's interested in more than a fling?" Rowan asked.

"Yes," Callie said softly. "I think he is. Once this whole horrible business is sorted and we can get back to normal."

Neve opened her mouth to answer, but at that moment Rowan's phone rang. They all stared at it.

"Go on," Callie said with excitement. "Answer it!"

Rowan did so, her face growing pale. Callie could understand her worry—even in this day and age, childbirth was never risk-free, and there were always things that could go wrong.

"It's Liam," Rowan mouthed. Her eyes widened as she listened, and then her face broke into a huge grin. "It's a boy!"

"Woo-hoo!" Callie yelled, and they all stood and high-fived, cheering and jumping around.

"He's eight pounds six and doing well," Rowan announced once she'd hung up. "And Willow's fine too. A bit tired, but fine. I'll go and see her later."

"We'll all go tomorrow, too," Neve said.

Callie hesitated, not sure if Gene would let her leave the house to visit her friend in hospital. Frustration filled her. Fuck this stupid situation! How long was she going to have to be a prisoner in her own home?

She opened her mouth to tell the others that she wouldn't be able to go with them, but the words faded on her lips and she frowned, looking down the garden. Julia's phone had rung a few seconds ago and she was holding it to her ear, listening. Callie hadn't taken any notice because the agents were on the phone practically all the time. But something in Julia's face made her catch her breath.

The other girls stopped talking, and automatically got to their feet as Julia finished her call and walked up the garden toward them. Her eyes shone.

"There's someone to see you," she said, a hint of her smile on her lips.

Callie frowned and turned at the sound of a commotion at the front of her house. And then the front door opened and Gene came striding in, Phoebe right behind him.

He scanned the room, saw them in the garden, and came over to the door. It was as if he didn't see anyone else—he looked straight at Callie, his eyes blazing bright with excitement and triumph.

"They got him." His face broke into a grin. "They got Kirk."

Everyone cheered, including Phoebe and Julia, and behind them so did Ian and the other two agents who'd followed Gene in.

"It's over," he said to Callie, walking closer to her. He looked into her eyes, his own filled with such love and affection that it took her breath away. "How does it feel?"

Callie burst into tears.

Everyone cooed, "*Awww*," the girls covering their mouths and giving sympathetic laughs.

"Oh, sweetheart…" Gene put his arms around her, and she sobbed into his shirt. "I didn't mean to have that effect."

"Sorry," she said, trying to stop, but the tears just kept on coming.

"It's all right." He rubbed her back. "You've had a hell of a few weeks. I think you're allowed."

Her mother came up to her and touched her arm. "I'm so sorry to have put you through all this," she whispered. "The last thing I ever wanted to do was put you in danger." She kissed Callie's hair, then said to the others, "Why don't we go inside and leave them for a moment? I'm sure Callie has a bottle of wine we can break open."

Everyone went inside, leaving Callie and Gene alone on the deck, warmed by the afternoon sun.

Gene held her for a while, waiting for her sobs to quieten. Gradually, the emotion drained away, and she rested her cheek on his chest, listening to the others talking and laughing inside, and watching the fantails jumping about in the lemon tree.

He moved back a little, lifted her chin, and wiped her face. "Okay?" he asked.

She sniffed. "I must look awful."

"Well, I've seen you covered in blood and waking up straight after an operation. If anything was going to put me off, I think it would have done so by now."

Her lips curved up. His eyes were full of admiration, and something she hadn't expected to see—hope.

"Is it really over?" she whispered.

"It's over. Kirk's henchmen won't be interested in carrying on his personal feud now he's gone. And he's going to be in prison for the rest of his life."

"I can't believe it." She felt as if there had been storm clouds on the horizon for such a long time, and now they'd suddenly gone away and the sun had come out. "Does that mean…?" She could hardly bear to form the words.

Gene's face looked solemn. "Callie Summer, would you like to go to dinner with me tonight?"

Her lips curved up. "A real date?"

"A real date."

"Can we hold hands?"

"We can even snog at the table if you like."

She chuckled, then placed her hands on his chest and played with the button of his shirt. "And can you come back to my place... and stay the night?" She lifted her gaze to his.

"If you'd like me to." His voice was suddenly husky.

"I'd like that more than anything in the world. To sleep next to you. To wake up with you."

He cupped her face. "Then it's settled." He lowered his lips and kissed her.

Inside, everyone cheered. But Callie ignored them all and kissed him back.

Epilogue

"A kids' Easter egg hunt," Callie said. "I cannot believe we got talked into this. Whose daft idea was it again?"

It was about a month later, and Callie was helping out with a large group of other friends at a kid's birthday party in the middle of Wellington. The party was in a local play den that consisted of a large area devoted to ball pits, bouncy toys, miniature climbing frames, slides, and lots of other things for kids to play on. There was a small café attached where parents could get a drink and a snack and have a well-deserved break while their children ran off some energy. The adults had hidden hundreds of tiny chocolate eggs all across the play den, and the place filled with excited screams every time one of them was found.

"It's complicated," Rowan said. "You remember Rhett?"

Neve stared at Rowan. Rhett had been the best man at Willow and Liam's wedding, and he and Neve had had a brief fling five years ago.

"What?" Neve demanded, her face like stone.

"Um, well, Rhett's got a sister, Ginny, and she's got three kids, and the eldest is six today. The thing is, Ginny's husband left her at Christmas, so she's on her own. She wanted to give Tom, the boy, a party, but she needed some help, so I volunteered us."

"Without telling me Rhett was going to be here?" Neve said fiercely. "Rowan!"

"You can't go now," Rowan said desperately. "Think of Ginny."

Neve gritted her teeth. "I'll stay," she conceded, as Callie had known she would. "But don't think I'll forgive you easily for being so flipping sneaky about it." She walked off, in the opposite direction to where the guys were playing with some kids in the ball pit. Rhett, who'd been watching her, shrugged and turned away.

Rowan stuck her tongue out at Neve's back. Callie chuckled. "I do wonder what happened between her and Rhett. Clearly he got under her skin."

"I expect she scared him off," Rowan grumbled. She sighed and brought her gaze back to Callie. "Anyway, how are you? How's the shoulder?"

A week ago, Callie had moved out of the house they shared and in with Gene. It seemed silly not to when they were spending every spare moment they could together, and neither of them wanted to go home at night.

"Good." Callie rotated her arm and winced. "Well, about eighty percent better. Not quite there yet, but on the mend."

"Getting plenty of exercise?" Rowan said airily.

Callie smiled wryly. "A bit." Then she giggled. "Okay, a lot. The man's insatiable."

Rowan gave an envious sigh. "I am so jealous. I haven't had any for soooo long."

"You have to get out a bit," Callie said. "You said yourself that you won't meet Mr. Right sitting in your living room."

"Yeah, I suppose." Rowan's smile faded and she looked away, across at the kids having fun.

Callie frowned. She decided she'd have to make the effort to try to get Rowan to go out. She had no doubt that Neve would eventually meet someone who'd knock her socks off, and Bridget was far too nice to never settle down, but Rowan was clueless when it came to men. She had no idea what made them tick, and the relationships she'd been in had all ended with a whimper rather than a bang, with no man being the romantic hero that Rowan dreamed of.

Callie glanced around, suddenly missing Gene. "Where are the guys?"

"They're all in the ball pit," Rowan said, amused. "Look at them. Men never grow up, really, do they?"

Callie followed her gaze to the ball pit, and started to laugh. Gene, Hitch, Rhett, and several others were up to their necks in colored balls, surrounded by kids who appeared to think that burying the guys was the most fun thing they'd ever done in their life.

Gene caught her eye and got to his feet, picked up Tom—the birthday boy—and carried him like a rugby ball to the edge of the ball pit, where he gently tossed him back into the plastic balls, the boy screaming with laughter all the way. He began to walk over to Callie, but paused to pick up a tiny girl who'd fallen over, setting her back on her feet and making sure she was all right before he carried on.

"Well, well," Callie said with amusement. "You seem to be enjoying yourself."

He gave a nonchalant shrug. "Well, you have to help out, don't you?" His teasing smile told her how much fun he was having.

"Hitch!" Rowan shrieked. "Put him down!" She went marching off to berate the unfortunate Hitch, who had shouldered Tom and was galloping around the play den. She scolded him for risking the boy's safety, and he lowered the boy to the floor. Rolling her eyes, she turned to leave. Hitch smacked her backside, sending her on her way. She stopped, her eyes nearly falling out of her head, then walked on sedately to the café without looking back.

Gene looked at Callie, and they both burst out laughing. "He likes her," Gene said. "A lot."

"Hmm." Callie studied Rowan's scarlet cheeks as she bought herself a cup of coffee. "Does he now?"

Gene slid his arms around her and turned her to face him. "You okay?" He kissed her nose.

She kissed him back, snuggling into his embrace. "I'm fine, thank you. You?"

"I'm having a great time." He looked across at the little girl he'd helped up, making sure she was all right. "I want one."

Callie stared at him. "What?"

He shrugged and looked back at her. "I want one. A kid. With you. What do you think?"

Her jaw dropped.

"We'd have to get married first," he said. "Of course."

"Gene!" Callie could barely breathe. "Oh my God!"

"What? Don't you want to marry me?" He nuzzled her ear and kissed her neck.

"I... Oh! Is this a proposal?"

He kissed along her jaw to her mouth, then pressed his lips to hers for a long moment. "Maybe," he whispered when he eventually pulled back. "I know you don't want to rush into anything. I'll do it properly when you're ready. A ring, down on one knee, the whole works. The urge kind of took me by surprise." He kissed her again. "I love you, Callie. We can take our time, because we have the rest of our lives together, but the point is that I know I want to spend the rest of my life with you."

She had to be careful or she was going to cry in front of twenty six-year-olds. "I love you too."

"So when I do ask you to marry me, do you know what your answer will be?"

She blinked furiously and nodded. "Yes. I know what my answer will be."

His lips curved up. "I'm crazy about you, Callie Summer."

"I'm crazy about you too," she whispered back.

"Gene!" It was Hitch, yelling from the ball pit. "Put her down and get your butt back in here! I'm under siege!" He disappeared beneath a mountain of balls poured on his head by a couple of the kids.

Gene laughed. "I'd better rescue him." He kissed her nose. "Love you."

"Love you too."

She watched him leap into the ball pit and disappear beneath the balls, making the kids squeal as he hunted for them beneath the surface like a shark.

"He's quite a guy." It was Rowan, who'd sidled up with two cups of coffee. She handed one to Callie. "I'm so pleased for you."

Callie blinked away her tears and gave a bright smile. "What about you, Rowan? Have you ever thought about dating Hitch?"

"Hitch?" Rowan stared at her. "He's like a brother."

"He's not, though. And he likes you."

Rowan blew a raspberry. "Yeah, but not in that way. He'd never be interested in me." She spoke a little wistfully, obviously thinking the gorgeous Hitch was out of her league.

Callie just smiled and blew on her cup of coffee as she watched Gene play with the children, and began to scheme in her head.

*

Read Rowan and Hitch's story in Tempting Autumn,
The Four Seasons Book 2

The Four Seasons

Book 1: Seducing Summer
Book 2: Tempting Autumn
Book 3: Bewitching Winter
Book 4: Persuading Spring

If you'd like to be informed when my next book is available, you can sign up for my mailing list on my website, http://www.serenitywoodsromance.com

I also send exclusive short stories and sometimes free books!

About the Author

Serenity Woods lives in the sub-tropical Northland of New Zealand with her wonderful husband and gorgeous teenage son. She writes hot and sultry contemporary romances, and she would much rather immerse herself in reading or writing romance than do the dusting and ironing, which is why it's not a great idea to pop round if you have any allergies.

Website: http://www.serenitywoodsromance.com
Facebook: http://www.facebook.com/serenitywoodsromance
Twitter: https://twitter.com/Serenity_Woods

Made in the USA
Columbia, SC
30 April 2024